THE REAPER'S
SCYTHE

MICHAEL ANGEL

The Reaper's Scythe

ISBN-13: 978-1079603804

Paperback Edition of The Reaper's Scythe printed in the U.S. and published by Banty Hen Publishing, July 2019.

For more about Michael Angel, please visit MichaelAngelWriter.com.
For more about Banty Hen Publishing, please visit our website at:
BantyHenPublishing.com.
Cover art by DerangedDoctorDesign.com.
Editing/Proofing by Leiah Cooper, SoIReadThisBookToday.com.

THE PLAGUE WALKER PANDEMIC MEDICAL THRILLER NOVELS

The Devil's Noose
The Reaper's Scythe
The Blood Zone

The Plague Walker:
(A Leigh Austen Short Medical Thriller)

FANTASY & FORENSICS BY MICHAEL ANGEL

Book One: Centaur of the Crime
Book Two: The Deer Prince's Murder
Book Three: Grand Theft Griffin
Book Four: A Perjury of Owls
Book Five: Forgery of the Phoenix
Book Six: Assault in the Wizard Degree
Book Seven: Trafficking in Demons
Book Eight: A Warrant of Wyverns
Book Nine: The Conspiracy of Unicorns
Book Ten: Dragon with a Deadly Weapon

Forensics and Dragon Fire
(Fantasy & Forensics Novella)

DEDICATION

To Kristine Kathryn Rusch:
It took me way too long
to listen to your advice.
Better late than never!

To Dorothy Papin:
Your love and support
are all I need.
You are my muse.

To Alan:
Once again, this book exists
only because of your
willingness to pass on
your hard-won wisdom.

CHAPTER ONE

Surinamese Rainforest
Brokopondo Administrative District
Upper Reaches of the Kutari River

The jungle was starting to darken when Lucas spoke up.

"We should head back," he urged, even as they continued down the barely-there dirt trail. "Even if the pigs really are there, I doubt they're safe to eat."

Imro let out a grunt. He shifted the grip on his 12-gauge as he pushed through a tangle of vines. The man's knuckles were as dark and worn as the wood that made up his shotgun's stock.

"My brother says he saw them," Imro finally said. His Sranan accent smoothed *brother* into *brudda*. "That damn good enough for me. 'Sides, say we come back to camp empty-handed, you t'ink anyone going to be happy about their empty bellies?"

"That's right," Maikel called back from up ahead. "Maybe if they hungry enough, they gobble you up instead!"

Maikel laughed and made a wet smacking sound with his lips.

Jaime Lucas shook his head and didn't bother saying anything in reply. He'd arrived by way of Philadelphia three years ago as a volunteer with the Peace Corps. In time, he picked up the country's English-based Creole language.

He also picked up a bad case of gold fever.

The rumors spoke of a place downriver that glittered with bright golden flakes. The location was achingly remote, especially on foot. But Lucas and a dozen other men reached the place, panning the sandbars from first light to sunset.

Eventually the stores of beans, rice, and tinned goods ran low. Lots were drawn, so the three least lucky were sent off to hunt for bush meat. So far, pickings had been sparse.

Then Maikel climbed a tree and spotted them with his field glasses.

A group of dead peccaries lying in a distant clearing up ahead.

Lucas didn't like it one bit. Yes, the jungle's 'skunk pig' was good eating. Up to sixty pounds of meat lay under a peccary's collar of bristly hair.

But *something* must have killed these animals.

Worse, the rainforest made sure that every scrap of free flesh, skin or bone got recycled by a thousand tiny mouths. That nothing had yet come to touch these pigs did not make sense to Lucas. He had an uneasy feeling that settled into his temples like a dull ache.

They passed into a dense thicket of vegetation. Maikel made his way through without breaking pace. Imro merely slowed to make sure nothing fouled the barrel of his weapon.

Lucas was forced into a crawl to get under the worst of it. He fought to keep the supply pack from being yanked off his shoulders. Ropey vines clutched at him like half-dead things.

Maikel froze. He raised one spindly arm to point ahead. His index finger quivered.

"What are you doing?" Imro demanded. "Stop playin' at sticks, or I'll–"

"The *pakira*..." Maikel gasped, using the local word for peccaries. "They gone."

"You gone cray? What you mean, gone?"

Imro pushed past his brother. He brought his shotgun up, but no targets presented themselves. Lucas followed on his heels and stared wide-eyed at the scene.

The rare open patch of rainforest floor lay bare, save for the clumps of weedy ground cover that sprouted wherever sunlight could touch the earth. Imro knelt by one of these patches and put his nose within a palm's breadth to sniff it.

Lucas watched without comment. Imro had been a tracker and poacher before joining the gold panners. He'd put three children through school in Paramaribo by selling feathers from birds as elegant as they were endangered to select European couturiers.

"My brother's right. The pakira were here," Imro finally declared. He motioned to one side with the shotgun's barrel. "T'ink they go that way. Come on."

"Hold up," Lucas protested. "Something is very wrong here! Did the pigs just decide to take a late afternoon nap and then get up again? They're probably sick."

Imro whirled to face him.

"Yeah, they might be sick with the dropsies. Out here, you see any market? We need food to bring back! If the meat's got a sickness, the fire burn it out 'fore you eat it! You still got a problem dwellin' in your head?"

"No," Lucas finally said. He'd never seen the big man show more than mild annoyance before. "No problem."

"Mikael," Imro called. "You see where pakira go?"

His brother nodded.

"Good. Lead on then."

The three men continued down the path as dusk deepened around them. The sounds of night animals readying for their time began to filter through the underbrush.

The bruised purple of the sky changed to a strange, still gray. The gray of a vaulted marble ceiling in a room lit by a guttering candle. A strange heaviness filled the air, smothering the sounds of everything but the cautious *crunch* of their footfalls.

Finally, Lucas couldn't stand the silence any longer.

"We're going to have a hell of a time finding our way back."

"You frightened by the dark?" Imro sneered.

Under the insult, Lucas heard something else in the older man's voice. A tension that veered perilously close to outright fear. It stole his breath as realization came to him.

Imro and Mikael don't know what's going on either.

Lucas glanced about. A mist had wafted out of the trees ahead and settled around them in a dense gray mass. The plants about them had changed as well.

Their leaves were waxy with a gray tinge. Ground ferns, oil-palm leaves, hanging thorn vines, all looked as if the green had been blanched out. He shied away as he tried to avoid the strange vegetation's touch.

He almost ran into Imro's broad back. The older man had halted to stand next to his brother. The two men stared out into the rapidly darkening jungle ahead of them.

"What in the word of the Christ-child is that?" Mikael whispered.

Lucas bit back the obvious question and simply listened. He strained to pick out anything at all. The mist made his ears feel as if they had been stuffed with cotton batting.

Then he heard it.

A deep, gut-churning *throb* in the distance. Another. Then another.

There was an edge to the sound that raised gooseflesh on the nape of his neck.

"That's a heartbeat," Imro breathed. "That's what it is."

"Jungle got no heartbeat," Mikael whispered back. "Can't be."

"Can't see anymore. Need the light up in here."

Lucas shrugged off his pack. He set it down on the ground before him, unzipped the top compartment, and pulled out a metal-skinned flashlight. He passed it over Imro's shoulder.

The older man grasped the flashlight's handle with his right hand. He shifted the shotgun to hold it in the crook of his left arm. With a jab of his thumb, Imro flicked it on and trained the beam on the heaviest bank of mist ahead.

Eyes gleamed back at them. Snarls filled the air as forms erupted out of the mist. Fear turned to horror as time slowed to a crawl of terror-filled moments.

Imro opened his right hand so that he could bring the shotgun to bear. The flashlight hit the ground with a *clank*. It rolled and bounced so that the beam only caught snippets of motion.

Blaze of yellow and black and gray fur.

Mikael crouched down on his knees, as if begging for absolution.

The glint of wet fangs in motion.

A blur of motion as Imro's shotgun came up.

A jolt of hot orange light as the gun blasted into the mist with a *BOOM*.

Lucas' nerves gave way and he turned to run. He took maybe three steps before he tripped over a loop of creeper vine. Arms flailing, he fell face-first into the dirt.

A second *BOOM* from Imro's gun. Screams from both brothers. The screams were followed by horrible sounds that could only be described as *wet*.

The flashlight rolled to a stop. The beam came to rest on a patch of earth before Lucas' nose. Another wet sound, and something landed with a *plop* into the light.

He had to cross his eyes to make out the object. It was shaped like a horseshoe, studded with dirty knobs of white along its length, and it dripped ragged red at the ends.

Breath whistled out of his lungs as he recognized Imro's freshly separated jawbone.

Jaime Lucas' sanity fled like a thief in the night as he heaved himself up to flee.

With a *ping*, the flashlight bulb's filament snapped, plunging everything back into darkness.

Michael Angel

CHAPTER TWO

Republic of Suriname
Hoogeveen City
The Jaguarbosstraat (Jaguar Forest Street)

The attack came in the nameless half-hour between dawn and a tangerine-colored sunrise.

Nicholas Navarro paced the already-warm asphalt, cradling his M4 carbine in the crook of his arm. He was a tall man with the wide shoulders of a linebacker, buzz-cut hair the shade of strong coffee, and a jagged scar that wended down the left side of his face from his hairline to below the cheekbone.

His deep-set eyes swept the area for threats. The five other men that made up his squad did the same. Navarro had posted them in a loose defensive perimeter around the firm's secure personnel carrier and the nearby building.

In truth, the personnel carrier was simply a large truck that his employer, Motte & Bailey, had up-armored. The thing looked as if a street artist had welded a together a pile of scrap metal and ballistic glass.

But it would stop bullets. That was all anyone cared about.

As a private military contractor, Motte & Bailey was

budget-conscious enough to improvise when needed. Thankfully, what they slapped together *worked*. Otherwise, Navarro and his men wouldn't put their butts on the line, paychecks or no.

Hoogeveen City slouched to life around them like a drunkard waking up after an all-night bender. Butterfly jasmine blossomed in the tropical heat. The flower's sweet scent temporarily blotted out smells of auto exhaust and leaking sewer lines.

Street vendors began unloading their sidewalk carts. People emerged from row houses sporting chipped paint and barbed-wire topped fences to open shop fronts. Rust-spotted taxis coughed to life as they puttered along the potholed streets.

The uptick in activity always put Navarro on edge. He had two squads out today, both stationed in the more highly trafficked areas of the city. And today, the second squad had control over his eyes in the sky.

Hoogeveen had far too many shadowy groups circulating among the population for Navarro's taste. Most of the roving armed gangs were employed by drug cartels. Others were allied with a motley collection of smugglers moving gold, emeralds, weapons, or even exotic hardwood trees.

They all liked shooting at anyone protecting what remained of local government. And since Navarro was parked in front of the provincial governor's *palacio*, he had a bad feeling brewing in the pit of his stomach. He grabbed the tactical radio hanging from his belt and thumbed the transmit button.

"Sierra Two, this is Sierra One, come in," Navarro said, in a voice that carried the barest trace of a Western twang. "Gimme a SITREP."

A couple seconds passed before he got a static-tinged response. The leader of his second team, John Redhawk, was a man who rarely if ever minced words.

"This is Sierra Two. Nothing kinetic on the ground," came the reply. "Just as it's been over the past week."

Kinetic was the term used as a catch-all to describe any kind of violence or unrest. Nothing kinetic was welcome in a city prone to riots and shootouts. Navarro's gut unclenched a bit.

"You know I had to check. Don't want your squad falling asleep out there."

He got a short bark of a laugh in reply. "Falling asleep, my ass."

"What about Abbott and Costello?" Navarro asked.

"Abbott's not reading anything out of the ordinary. The usual Red Cross bird's heading past on schedule, that's all. Costello's still in search mode at the end of our Green Zone. Hold on, I'll get you an update."

Redhawk led his second squad, but the man's main talent was running drone surveillance. Abbot and Costello were a pair of 'extended loiter' unmanned reconnaissance aircraft. Each XLURA looked as if a block of video cameras had been duct-taped to ten-foot lengths of coat hanger wire and cellophane. But their AI algorithms made use of thermal updrafts to stay aloft for up to twenty hours. More importantly, they could make decisions to check out suspicious behavior on their own.

Navarro looked to the brightening sky as he heard an approaching aircraft. He recognized the familiar *thwap-thwap* of circling rotor blades. The rugged profile of a Bell transport helicopter came into view as it flew past overhead. The Bell's paint job set off the scarlet cross on the fuselage as it headed north towards Hoogeveen's harbor area.

The main door to the palacio opened and a man with thinning hair and a gunmetal gray suit emerged. He had a hatchet nose and a face to match, but he carried himself as if he expected the world to happily wait on him. The two squad members closest to the building pulled back to flank the man as he approached the armored truck. Another slid the vehicle's side door open for him.

Navarro doubted that anyone would serve Geoffrey Chadwick out of the goodness of their heart. The man had an unfailing belief that Motte & Bailey's protection meant that they served as his at-whim limousine service.

Chadwick placed one foot inside the vehicle before stopping in his tracks. His mouth crooked up on one side in an irksome grin. He leaned against the door and turned to Navarro.

"Well, now," Chadwick said. "It's a shame I can't collect on our gentleman's bet."

Navarro raised an eyebrow. "I'm sorry, I don't recall betting you anything."

"No, of course you wouldn't. You ground-pounders are too busy polishing your weapons in private to remember anything important."

The words were jocular, but the tone wasn't. Not for the first time, Navarro had to remember that this man's organization was a paying customer. So, he let it slide. Mostly.

"We do get busy, Mister Chadwick. Tryin' to keep people like you safe."

"Then perhaps you better sharpen your instincts. You said that I'd never make headway with Governor Murken. Well, he just gave my firm permission to extend our base contract. I'm a born negotiator, you know. This just proved me right, and you wrong."

What a stuffed shirt, Navarro thought. A fortnight ago, he'd given the man his candid assessment of the local governor. Daan de Murken was honest, at least for a Surinamese politician. If he was bribed, he *stayed* bribed. But without a healthy dose of self-interest and a suitcase filled with hundred-dollar bills, Murken wouldn't so much as lift a finger.

"Of course, Mister Chadwick," was all that Navarro said aloud.

Redhawk's voice crackled over the radio.

"Costello's reporting a heat signature," he reported. "It's coming from—"

"Get me back to base," Chadwick said, interrupting Navarro's thoughts and overrunning his squad leader's words. "Run the lights if you have to, I don't want to miss breakfast again."

"Hold on a moment," Navarro turned away. "Say again, Redhawk?"

"We've got a heat signature," his friend repeated. "It's

coming from the upper floor of a building four clicks east of you."

"Heat signature? From what?"

"Nothing good, I can tell you that. Now we're getting a bloom on the IR scanner."

"I'm not 'holding on' for anyone!" Chadwick demanded. "You will take me back to base immediately, as I'm not planning on–"

The rest of Chadwick's rant was lost as the distant *whoosh* of ignited propellant filled the air. Navarro spotted a bright flash and a dull gray cloud of smoke billow from the roof of a low-rise apartment building in the distance.

An arrow-shaped object launched upwards from the smoke cloud. It burned a white-hot arc across the sky.

Navarro's gut clenched again. *Anti-aircraft missiles? Here, in Hoogeveen?*

With a teeth rattling *BWAM!* the projectile exploded as it hit the Red Cross helicopter's tail boom. The rotor at the end of the boom wobbled ominously for a second. The aircraft hesitated in mid-air.

Then the small rotor flung itself free. With a metallic *whine*, the tail rotor fell from the sky. The razor-sharp blades sheared the head off a nearby palm tree and buried itself in the roof of a parked taxicab.

The helicopter went into a slow downward spin. It drifted behind some more buildings, out of view of Navarro and his squad. A second, more distant *boom* as it came to earth.

Navarro thumbed the radio again. "There's a bird down! Dammit, someone *shot* it down! Redhawk, your drones have a visual on the crash site?"

"Just a second," came the reply.

Chadwick had gone pale after watching the helicopter vanish.

"The base," he gulped. "I demand that you to take me back to base."

"The bird's gone down at Plaza Van de Slagers," Redhawk continued. "Edge of our Green Zone. At least the pilot brought it in upright."

"Survivors?"

"If it's upright, there's a fifty-fifty chance. We've got movement, though. I'm seeing at least one squad of armed men approaching the helicopter. I'd say cartel for sure."

Navarro didn't hesitate. "Right. I'm bringing Sierra One to the site, we're closer to that plaza than you."

"Understood."

"Are you listening to me?" Chadwick squealed. "We're under attack out here! I...I *order* you to take me back to base!"

"My only orders are to keep you safe," Navarro said tersely. "And I can't do that if I'm heading into a free-fire zone. You're staying here, Chadwick."

"Staying here? Are you crazy? Your charter is to protect *me*! There's no reason to–"

Navarro had to fight the urge to throttle the man. "That's a Red Cross bird out there. The cartels just forced it down, and if they don't shoot the survivors outright, they'll take them hostage. I figure that gives me a damn good reason to go out and stop them."

"You can't just–"

But Navarro wasn't wasting any more words on the man. He yanked Chadwick off the truck by the shoulder and shoved the man towards two of his squad members.

"Farris, Grimes!" Navarro barked. "Get him inside the palacio and secure the wing you pick. Keep him away from the windows."

With that, Navarro hurried up to the truck's cab. Opening the passenger side door, he took the seat next to his driver. His three remaining riflemen clambered aboard and slid the side door shut. He caught a last glimpse of Chadwick glaring hatefully as he was escorted back into the building.

Navarro put it out of mind. Lives were at stake in the here and now. He turned to the driver, a younger man who'd just left the military and joined the ranks of Motte & Bailey.

"Sims, right?" Navarro asked.

"Yes, sir." The young man said, swallowing hard as he

spoke.

"We've got people to rescue. Floor it!"

Sims slammed the gas pedal underfoot. The makeshift personnel carrier gave a grumbling wheeze as it lumbered down the street towards the crash site.

Michael Angel

CHAPTER THREE

Navarro spotted the trap just as the personnel carrier turned off the main boulevard and onto one of the town's secondary streets.

A pair of near-derelict vans emerged from the alleyways up ahead, one from the left and one from the right. Their front bumpers touched in the middle of the street as the drivers put them in park and then jumped out. A second group of men ran across the street just in front of the vans, dragging a rusty anchor chain and anchoring each end to a pair of the city's remaining lamp posts.

"Roadblock!" Navarro warned.

Sims eyed the sides of the road nervously. "I've got no room to swing this beast around!"

Of course not, Navarro said to himself. *That's why they put the roadblock* here, *and not on the main boulevard.*

"Bring us to a stop." Navarro ordered. "Then a three-point turn!"

The Motte & Bailey driver slammed a boot on his clutch, shifted, and then stood on the brake pedal. The big truck's rear end wobbled, threatening to skid to one side as it slowed. The cabin filled with the eye-watering scent of burning rubber and smoldering brake pads. At the last second, Navarro remembered to grab the seat belt, pull it across his front, and snap the buckle in place.

His breath whistled from his chest as the personnel carrier smashed into the stretched chain with a *jangle* of metallic links. That was followed by the *screech* of metal on metal as the pair of vans used in the roadblock shifted slightly from the impact. Navarro gasped for breath against the now-taut seatbelt as he spotted furtive movement from behind the roadblock.

"Reverse!" he croaked.

Sims had just grabbed the gearshift as two men dressed in dark blue coveralls climbed atop the roofs of the vans. Each carried an assault rifle. They brought their weapons up and unleashed a murderous burst of fire at the carrier's windshield.

"*Shit! Shit!*" Sims gasped, as he flinched under the hail of bullets.

The ballistics glass held. The attackers' bullets dug pits and spread cracks across the two-inch thick pane. Navarro gut clenched anew as particles of layered polycarbonate fell onto his chest and lap with tiny *plinks*.

"Get us the hell out of here!" he roared, as he looked around desperately for his rifle. The M4 had slipped out of his hands upon hitting the roadblock. The weapon now lay down by his feet.

Cursing, Navarro reached under his jacket and groped for his shoulder holster.

The personnel carrier shifted into reverse with a *clunk* of its abused transmission. Navarro's hand closed around the handle of his service pistol. He brought it out and lunged forward against the tautness of his seat belt.

He shoved the barrel of his firearm against the closest pit dug in the ballistic glass. The tip broke through the windshield with a *crunch*. Navarro squeezed the trigger four times.

His first three shots whistled past the cartel gunmen. The last caught the one on the right high on the forehead. The close-range impact jerked the man's chin skyward and turned the top of his skull into bloody mist.

With another *squeal* from the rear tires, the personnel carrier hurtled backwards. It jolted as it slammed over a curb and Sims was forced to brake. He spun the steering wheel around, shifted once more, and brought the vehicle forwards again.

Navarro continued to fire through the hole he'd made in the windshield until his magazine clicked empty. He didn't hit anything, but he made the remaining gunman jump back down for cover. The side mirror outside his door snapped off with a *pang!* as the carrier managed to scrape its way around, completing its turn and lumbering back up the street.

"Where to now?" Sims asked, as he squinted through the damaged windshield.

"Head up Jaguar Street until you get to a plaza with a statue in it," Navarro said. "Then hang a right."

"On it."

Navarro thought furiously for a moment. He knew the city reasonably well, but there was no way he'd send his vehicle back down a secondary street. Any more hits to the windshield would put it – and his squad – out of action. But the alternative would take them at least ten minutes out of their way.

He blew a frustrated breath through his lips. Then he grabbed the carrier's dash radio.

"Sierra Two, this is Sierra One."

"Copy," came Redhawk's laconic voice.

"Things just got kinetic. Almost got caught at a roadblock off Jaguar Forest Street. No casualties, but we've got to take the long way around. What's the ETA of our bad guys and that downed bird?"

A pause. Followed by a muttered curse.

"A minute or two, tops. They're less than a block away."

"Redhawk, we're at least ten minutes out. Your squad can get to the site before us. I hate to do this, but you've got the ball now."

"Copy that," Redhawk said. "Putting the drones on standby and taking my squad in."

"Good hunting. Out."

Navarro held the connection a moment longer. He heard Redhawk barking orders, collecting his squad. Last, the deep growl of an engine filled the speaker before the sound cut out.

Redhawk had five armed riflemen and a similarly armored personnel carrier at his disposal. He'd more than proven himself on a half-dozen missions in the Corps, and a dozen more with Motte & Bailey. The man knew what he was doing, no doubt.

Then what's giving me the damned shakes? Navarro tapped the GPS map screen mounted in the center of his vehicle's dash. A quick scan confirmed there was no shortcut from Jaguar Forest Street to Plaza Van de Slagers.

Navarro still wasn't fluent in Suriname's mixture of English and Dutch place names. But he knew this one. It sent an unwelcome shudder down his spine.

Plaza of the Butchers, he thought uneasily. *Well, if that's not an omen, I don't know what is. Redhawk, you're going to have your hands full when you get there.*

CHAPTER FOUR

John Redhawk's days on the Apache Salt River Reservation in Arizona had been spent either peering through binoculars or staring at casino security monitors. Both skills had come in handy when joining Motte & Bailey as a private security contractor. While in their employ, he'd learned to kill when under fire.

Redhawk wasn't a squeamish man, but he'd never warmed to the task. He preferred his role as a scout, whether on horseback or via robotic proxy. His already grim face took on a sterner cast as he contemplated what was to come next. He hoped that it wouldn't involve killing again.

But if it came down to it, he was ready.

He'd braced his laptop against the slope of the dashboard as the personnel carrier came to a stop at the side of the road. Before he closed it, he took one last look at the video feed provided by Costello as the drone continued to circle overhead. He turned to face his five squad members.

"Okay, the crash site's one block up and to our left," he began. "We've got four or five bad guys crawling all over the crash site. The good news is that they haven't thrown up any kind of perimeter barricade yet."

One of Redhawk's men snorted. "Seems odd for them not to do that. Sloppy."

"Maybe, but we're taking advantage of it." Redhawk first pointed to the man who'd spoken, then to the others in turn. "Mason, you're my second on this one. I want you, Dale, and Kenzie to take position on the northwest corner of the plaza when you get there. Ojeda, you and McCall are coming with me. We'll take the northeast corner. Watch your fire, they may have hostages."

Another of Redhawk's troopers spoke up. "Think these guys have any more rockets to shoot at us?"

"Doubt it. Then again, nobody thought they could bring down a bird in the first place," he replied. "You bring up a good point. Any of you see a rocket heading your way, then you damn well better *duck*."

Redhawk got a couple of dark chuckles from that. The truck's side doors slid open and the men got out. Each of Motte & Bailey's men wore a mix of dark green and gray fatigues over body armor plating. While more lightly equipped than an Army-equivalent squad might be, they each carried the short-barreled M4 carbine and enough ammo to last through a prolonged firefight.

They split into two squads of three as directed. They'd stopped on a street of green and white row houses split by a median of dead pampas grass and crumbled concrete. The smell of stewing pork, blooming orchids, and stagnant water hung in the air.

The few city folks who'd come out at the sound of the crash quickly vanished back inside as they caught sight of the armed men coming down the block. Several half-open stores and fruit carts used by the local street vendors stood empty and silent.

Redhawk said a silent *thank you* up to the Great Spirit of his ancestors. This situation already threatened to get messy, and having large numbers of civilians on the street would've quickly turned this into a catastrophe.

He gave a hand-signal to indicate that Mason and his two

companions should take point. They moved around the corner, vanishing as they took cover. Redhawk waited a few seconds. When he didn't hear gunshots, he motioned for his men to follow him. He came around the corner, dropped to a kneeling position behind a traffic barrier, and spotted the downed Bell helicopter up ahead.

As he'd seen on the drone monitor, the pilot had managed to bring the crippled bird down in an upright position. Because of this, the main rotor's blades hadn't sheared off on impact. Instead, the ends drooped from the rotor mast like the fronds of a date palm.

The landing skids were mashed flat against the concrete that made up the plaza's open traffic square. The pilot's windscreen lay broken. Shattered bits of glass glinted up from the pavement. The tail boom was nothing more than a smoking stump.

Three men in jet-black fatigues stood outside the wreckage, carrying assault rifles at the ready. Redhawk glimpsed two more moving about inside what remained of the fuselage. He frowned. The all-black outfits were an odd choice for the cartel to be wearing in a tropical climate.

He risked a second glance, which did nothing but puzzle him even more.

The black fatigues are weird enough, he thought. *But I could swear that they're wearing* gloves*! And what's up with the strange black cloth covering their mouths? How's that supposed to be a mask if I can see the top half of their faces?*

But he didn't have time to think on it any further.

"*Vijand!*" came the cry. "*Schiet ze neer!*"

The three gunmen outside the helicopter each dropped to one knee. They began spraying the area with fully automatic fire. Redhawk and his two men ducked as they heard the familiar *rat-tat-tat* followed by the warble of bullets ricocheting off the cement face of their traffic barrier.

Mason's men returned fire from their position across the street. Instead of the fully automatic streams directed at them, they limited themselves to short bursts that mostly drew attention. Redhawk took the opportunity, dashing towards the next vantage point, where a line of parked cars provided halfway decent cover.

Mouth dry and panting for air, he ended up crouched behind a derelict pickup truck covered in a leopard pattern of rust spots. Redhawk waited until his men were in position. Then he brought his carbine up, ready to provide cover in turn for Mason's men to move.

He blinked. The targets were gone. The black-clad gunmen were in full retreat. They ran for the safety of a large camouflage-patterned SUV that had pulled up on the far side of the plaza.

"Advance!" Redhawk shouted. Both his two men and Mason's trio broke cover and ran towards the crash site.

The last of the cartel's gunmen piled into the rear of the SUV as Redhawk reached the downed helicopter. Ojeda and McCall knelt and took a couple of shots at the vehicle. It didn't prevent the driver from gunning the motor and disappearing into the warrens of Hoogeveen's Red Zone.

"Cease firing!" Redhawk called, though the escape left a sour taste in his mouth. "McCall, I need that paramedic training of yours. If they left anyone alive, I need you to help keep them that way."

Mason stuck his head out of the bird's fuselage.

"We've got three alive in there. Two dead."

"Aw, hell." Redhawk spat off to one side. "Bastards."

"Looks to me like they died in the crash."

Amazed, Redhawk walked up and stuck his head inside the remains of the helicopter's cabin. The corpses of the pilot and co-pilot lay slumped over their broken control panels. Three people in the main compartment lay groaning and half-buried in the wreckage.

Redhawk's nose twitched as he smelled something sweet.

"Son of a *bitch*," he murmured, as he recognized the aroma of leaking aviation fuel. "This damn thing might blow us all to hell if we don't get out of here!"

CHAPTER FIVE

Redhawk forced himself to remain calm. Danger or no, he wasn't about to abandon anyone to a fiery death. He turned to address his men.

"I'm smelling gas. If it catches, this thing goes up like a fireball. Let's get these people out of here. Watch out for metal on metal contact. Try not to scrape, or you might set everything off."

His squad split into pairs as they pried loose bent seats or shoved aside fallen boxes of supplies. Ojeda helped Redhawk lift the man trapped directly behind the cockpit out of the wreck. The two carried him a safe distance away and laid him gently on the warm concrete.

"Check with the others," Redhawk said, as he knelt by the crash victim's side. "Give me a status on their injuries."

"On it." Ojeda dashed off.

Redhawk looked back to the crash victim. The man was thin, with a wispy beard and a now-tattered white hospital coat. A badge clipped to the coat bore the medical symbol of a rod with a snake curled around it and the name *JANSEN*.

"Talk to me, Jansen," he urged. "Help's on the way. Stay with me. Tell me where it hurts."

"Left leg doesn't want to move," Jansen said, with a cough.

"Easy now, help's on the way," Redhawk replied, as he placed a hand on the man's forehead. It didn't feel clammy, so shock wasn't an issue yet. "The cartel shot you guys down. They must've wanted something of yours pretty bad."

Jansen looked puzzled. "We're just a medical helicopter. And those men…they didn't take anything. They only sprayed us."

Redhawk blinked. Before he could say anything, Ojeda reappeared at his side.

"McCall's got the other two stabilized. One's in bad shape, though. Broken ribs and internal bleeding."

"As soon as Sierra One gets here," Redhawk said, "we'll secure the area and have them get the injured to a hospital." He looked up at the sound of an approaching engine. Navarro's personnel carrier was heading their way, looking as if someone had taken a sledgehammer to the front end. "Speak of the devil. Finally, a little good luck."

But something stopped him before he got to his feet.

What the hell's going on here? his brain demanded. *Why would the cartel go so far as to shoot down this helicopter without a damned good reason?*

"Wait a minute," he muttered, as he looked back to Jansen. "What did you mean, they 'sprayed' you?"

"That's what they did," Jansen said plaintively. "They held up a spray bottle and doused us with something. They were doing the same thing to the inside of the helicopter, until you showed up."

Redhawk began to get a very bad feeling about this.

"They might have left a contact poison behind," he said aloud. "Jansen, think: Did they say anything to each other? Anything?"

"I couldn't make it out, it was gibberish," the man complained. "I speak Dutch, but I can't make out everything the way they say it down here."

"Tell me the gibberish, then!"

"Right as they left, one said something like, '*Let's see how they like their new blankets.'"*

The newly arrived personnel carrier pulled up at the edge of the plaza with a hiss of abused brakes. Navarro got out of the passenger side of the cab while two more of his men emerged from the sliding door at the rear. The big man ordered his two subordinates to take position at the nearby intersections to watch for any approaching traffic. Only then did he start jogging towards the crash site.

Redhawk sat back on his heels, his mind awhirl. The words that Jansen overheard sounded like nonsense, that much was true. But it wasn't nonsense speech. It conveyed meaning, purpose.

Let's see how they like their new blankets.

Who was *they*? If the bad guys meant the crash victims, then nothing visible had been left.

But what if *they* meant the *rescuers*? If so, did that mean the crash victims had *become* the blankets left to be picked up?

It hit him in a flash.

Redhawk stared at his palm, where he'd touched Jansen's forehead. As if in slow motion, he stood up. Navarro waved to him, called out to him. Maybe twenty yards separated the two men.

Redhawk brought up his carbine. He shouldered it and aimed at his friend. Navarro slowed to halt, eyes wide, and put his hands up.

"If this is about that night with your niece," Navarro said hesitantly, "I'll swear on a whole stack of Bibles that I was a complete gentleman–"

But Redhawk wasn't listening. Once again, the sound of the blood rushing through his ears with an incessant beat blotted out almost everything else. That, and the feeling of something terrible coming their way, like a wave rolling towards a beach at night.

He spotted movement off to one side. McCall and Kenzie had put together a makeshift stretcher. They carried one of the crash victims, a woman with a bloodied mop of brown hair, towards Navarro's vehicle.

Redhawk raised the barrel of his weapon and squeezed off a burst into the air. Navarro's men whirled about, sighting on him. Everyone stopped in place as his voice boomed out across the plaza square.

"Sierra Two! Return to within ten meters of the crash site. Bring all the wounded back."

Kenzie, who was holding one end of the stretcher, gave him a puzzled look.

"Back? I thought we had an explosion hazard."

"We do. But we've got a worse problem on our hands."

"Have you gone nuts?" McCall burst out, from where he had the other end of the stretcher. "We're going to lose this woman if she doesn't get into surgery in the next twenty minutes, tops."

Redhawk looked at him. His voice shook. "You heard me."

Navarro slowly put his hands back down. "McCall, you've got your orders. None of us give 'em without good reason."

Together, Kenzie and McCall turned the stretcher around and headed back towards the downed bird. Redhawk lowered his carbine and then rubbed at his eyes. He let out a couple of deep, shuddering breaths. Navarro waited a moment as his friend got his emotions under control before speaking.

"Talk to me, John," he said, in a quiet voice. "If I had a brother, I'd trust him like I trust you. What's going on?"

"When my squad got here, the cartel had five men already at the bird. We chased them off, but it was too damned easy. A couple shots, and off they went."

"Okay, go on."

"We found three survivors in the wreck. But just now, one of them told me that the bad guys sprayed them with something. Then, just as they're bugging out, they say: *Let's see how they like their new blankets.*"

Now Navarro was the one who gave him a puzzled look.

"Don't you get it?" Redhawk finally burst out. "That's what the British said when they gave smallpox-contaminated blankets to tribes of Native Americans, back in colonial times. Tribes like *mine!*"

Navarro stared at him for a moment.

"Jesus," he breathed. "All right, I think you're on to something. Just sit tight."

Redhawk hung his head and went to join his men. Navarro jogged back to his personnel carrier. Sims already had the radio unit ready and handed it to him.

"Sierra Base, this is Sierra One," Navarro said. "Sierra Two has a possible NBC exposure, request assistance."

The reply came after a startled silence. "We read you, Sierra One. Negative on the assist for Nuclear-Biological-Chemical contamination. There's nothing in our local inventory designated for an NBC event."

Navarro cursed. "Then contact the Suriname government, there's got to be a fully equipped hospital somewhere in this country! And send me another personnel carrier with an additional squad of men. Bring at least three or four dozen interlocking steel barricades. I need to secure this plaza against incoming vehicular and foot traffic."

"We copy that. Call it fifteen minutes inbound."

"I also need a paramedic team equipped for on-site injuries as well as contagious diseases, and I need them ASAP. If you can't get them, send me a crate of medical supplies and I'll figure out a way to get those to the crash site."

"Copy. The main Paramaribo hospital has been notified. Anything else?"

I need one more thing, Navarro thought. *I don't think she'll be pleased at my dragging her into this, but I'm at the end of my rope here.*

"Yeah, there is. I need you to escalate this to a November Charlie. Run it all the way up to the top of the leadership chain. Let them know the situation, and tell them one thing."

"Go ahead, Sierra One."

Navarro blew out a breath, as if gathering in his will.

"Tell them I need Doctor Leigh Austen down here in the next twenty-four hours," he said plainly. "Otherwise…we might be looking at a hell of a lot of dead people out here."

Michael Angel

CHAPTER SIX

Beacon Wood Gated Reserve
Estates Country Club
Potomac Falls, Virginia

The last notes from the grand piano lingered in the air as Joseph Widerman finished his piece with a little flourish. Leigh Austen and the other guests applauded enthusiastically, as Widerman had been a concert pianist before founding Whitespire Labs. The applause continued as he stood to adjust his yarmulke and prayer shawl. He then gestured to Austen, encouraging her to stand.

The applause swelled as she did so. Austen blushed to the roots of her shoulder-length auburn hair. In a sense, she'd been responsible for the melody they'd just heard. When Widerman had been accidentally exposed to the deadly Crucero virus, a split-second decision of hers had saved the man's left hand and his ability to play.

Even so, Widerman's experience had earned him a six-week stay in Stoney Lonesome, the nickname for the lab's medical isolation ward. His hot-zone level exposure required 24x7 care from nurses and doctors wearing Class 4 safety suits. In the case of his death, he'd have received a HEPA-filtered incineration, a ceremonial ash holder for his wife Elaine, and a page in his own company's 'Lessons Learned' manual.

Austen put that awful scenario out of her mind after the audience dispersed and the bat mitzvah after-party began in earnest. Widerman's thirteen-year old daughter had read flawlessly from the Torah earlier in the day. Afterwards, the entire entourage had left the synagogue and re-convened at Widerman's country club for a *kiddush* luncheon.

She wandered through the richly appointed hallways towards a dining table piled high with cold cuts, challah loaves, stuffed cabbage rolls, and a smoked fish platter in seven different mouthwatering shades of pink. Austen considered getting in line when she felt a pair of eyes on her.

She spotted a dapper-looking man gazing at her from across the room. Austen was a tall woman, and (according to Elaine Widerman) only five pounds too skinny to be attractive. Yet it wasn't all that unusual for a man to be eyeing her.

He had a pleasant face and bright eyes that could have belonged to a man anywhere from thirty to sixty years of age. His features were set off by a blond mustache trimmed to the same exacting standards as his crease-free khaki suit and pants. The man moved towards her, carrying himself with the unhurried gait of someone who came from old money.

"Doctor Austen, I presume?" the man asked. His voice carried the urbane British tones of a BBC newsman.

Austen gave him a wry look. "Well, I'm not Doctor Livingstone. And I don't think we've met before."

"We haven't until now. And I'm afraid that I must confess something." He leaned in slightly as he stage-whispered, "I'm a party-crasher."

"If you're from the CDC, then I'm not interested in working for–"

"The Centers for Disease Control and Prevention? Alas, I don't run a federal agency. I only work for them on occasion. To be honest, I represent a much less humanitarian organization."

Joseph Widerman came up to stand next to Austen. The man had a bony face dominated by a pair of tortoiseshell glasses. After his recent illness, Widerman's frame verged on frail. But his voice remained as strong as ever.

"Is everything all right, Leigh?" he asked pointedly.

"Everything's fine," she replied. "I was just chatting with this gentleman here."

"So I see." His eyes fixed on the newcomer. "I know every person here for my daughter's ceremony. Except one. Who might you be?"

The man made the slightest bow. "My name is Niles Bailey. I apologize for the intrusion, but I'm here to speak to Doctor Austen about something rather urgent. For some reason, I wasn't able to reach her by phone."

"Elaine and I asked that everyone leave their cell phones at home. If you have important business to discuss, please do it quietly."

Bailey flashed a quick smile. "We shall be as unassuming as church mice. Do join me, Doctor Austen."

With that, Bailey gently but firmly took Austen's arm. He steered her away from the table and towards the doors at the far end of the hall. His voice remained calm and jovial, but his words made the hair on the back of her neck stand on end.

"The 'urgent matter' I referred to involves a potential threat to world health. To be more precise, a potential *catastrophe*. It involves the country of Suriname. Are you familiar with the place?"

"I know it's in South America, just outside the Caribbean. When I was working for the CDC, my friend Daraja said it was one of the few places she wouldn't go."

"Did she give a reason?"

"She said that the coast was quite nice, but that the interior is as lawless as the Wild West."

"Yes, that happens when there is too much money to be made. And not enough morality to keep those making it in check."

"So, now there's an outbreak down there?"

"To be precise, it appears to have been a bioterrorist attack."

She stopped and stared at him for a moment. Her voice went up a notch.

"Then why are you coming to *me*? You need to get the WHO on this, and then the CDC!"

A couple of the guests turned curiously to look at them. Bailey nodded politely as they walked on by. "Please, Doctor Austen. A little more of the 'inside voice', if you would be so kind."

Austen felt herself blushing once more. "I'm sorry, Mister Bailey. It's just...in these cases, the local health officials are supposed to contact the World Health Organization before anything else can happen."

"The local health officials you speak of were the ones injured in the attack. And as for pulling the fire alarm on our own, things get a little more complicated. I felt that a private contractor could handle things better and contain the outbreak on their own."

Austen's voice went flat. "You're asking *me* to step up for this, aren't you?"

"I need a field epidemiologist. Someone experienced in handling emergent diseases outside of a laboratory. And someone who wouldn't mind making a substantial sum of money in the process."

Bailey whispered a sum in her ear. It was enough to pay off the mountain of loans she'd taken out to finish college and graduate school. And yet, all the offer did was firm up her resolve.

Austen knew how badly a field team could fare in an unstable or war-torn country. Her mind flitted back to the outbreak of Black Nile in Africa. The stench of bodies that had greeted her when she'd arrived. The sight of the entire medical team wiped out by the killer virus.

Her insides chilled as she thought of more recent memories. The dusty wastes of Central Asia. The staggering depths of an open pit mine. Being engulfed in the alien embrace of a horrific life form responsible for wiping out the dinosaurs.

She shook her head. "I barely got out of my last overseas assignment alive. I'm not about to chance repeating that experience, thank you very much. The answer is *no*."

"Then you should know more details about the incident," Bailey went on. "Early this morning, a medical helicopter was shot down in the city of Hoogeveen. The three surviving physicians were sprayed with an unknown pathogenic compound, infecting both the doctors and the team sent in to rescue them. Among the infected is a gentleman by the name of John Redhawk. I believe that you know him from an incident in Ozrabek, Kazakhstan."

Austen's throat went dry. She had to swallow before answering. "I know him."

"His condition, as well as the other people involved, has already deteriorated rapidly. Mister Redhawk's commander specifically asked for you. He feels that you are the only person able to save his friend. That commander is Nicholas Navarro."

"Nick?" The name fell from her lips like a gasp.

"Yes, that would be the colloquial version of the name 'Nicholas'. He asked for you in part because you earned his trust during the Ozrabek incident. It remains to be seen if that trust was correctly given."

Austen looked away for a moment before answering.

"For a proper British gentleman, you sure fight dirty."

Bailey's eyes didn't leave hers. "Indeed. Will you come? I can get you to Suriname before the sun sets, but only if we leave promptly."

"By sunset? How are you going to–" She blinked as the man's name finally sank in. "Niles Bailey. You're one of the two founding partners of Nick's 'private security' firm, aren't you?"

"I have that dubious honor."

"I'm a little surprised," she admitted. "No offense, but you run what many people would call a mercenary army and private air force. And yet you look...rather ordinary."

"Not everything is like in the movies. Which is unfortunate, as I'd like to wear an eye patch. That way, if Hollywood makes a film about my life, I should hope they hire Samuel Jackson to play me."

"All right," Austen finally said. "Count me in. I'll need more details about the attack and Redhawk's condition, for a start. And I need to know who else I can bring in as support."

"There is time enough to fill you in during your journey," Bailey said, as they came to the end of the hall. "Our ride is here."

He held open the front door and they emerged into the bright sunlight. Widerman's party guests came running to the windows as an impossibly sleek helicopter appeared over the treetops. It extended a triple set of wheels and landed in the parking lot. The three-pointed Mercedes star gleamed from the polished silver fuselage.

Austen raised an eyebrow. "Not everything is like in the movies?"

She got a shrug in return from Niles Bailey.

"Very well, *some* things are like in the movies. Do indulge me."

With that, he escorted her towards the waiting aircraft.

CHAPTER SEVEN

The helicopter hurtled across the sky at a speed that turned the Virginian countryside into a gray-green blur. Bailey motioned for Austen to slip on a pair of headphones so that they could talk easily over the whine of the aircraft's rotors.

"We don't normally travel this speed at low altitude," Bailey said. His voice sounded rich and smooth even through the headphones. "Not without good reason. In your case, you'll need the extra time to get to Dulles International."

"You're not taking me directly to the airport?" Austen asked, surprised.

"I'd have *preferred* to bring you there. However, Nicholas Navarro was very insistent that we drop you off at your personal residence. Would you have any idea why?"

Austen did her best to maintain a poker face as Bailey asked his question.

She wasn't all that sure about Niles Bailey. But when she'd first met Navarro, the big man inspired her trust. She'd trusted him with one of her closest secrets, and here was proof that he'd kept his word.

Bailey doesn't know about DiCaprio, she realized. *And Nick knows that I've got to try and reach him, no matter what.*

DiCaprio was a very strange, very useful 'gift' from Austen's uncle, Senator Bainbridge. She thought of DiCaprio as a 'he', but she really had no idea if DiCaprio was male or female, let alone who he worked for. All Austen knew was that whatever question she sent to DiCaprio, she'd get an answer.

That answer might be hard to understand at first. Sometimes, it was couched in fortune-cookie style riddles. But DiCaprio had never been wrong. *Ever.* Because of that, Austen found herself relying on this personal oracle more than she cared to admit.

Austen realized that Bailey was waiting for an answer to his question. She blinked and gave him the first explanation that came to mind.

"Nick's right, I've got to stop at my house first. I've got certain tools and protective gear I want to pick up. It's more for luck than anything else. Field epidemiologists are quirky like that."

Bailey gave her a skeptical look. "I'm finding it hard to believe that a profession steeped in science relies on...well, it seems like rank superstition."

"And just how many people from my profession have you worked with?"

A dry laugh. "Touché, Doctor Austen."

He reached into a compartment, pulled out a black leather folder and handed it to her. "This contains the information you shall need."

Austen opened it. One of the folder's pockets came pre-stuffed with business cards and documents. The other held a number of documents, the top sheet listing out her flight plan. A Boeing 737 would take her from Dulles to Puerto Rico. From there, she'd board a cargo transport plane bound for Hoogeveen City in Suriname.

"The business card on the top left lists the number for a limo service," Bailey instructed. "They'll be transporting you to the airport as soon as you call them. You have three hours to get there from when we drop you off."

Austen nodded. "That gives me plenty of time."

"Not as much as you'd think. The next card down lists the name, location, and entry code for a secure network pod I've reserved for you at the Dulles International Terminal."

"A network pod? What do I need—"

"You'll be downloading files on the current situation in Suriname and the nature of the attack." Bailey glanced out the window for a moment before continuing. "Afterwards, go ahead and get hold of the personnel you want to join your field team. M&B will cover the cost of transportation and pay them seventy percent of the hourly salary I quoted you."

"It's short notice, but with what you're paying I should be able to find someone."

"Good. Once in Suriname, let me know if you need medical supplies and equipment. But I should warn you in advance that I won't be able to get you everything you need. Perhaps not even much of it."

Her brow furrowed. "That seems...odd. Especially coming from someone who can hire support personnel and transport aircraft from half a hemisphere away."

Bailey let out a long-suffering sigh. "As I alluded to earlier, I represent a less than humanitarian organization. Are you familiar with the term *ROE*?"

She shook her head.

"That is a document stating the Rules of Engagement when it comes to military conflict. Organizations like mine are placed under strict contracts – ROEs, if you will – when hired by the United States government. Specifically, those parts of the government which prefer to remain in the background."

"I once heard these areas called 'Gray Zones'," Austen said. "Areas where intelligence services are doing things they don't want the average person to know about."

"Then Suriname is in the grayest of those zones. The country has become a hub for drug cartels and smugglers bringing across all sorts of nasty things across international borders. The State Department has, like a good chess player, positioned a counter-force project in the area called 'Deep Six'."

"To 'Deep Six' something means to bury it," Austen observed wryly. "Someone at State has a sense of humor."

"Indeed. My company's ROE centers around protecting this asset and to keep it from prying eyes. We're not about to bring in anything that would make the World Health Organization's medical investigators sit up and take notice."

"You're saying that bringing in the WHO would shine a little too much light down there." Austen frowned. "If so, then I don't like it. You'd be gambling with hundreds or even thousands of lives. A possible pandemic's not worth keeping your pet project a secret."

"Doctor Austen," Bailey said sternly, "I must remind you that this is *not* my pet project, nor my rules. I don't like this any more than you. As it is, I'm skating on the thinnest of ice just by revealing the presence of Deep Six to you. And by bringing you down to identify and stop this biological agent quietly, before it becomes a serious problem."

"And if I'm unable to do that?"

"Then I might have to ask you to bend your own rules, just as I've bent mine. For example, if you cannot save the infected, then a swift and graphic demise of some of your patients might be in our best interests."

Her eyes widened at that. "What the hell are you saying?"

"I can't bring in the WHO without violating the terms of my contract." Bailey continued. "Perhaps you can, but only if the Surinamese government allows it. And that will be difficult without dead bodies on the ground."

"You must be joking. Tell me you're joking!"

Bailey shook his head. "Billions of dollars in drugs and illegal goods find their way across this area, Doctor Austen. Hoogeveen is also a stopping point for most of the Caribbean cruise lines. The local governor isn't about to jeopardize either of those revenue streams."

"Surely they can't be that stupid—"

"Doctor Austen, when bribe money flows as easily as water from a tap, only the instinct for self-preservation can best it. Your specter of a bioterror outbreak will be more convincing with dead bodies, not suffering patients."

Austen couldn't help but stare for a moment. Niles Bailey's suggestion repulsed her.

The helicopter slowed to a hover and lowered its tri-wheeled landing gear. That was followed by a dull *bump* as it touched down in the traffic roundabout down the street from Austen's home.

"I don't think you want to know what I think of you right now," she finally said.

"Whether you think I'm a devil or a saint, I only speak the truth. A few deaths now might save more people later."

She had nothing to say to that. Instead, she slipped off her headphones, unlocked the aircraft's passenger door, and disembarked. Several of her neighbors emerged from their homes and watched in astonishment as the helicopter sitting in their traffic circle took off again.

Austen jogged towards her house, only stopping as she reached the front door. She groped for her keys even as her mind continued to run full tilt.

I'll be damned if I let anyone die if I'm able to save them, she thought furiously. *God help me if it ever comes to that.*

No, another part of her mind corrected her. *If it comes to that, God help us all.*

She unlocked the door, pushed her way in, and made her way towards the study. There, she'd log into a terminal safeguarded by an encryption device that cost more than she made in year. It was the only place in the world she could contact DiCaprio and ask for his advice.

Austen let out a *squeak* of surprise as she entered the study.

Her computer screen wasn't in its dimly lit screensaver mode. It displayed a two-line text message in a simple white square.

YOU HAVE A CONTACT FROM THE USERNAME: DICAPRIO.

WOULD YOU LIKE TO READ THIS MESSAGE: YES/NO?

Michael Angel

CHAPTER EIGHT

The airport tram came to an abrupt stop as it reached the International Flights terminal. A pair of frosted glass doors slid open, allowing Leigh Austen to exit. She adjusted her denim travel jacket and double-checked the information from a card in the black folder.

She turned down one of the alcoves off the main concourse. A series of oval structures roughly double the size of a walk-in closet sat inside a gated area labeled *ZippyTel Office Pods – Work in Style!*

Austen went up to one of the pods, which had a numerical touchpad and a screen flashing the words *OPEN FOR BUSINESS*. She tapped in the code listed on one of the cards Bailey had given her. A small door swung open with the hiss of compressed air. Inside lay a small but well-equipped miniature office space, with an array of computer screens and every teleconferencing system she'd yet seen on the conference circuit.

"Okay, this is interesting," she remarked to herself, as she stepped inside.

The door closed automatically behind her. The sounds of the busy terminal outside vanished as if someone had turned off a switch. She settled into the chair before the screens, its contours holding her like a glove made of butter-soft leather.

I've got *to get one of these,* Austen thought, as she stretched out comfortably. *Then again, I might fall asleep in this thing unless I get to work.*

Using the directions printed on a sheet in Bailey's folder, she logged into the computer and proceeded to call up the information on the bioterrorist attack. As she did so, the lights in the pod thoughtfully dimmed so that she could see the monitor's images better.

Whoever had done the report for M&B had been extremely thorough. The crystal-sharp text included links for her to read on the history of Suriname and the current problems facing Hoogeveen City. Many issues were being solved (or made worse, depending on how one read the report) by the current Provincial Governor, Daan de Murken.

At least three major drug cartels were known to be operating out of Hoogeveen, with the Viezeman, Waalwijk, and Arakaka Cartels dominating the *kinetic* forms of urban crime. Austen frowned as she came across the term. It was a remarkably sanitary way to call something *violent* without sounding too scary. Bureaucrats in epidemiological science sometimes called those killed from epidemic disease *metabolically challenged.*

It left a sour taste in her mouth.

The report then detailed the events of the attack earlier that morning. Hoogeveen MedFlight 3209 was making its tri-weekly run transporting medical personnel across the city when it had been shot down, likely by an anti-aircraft missile. The event left two dead and three injured, one critically.

Austen sat up. Now things started getting interesting.

One survivor reported being sprayed by an unknown substance. Squad Leader Redhawk had notified Navarro, who cordoned off the scene until a barrier system had been put in place. It had taken two solid hours to set up a secure form of transport to bring the three survivors and the six members of Redhawk's squad to a medical isolation ward.

"Secure form of transport?" Austen said to herself. "What the hell does that even mean? What level of secure isolation did they set up? And how did they decon the crash site?"

What she read next moved from disturbing into the realms of the impossible.

All nine patients began reporting a creeping numbness. It started with their outer extremities and then progressed to their limbs. Partial paralysis was reported among the three injured medical personnel only three hours after the attack. Similar weaknesses began affecting Redhawk's men shortly thereafter.

Austen's heart sank as she scrolled through a whole list of growing symptoms. Persistent nausea. Vomiting, with signs of elevated bile production. Shooting pains with no visible wounds.

"This can't be something biological," she muttered. "The speed...what the hell creates symptoms like these so fast?"

Finally, she found what she was looking for, clearly stated in black and white. M&B hadn't included more than basic protective equipment in case of a biological attack. Yet they did have swabs to test for common substances used in chemical attacks, from chlorine residue to nerve gas. All tests came up blank.

Except for the extreme speed, the symptoms pointed to a biological weapon. Chemical weapons were brutally simple in their lethality. There was no subtlety to their effects.

The corrosion of mucous membranes took place in an instant. Lungs burned from the inside out. The jellied surfaces of the eyeball melted. Skin bubbled up and sloughed off like loose bark off red-fleshed tree limbs.

Still, she had to rule out all the possibilities. And she had to find out who could join her on ridiculously short notice.

Austen ran her hands through her hair as her mind ran through her list of possibilities. In the meantime, she dug in her pocket and brought out her key ring. A miniature flash drive sat next to the house keys. She plugged it into an available port and downloaded all the information she'd been given.

Activating the speakerphone system, she dialed in the first number on her list. The phone rang several times before going over to voicemail. The same thing happened for the next number she called. Finally, she got an answer on the third number.

"Well, if this doesn't take the biscuit!" Doctor Edward Preble exclaimed. "I didn't recognize the number. You're not still at work, are you?"

Austen relaxed as she heard her friend's warm, impeccably British tones over the speaker. Preble was a longtime friend of hers, and one of the world's best toxicologists. Since it was mid-evening in London, she'd been gambling that he'd be home.

"No, nothing like that. Things just got a little more…well, complicated over here on this side of the pond."

"Oh, dear. The last time I heard you say those words, everything was about to go pear-shaped over a new breakout disease."

She let out a tired sigh. "You might not be far off the mark, Ted."

Austen briefly described the events in Hoogeveen City, walking through the timeline and the symptoms observed. Preble restricted himself to only the most basic of questions until the very end.

"Bloody hell," he finally said. "You could be describing symptoms of everything from lead to mercury poisoning. Even the speed the symptoms are manifesting fit a mixture of toxic metal exposures. Is there any heavy industry based out of Suriname?"

"I'll double-check, but the M&B files are pretty detailed. Aside from illegal drug smuggling and some back-country mining, Suriname's main moneymaker is tourism."

"And the tests performed by M&B's people came back negative as well. Think you can perform those again, double-check the results?"

"Actually, I was hoping you could come and do that in person, Ted."

"Leigh, you know that I'd drop whatever I had in hand to come running," Preble said. "But I'd be nine-tenths hindrance to you and only one part help right now. Mister Parkinson and I are still locked in our deadly dance together, you know."

Austen knew. Ted had come down with Parkinson's Disease only a few years ago, and the degree it affected him continued to mount. When they'd last worked together, he'd had trouble walking without a cane.

"How bad is it?" she asked.

"Things seemed to be getting better around the holidays. Then they turned on a five-pence last week. I took a tumble. Now I've got a leg in a cast *and* a bloody awful looking orthopedic boot. Neither of which are going to be helpful out in the field."

"Ted, I won't ask you to come out with me," Austen finally said. "But perhaps you'd be willing to review any results I come up with?"

"Of course, so long as you have access to some kind of communication better than smoke signals. What else can I do to help?"

"Would you know of anyone who could join me in the field in a hurry? As in, dropping everything right now and running for the airport kind of hurry?"

Preble blew out a breath. "As a matter of fact, there might be. I just spoke with a very nice young lady named Emily Piper. She's a former grad student of mine. Background in pathology. She was pursuing an advanced degree in tropical diseases at Dade University in Miami."

"What do you mean, 'was' pursuing?"

"She ran afoul of some of the university's bylaws," Preble said carefully. "That's why we were talking – she wanted to ask if I could provide a professorial reference. Because she's looking for a job instead of schooling."

"I can't be too picky. If she's got the background I need,

then I want her on the next plane to Suriname." Austen passed on the charge codes from Motte & Bailey's folder. "If she's looking for experience and a chance to earn some cash, this could be her ticket."

"She'll take it," Preble assured her. "Something tells me that she might even find it fun."

Great, Austen thought. *All that tells me is that Emily Piper hasn't done any fieldwork yet.*

A three-tone chime sounded in the little office pod.

"Attention," said a sultry female voice, "You now have ten minutes to arrive at the boarding area for your outbound flight to San Juan, Puerto Rico."

"That's my plane," Austen said. "I've got to go. Cross your fingers that this grad student takes us up on the offer."

"Of that you can be sure. Safe flight, contact me when you need my help."

She shut down the line, disconnected her flash drive, and stuck it in her pocket. Then she pressed the button to open the exit door. The sounds of the busy terminal flooded in with a rush of noise.

Austen took a breath, as if she were about to plunge into deep water. Then she strode out to blend in with the busy mass of people as she rushed to make her flight.

CHAPTER NINE

Surinamese Rainforest
Suriname – Guyana Border Zone

The mist hung about the compound like a sodden blanket. It was comfortingly warm, but that was where the good qualities ended. It rusted out metal catwalks. It contaminated processing equipment with mold. Worst of all, it made Erich Zann's collar stick to the back of his neck, which irritated him to no end.

The manufacturing staff kept the machinery noise to a minimum. His personal servants scurried out of the way or kept their eyes averted from his at these times. People at the plant knew that an irritated Zann meant bad things.

Unhealthy things.

In fact, three solid weeks of mist had made things downright *lethal*.

Zann let out a breath and dropped back down into his combat stance. It came second nature to him. He and his brother had grown up as a back-alley scrappers on Rotterdam's brownstone streets. He'd enforced deals and broken the odd kneecap or two for the local drug kingpins. He'd even boxed for a living throughout the former Soviet fiefdoms in Eastern Europe. All the while, he'd risen through the ranks of criminal enterprises until he'd come out on top.

He'd kept up his fighter's build. With all the mist, he hadn't lacked for exercise.

Zann moved forward. Hand clenched around the flexible band of his protective wraps. He slammed his fists into the punching bag with a series of sharp, crisp punches. Each impact made an eye-wincing *whap!* or a tooth-rattling *crunch!* as if his arms and hands were solid rods of steel.

Three people remained inside Zann's personal training room as he worked out his frustrations, hitting the bag ever more viciously as the minutes wore on. Two were security guards, who watched impassively from the doorway. The third wore a researcher's white coat and a singularly glum expression. He stood close by the swinging bag, looking ever more alarmed as the session went on.

"You know what I detest the most about this mist?" Zann remarked, as sweat glistened off his muscled upper torso. "Any idea at all, Doctor Tiwari?"

"I…I had heard that it was the way it made your collar stick to your neck," the poor man ventured.

"No. It's not that." Zann punctuated each sentence with another vicious punch to the bag. "It's. The damn. Noise. From the creatures outside."

"The noise?" Tiwari's square-rimmed glasses threatened to slide off his nose. He pushed them back up and did his best to ignore the stains that began soaking through the bottom of the punching bag. "But there's nothing I can do—"

"I disagree." Zann finished off his workout with a last flurry of blows. He motioned for Tiwari to follow him towards the room's outside window. "Don't you hear it?"

Even through the thick glass, it was audible. From out in the mist came the sounds of hungry predators snarling, howling, and hissing.

"Yes. I hear it."

"They're out there, baying for blood. Your work was

responsible. I want you to find a way to keep them quiet."

Tiwari knew better than to argue. "I'll need to get back to my lab."

"That's a good man. I like a positive attitude."

The doctor swallowed hard. "I need more personnel to do what you want."

"Really? Then perhaps you had better stop disappointing me."

Zann nodded to his men. They went over to the punching bag, which now dripped a thick, viscous red from the bottom. One steadied the bag while the other tugged at the zipper running down the length of one side.

A broken human form slumped out of the bag and landed on the padded floor with a boneless *plap*. Blood streamed from the nose, mouth, and ears of a face beaten to a formless pulp. One of the guards pressed fingers to the form's neck for a moment. He looked up and shook his head.

"How about that," Zann remarked. "It looks like you *are* short-handed in the lab again."

Tiwari made a sound close to a sob.

"Only my respect for your work has kept you out of the bag," Zann went on. "That, and my recent good mood. The first phase of the plan seems to be on schedule, and your work was in part responsible. You may thank me now."

"Thank you," came the dutiful reply.

"Yet, since your recent lab work has been so shoddy, you cannot remain completely unpunished. I'm giving you a new chore, starting today." Zann pointed down into the courtyard below. Even at a short distance it was hard to see through the moisture condensed on the window pane. "There is a barrel of wet food down there. Offal from our kitchens. Drag it to the gates and shovel it to the mob of creatures outside. You will complete this task at least twice per day from now on."

"But Mister Zann," Tiwari lifted his spindly arms. "I can hardly drag something so heavy."

Zann turned away from the window. He grabbed his shirt in one hand, a towel in the other. He spoke offhandedly to

Tiwari over his shoulder.

"You shall find a way, I'm sure. Go. Now."

Shaking, the doctor moved towards the exit. The two guards watched his fear with scarcely concealed amusement.

"Oh, and one more thing."

"Yes, sir?"

Zann's voice went as cold as ice. "No more objections. Otherwise, instead of serving the wet food...I'll make sure your next assistant gets to *be* the wet food."

Tiwari fled out the door to the sound of the guards' rough laughter.

CHAPTER TEN

Hoogeveen Regional Airport
Republic of Suriname

The pilot brought his plane down on the runway as if he were trying to stamp his name on the battered asphalt. Austen winced at the teeth-rattling *BUMP* and felt her lap strain against the worn safety belt. The plane shot along the length of the runway and pulled up within a hundred yards of a dilapidated freight terminal.

The pilot barely turned his head to shout at her. "*Kom op! Ga weg!* No time! You, get off, now!"

"Right," Austen muttered, as she undid her belt and grabbed her lone suitcase. "Thanks for flying a-hole airlines, please come again."

She made sure to exit out the rear door of the twin-engine Viking Otter, as the pilot kept the propellers running. She shuffled her way past boxes, piled auto parts, and a rack of Sebright banty hens. During the trip, the pint-sized chickens kept up a steady stream of aggravated *squawks* with each mid-air bounce or jolt.

A group of sweaty uniformed men trundled up in one of

the airport tugs. They began unloading the plane and tossing boxes into an attached luggage bin. The pilot leaned out the window of the plane and urged them on with some choice swear words.

Austen picked up her bag and made her way towards the main passenger terminal. The setting sun's reflection made all the terminal's windows look as if they were ablaze. She raised a hand to shield her eyes from the glare and made out a makeshift customs area that had been set up under a raised tarpaulin.

A series of rope barriers hung between stanchions had been set up to channel people into a snake queue. But there was only one other person in line, and she was busy berating the customs agent as he went through her bag. Austen walked around the empty queue area, taking note of the pair.

The customs official was a sleepy-eyed man who absently pawed through the open suitcase. He said nothing but quietly rubbed his thumb and forefinger, as if expecting a bribe. The woman on the other side of the desk ignored the gesture. Instead, she kept glancing at her phone and reading phrases off the screen.

The woman was young and on the tall side. Her body was made up of bony angles under a set of cargo pants and a sleeveless tee shirt. Austen noted the shirt's *MERV 20 OR BUST!* logo, and then reflected on what she saw.

That looks like me at nineteen, she thought. *Only I didn't go in for the pink highlights.*

The hair in question had been shaved down to the scalp along the left side of the woman's skull. On the right, she'd let it grow out into a mane that swept down to her shoulder. Embedded in her light brown hair were strawberry-colored stripes.

"*Déjame hablar con tu jefe,*" she complained. "*Ahora!*"

Austen set her suitcase down before walking right up to the customs desk.

"Excuse me," Austen said, before pointing between herself and the young woman. "*Medisch. Ik en haar.* Okay?"

The man's sleepy eyelids rose a jot at that.

"*Het spijt me*," came the reply. The man nodded to each them before retreating from his desk and heading back into the terminal.

"You must be Emily Piper," Austen said, as she turned her attention to the woman. She extended a hand. "Doctor Leigh Austen. Thanks for coming on such short notice."

"Um, sure!" Piper shook the proffered hand. "Thanks for the assist, Doctor Austen. How did you know that guy didn't speak Spanish? And come to think of it, how did you know who I was?"

"First off, just call me Leigh. As for what to say, I know a little bit of Dutch. Suriname's technically in Latin America, but it's the only part settled by the Netherlands. I just told him that you and I were doctors, here to help the sick."

"I, ah, just go by Piper." The younger woman put her phone away and shook her head in disgust. "So much for the Latin America language app."

"As for who you were," Austen continued, "your tee-shirt told me. MERV-20 is a measure of air purification, the type used in hospital clean rooms. Who else but a medical person would even get that kind of joke?"

"I guess I get to play Watson to your Sherlock Holmes, then," Piper said. "Color me impressed."

"Watson or Holmes, I'm going to need all of your deductive reasoning to help me identify our bug here," Austen pointed out. "Did Preble fill you in on the details of what we're facing?"

"Ted passed on everything that you told him, at least. I still don't understand why we're not taking this to the WHO right away."

"Yeah, that gets into some of the gray areas of what we're doing, and who we're involved with," Austen admitted. "I hear that it's like this country we're in now. Things get a little tricky."

"Gray or not, I needed this job. I'm just glad you chose me for this."

Just as Piper finished speaking, Austen heard the *pok pok* of semi-automatic weapons fire. She immediately dropped to her knees, squatting by the shelter provided by the customs desk. Piper hesitated until Austen grabbed her arm, yanking the younger woman down next to her.

A squad of green-and-red clad security guards emerged from the terminal behind them. They brought their weapons to bear as the pilot of the twin-engine Otter gunned his motor and swung his plane around in a tight circle. The cargo handlers dashed for cover and trundled off in their tug.

That explains why the pilot acted the way he did, Austen realized. *This is what the military would call a* hot *landing zone.*

Glancing around quickly, Austen spotted where the initial gunfire came from. Several black-clad men had dismounted from a pickup truck along the far side of the runway. Their target wasn't the terminal, but a smaller single-engine plane taxiing on the nearby tarmac. The muzzles of their assault rifles blazed a brilliant red as they unloaded on both the plane and the men opposing them.

The recently unloaded Otter managed to claw its way into the sky. Gunfire continued between the terminal's security guards and the attackers from the truck. Piper peeked out from behind the desk. She stared transfixed as a wisp of smoke came from the smaller aircraft still on the ground. Two men next to the plane ran for their lives as the plane burst into flame with a chest-sucking *WHUMP!*

"I did *not* sign up for this!" Piper shouted, her voice on the edge of panic. "No one told me that I'd be getting shot at!"

You'd be surprised how often that happens in this line of work, Austen thought.

Aloud, she said, "They're not gunning for us! Just stay low for right now!"

Suddenly, she heard a new sound. The grumbling whine of yet another approaching airport tug. The low-slung vehicle pulled to a stop in front of the customs area, putting its bulk between the two women and the raging gunfight.

The driver's side window slid down. A huge man with a

blocky head and bushy cocoa-brown eyebrows peered out at them. He extended a hairy, well-muscled arm in a beckoning gesture.

"*Vot vy dvoye!*" the man declared, in a deep bass voice. He switched from Russian to slightly fractured English as he continued. "What are you waiting for? Written invitation? Get in!"

Michael Angel

CHAPTER ELEVEN

Austen recognized both the man's face and voice in an instant.

"October!" she exclaimed.

Piper looked astounded. "You know this guy?"

"Yes, and he's our ticket out of here. Come on!"

The two women grabbed their bags and ran to the waiting airport tug. They piled into the rear compartment of the vehicle's cab, doing their best to stay low as the gunfire across the tarmac continued. October mashed the drive pedal underfoot as soon as he heard them close the door.

"*Bozhe moi!*" he cursed, as a stray bullet deflected off the front passenger side window, spiderwebbing the glass.

A few seconds more, and the tug made it out of the free-fire zone and around the corner of the main terminal building. October didn't let up on the drive pedal. The tug's electric motor squeaked and hummed in protest as he brought the vehicle into the shadow of an outlying storage shed. He parked it next to a dull gray armored truck and shut off the motor.

"Okay," he announced. "We have better ride now. More comfortable. For me, anyway."

Austen got out, but she couldn't help but watch as October

shifted and squeezed his bulky frame out of the confines of the tug's tiny driver's compartment. The big man had been forced to drive the vehicle with his knees resting high up on the dashboard.

"*Eto bylo uzhasno*," he grumbled. "Now I know what caviar feels like inside tin."

Austen couldn't help but grin. "It's good to see you, October."

"That is double for me." The Russian swept her up in a bear hug that would've done a grizzly credit. "No, is *triple* for me. We survive the drop of Thor's Hammer together!"

"Thor's Hammer?" Piper asked, as she shakily stepped down from the tug's cabin. "You mean you two survived something worse than what we just left?"

Austen tried to reply, but October's friendly grasp made it difficult to breathe. She heard a truck's cab door opening and closing, then the sound of a second familiar voice.

"Hey, big guy," the voice said. "Don't forget, Leigh's still going to need those ribs when you're done greeting her."

"Ha!" October let out a baritone laugh as he put Austen down. "Do not worry, Nicholas. *Semeynoy* Austen means more than *kletska* and vodka put together."

"More than vodka and dumplings? Well, that's higher than I'm ever going to rate with you." Navarro admitted, before turning to Austen. "It's good to see you again, Leigh."

She hesitated, but only for a moment. "Likewise, Nick. It's been a little while, hasn't it?"

"It has. Wish the reunion was under better circumstances."

"You and me both." Austen gestured between her three companions. "Emily, this is Nicholas Navarro, the lead military contractor for Motte & Bailey down here. October Shtormovoy is his Ground Perimeter Security Specialist. Nick, October, this is Emily Piper. She's got a background in pathology and tropical diseases. Ted Preble recommended that she join me down here."

"*Dobryj vecher*," October said, nodding towards the young woman.

"I, ah, just go by my last name," Piper said, in a steadier voice. "No 'doctor' or anything. At least for now."

Navarro nodded his approval. "Preble's recommendation is a damned good credential in my book. Leigh, is Ted joining us too?"

"Not in person," Austen answered. "But if we've got a network connection, he can consult remotely."

"That's something, anyway. Let's go, we've got to get back to our Green Zone." Navarro led them over to the truck and slid the side door open. "Welcome to M&B's taxi service."

Austen and Piper quickly climbed aboard. Navarro went around to the passenger side of the cab, while October elected to drive again. This time, the big Russian was able to slide the seat back enough to fit comfortably. He started the engine and eased the truck out onto the road leading away from the terminal and into Hoogeveen City proper.

The younger woman craned her neck to look out one of the armored windows. She spotted the column of smoke from the plane set on fire by the gunfight. She only caught a quick glimpse of the runway. While the shooting had stopped and she didn't see any bodies, the plane simply sat on the tarmac, blazing away with no one to put it out.

"Yeah, I have to ask about this," Piper finally said. "Maybe all three of you are used to getting stuck in the middle of a firefight, but it's a new experience for me. What the hell just happened back at that airport?"

October let out a grunt. "Is obvious. One group of people wanted another group dead. Why else bother shooting at each other?"

"Outside our Green Zone, this part of Suriname is run either by government troops or gunmen from one of the cartels," Navarro elaborated, as October turned down one of the main boulevards. "It's possible that the pilot of that plane didn't bribe the right people to use that runway. Maybe one of the cartels didn't want something on that flight to arrive."

"But...that's the flight I came in on," Piper said timidly. "Were they after *me*?"

"Don't take this the wrong way," Austen pointed out, "but neither of us rate high enough for the cartel to take notice. Or care, for that matter."

"I'm not so sure about that," Navarro put in. "Piper, what was your flight's number?"

"Just a sec," she replied, as she dug in a pocket of her cargo pants and pulled out a ticket stub. "Flight 733. I caught it out of Trinidad."

"Interesting," October rumbled. "Could be chance."

Navarro shook his head. "Once is chance. Twice is a warning. Three times, and you better start shooting back."

"What are you talking about?" Austen demanded.

"That flight carried all the equipment and protective gear I'd ordered brought in from out-of-country. I'd placed that order because the truck carrying what we needed from Paramaribo's main hospital was hijacked en route to Hoogeveen."

Austen sat up straight at that. "What about Hoogeveen's local supplies? The Red Cross had a trauma clinic out here."

"Those supplies were on the bird the cartels shot down," Navarro said grimly. "Whatever wasn't destroyed during the crash is in ashes now. We had to burn the wreckage in order to sterilize the site. There was no other way."

She gave him a look. "Nick, you're telling me that we're on the hunt for a dangerous microorganism...and we've got *no protective gear?*"

Navarro's face reddened. "We have face masks. And gloves."

Piper slumped back in her seat and let out a groan. "I did *not* sign up for this."

Austen said nothing as Hoogeveen City loomed up ever closer in the truck's bulletproof windshield.

CHAPTER TWELVE

The up-armored truck arrived at Hoogeveen City's harbor in the middle of the last thing Austen would have expected: a raucous party.

October pulled into a covered parking space painted to look like a tiki hut and placed the truck in park. Austen slid open the side door. The smells of fresh coconut and grilled shrimp filled the air, as did the lilting sounds of calypso music.

Across an expanse of grass studded with palm trees lay a cheerfully decorated plaza, packed to the gills with people. Beyond the plaza, a wide wood-and-concrete pier jutted out into the harbor. Long white cruise ships from multiple lines were docked along the pier like luxury cars in a dealer's showroom.

"To answer your next question," Navarro said, as he opened his door, "You're looking at Hoogeveen City's number-one legal source of revenue. Tourism."

"You've got to be kidding," Piper remarked. "I guess we should've come by boat, not plane."

"The cruise ship terminal's a 'hands off' area for the cartels and smugglers. An attack here would piss off about a dozen countries, bringing more heat than anyone wants to

Hoogeveen."

Austen watched a couple moments longer. People lined up for dinner served straight from makeshift gas grills or danced under the purple tropical twilight. Musicians cranked out music from steel drums even as lines of somewhat-sober people wobbled their way back up the cruise ship gangways.

"You answered the first of my questions," Austen said, as she got out. "But I do have more. For starters, what are we doing here?"

October chuckled. "She is not going to be liking the answer."

"Hey, it was the best we could do." Navarro turned back to Austen and pointed to one last cruise ship, docked by itself along an adjoining wharf. "That's the *Stella Maris*. She clipped a reef a few months ago, damaged one of her propellers. The cruise line reduced personnel to a skeleton crew. Then they parked her here for the rest of the year until they straighten out the insurance claims. I got M&B to commandeer the vessel and turn her into a floating isolation ward."

Piper stared at him. "Are you nuts? That thing is docked a hundred yards at the most from crowds of people!"

"We moved our injured and infected people here in a secure truck, like this one. They were brought on board before the party got under way. The vehicle was washed down in bleach afterwards. All the portholes below deck are locked tight, and access to the ship is controlled by my men. That's all we could do."

"You did good," Austen said, considering. "Pretty darned good, actually."

"It is?" Piper's brow furrowed. "I mean, it's just a big *boat*."

Austen shook her head. "It's a medical center now, not a boat. A center surrounded by water, self-contained, and with limited physical access. Those are all pluses in my book, but I've got one more concern, Nick."

"All right," came his reply. "Shoot."

"The windows – the 'portholes', in this case – they're secure. But what about the ship's ventilation system?"

"The exteriors vents are just basic carbon-weave. But the interior ones that feed into them are HEPA filtered."

"Then we're not going to be venting contaminants anywhere near that crowd," Austen said, satisfied. "What about medical care? If the only medical people around are among the wounded, who's taking care of them? Especially if we're short on protective gear?"

"I guess you could say we got lucky. McCall, one of Redhawk's riflemen, is a former paramedic. He's already among the infected, so he wasn't so worried about the shortage of protective gear. But he's going downhill, fast."

Austen pursed her lips and thought for a moment. "All right. No matter the risk, I've got to see what's going on with our patients."

"Great," Piper said, as she prepared to step out of the truck. "Can't say I'm looking forward to this, but I'll head in with you."

"No, you won't be going in with me."

The younger woman flipped back her shag of tinted hair and gave her a defiant look. "As if! Look, I'm new to this, but you're going to need an extra pair of hands–"

"I need your extra pair of hands elsewhere."

"Oh, come on!"

Austen ignored the objection. "October, has M&B been operating down here a while? Long enough to have some kind of forward operations base?"

"Is classified subject," October replied. "Am not supposed to say 'six months'. Or that we have well stocked 'forward base'."

"We've got supplies and housing for up to a hundred contractors at any given time," Navarro agreed. "What do you have in mind, Leigh?"

"Piper, I want you and October to head for that base. Start going through M&B's inventory of cleaning supplies. Clothing. Kitchen supplies. Even the motor pool."

"All right," Piper said sullenly. "I don't get it, though."

"When you're in the field, you've got to improvise. And

you have to open your mind." Austen tapped her temple with a finger to emphasize the point. "Stop thinking about 'hazmat suits' or 'sterilized equipment'. Start thinking about barriers we can wear. Think about disinfectants we can use on anything from cloth to steel."

"I already brought in containers of bleach and scrubber pads," Navarro said. "And like I said, we have face masks and gloves."

"We'll need more. Piper, I'd just raid the cleaning supplies in general. Anything that can dissolve the fatty membranes of most viruses and bacteria will work, from rubbing alcohol to bleach. Then I'd go to clothing."

"Right, I see what you mean about the bleach," Piper said. "Why should I check clothing?"

"This is a tropical country. See if M&B included polyvinyl rain ponchos as part of their kit. If they don't, go raid the kitchen. Even a plastic garbage bag makes a better barrier than a porous cotton shirt."

"What about the motor pool?"

"They've got solvents we might be able to use. Better yet, they're likely to have safety goggles. We need eye protection. Airborne particles can attach to the moist surface of the eyeball. Got it?"

The younger woman hesitated a moment. "Okay, I got it. But…is this going to be safe?"

"There's no real 'safe space' in a hot zone."

"I don't mean that." Piper cast an apologetic glance towards Navarro. "Look, I'm sorry if this offends you, but you're a bunch of *mercenaries*, right?"

An awkward silence fell amongst the group for a moment.

Finally, October let out a boisterous laugh.

"She has good point!" he crowed. "We are bunch of killers, Nicholas!"

Navarro didn't smile. His expression remained neutral, but his voice took on a chilly tone.

"This is what some people might call a 'teachable moment'. I deal with this every time I'm called before a committee of politicians, but they rarely pay attention. Will you try to listen?"

Piper nodded. Her eyes flicked fearfully to the painful-looking scar that wended down Navarro's face as the man spoke again.

"M&B's employees prefer the phrase 'private military contractor'. Myself, I like the term 'security contractor'. That's because a mercenary is paid to *fight*. People like me and October are paid to *protect*.

"We don't generally go looking for trouble, but we'll shoot back when needed because it's our job. We try to do the right thing. Consider the people Redhawk and I tried to rescue from that copter crash. They're medics from the Red Cross. Last I checked, the Red Cross hasn't sent us one thin dime."

"Sorry," Piper finally said, abashed. "It's just…well, I didn't know."

"Is all right," October promised her. "If anyone looks at you with crossed-eyes, I will use their head as basketball!"

"Good luck in your scavenger hunt," Austen said. "Bring back whatever you can. I've got a hunch that we'll need every bit."

She slid the side door closed. October backed out of the parking space and the truck grumbled off into the evening traffic. Austen inhaled, taking in the scent of tropical orchids and freshly made piña coladas. She realized that these might be the last pleasant smells she encountered for a long while.

"Thanks," Navarro said, startling Austen out of her reverie.

"For what?"

"For telling me that I 'did good'. I feel like I've been flying blind. I needed advice, Leigh. I needed someone like you here."

She gave him a curious glance. Navarro's face remained poker straight.

"We both need advice, Nick. DiCaprio gave me some before I left." She nodded towards the *Stella Maris*. "Come on, I'll tell you what he said on the way. You're not going to like it."

"Why not?"

"Because I'll be damned if I understand a single thing that DiCaprio told me."

Navarro cursed. "I was afraid you'd say that."

Austen strode off towards the wharf, Navarro falling in at her side. The two moved through the drinking and carousing cruise ship passengers, completely unnoticed by the reveling crowd.

CHAPTER THIRTEEN

Austen and Navarro emerged on the far side of the crowd and moved to cross the space between the wharves. The wharf behind them had a veritable flotilla of medium-sized cruise liners docked in each open space. As the evening darkened, each ship lit up festively from stem to stern in a rainbow of party lights and dance music.

By contrast, a relatively small ship lay tied to the wharf before them. Drab white lights illuminated a single deck from bow to stern and a basic wooden gangplank. A small group of men dressed in civilian clothing guarded this entryway.

Navarro slowed his pace so he and Austen would have more time to talk.

"I hoped Niles Bailey would give you time to reach DiCaprio," he said. "Sounds like it paid off."

"Better than you know," Austen agreed. "This time, I didn't even have to contact him. DiCaprio contacted me."

Navarro did a double take. "*He* contacted *you?* How?"

"He sent me a message on the same computer I normally use to contact him. I didn't know he could do that."

"What do you suppose it means?"

"I don't know, but if I had to guess…DiCaprio's saying,

'Pay attention to this, it's important.'"

They paused inside one of the circle of lights cast by the dockside lamps. Leigh reached into a pocket and pulled out a folded sheet of paper.

"Good luck with this one," she warned, as Navarro took the sheet and unfolded it. "DiCaprio may be a 'backchannel' source embedded with State or Defense, but I wish I knew why he writes like this."

"Might be the only way to keep his cover. Security through obscurity is a real thing." Navarro read the lines with a scowl. "Then again, maybe he's just gone nuts. Any idea what this means?"

"Your guess is as good as mine."

"Great." Navarro re-read the note.

Five Creoles speak where still waters run six fathoms deep.
The black masks will tell you where to start.
Stay the course when things get tough.
Beware the beat of the jungle's dark heart.
Save those you can from the burning star.

"Okay," he said, as they resumed their pace. "I've got an educated guess for the first line, anyway."

"You do?" Austen quirked a grin at him. "And here I thought I was the smart one, and you were the tough one."

"You're a damn sight tougher than me," Navarro said, as they came up to one of the M&B guards. A look of recognition passed between the two men, but he still gave the pass code. "Tango Lima Two."

A nod, and the men stepped out of the way. Austen noted that each man wore a holster under his clothing. They watched the party going on in the distance with disapproving eyes.

She looked over the *Stella Maris* as they made their way up the gangplank. The sleek vessel stretched for more than one hundred meters in length. It was on the small side compared to the 'floating hotels' that plied the seas now.

However, the ship still had a bridge-forward design, where

the multi-story bridge structure had been placed up close to the bow. A huge teardrop shaped swimming pool sheltered in its lee on the midships deck. In the deepening dusk the water looked inky black.

"Suriname is a real witches' brew of a country, and the languages reflect it," Navarro said, as they stepped onto the ship's deck. "Outside the cities, most people speak a variant of English-based Creole. There are five recognized dialects. So, DiCaprio's describing Suriname for sure."

"I follow you so far," Austen said, as they turned and headed for the bow. She noted in passing that reclining chaise lounge chairs still lined the pool in neat rows.

"What's more, 'six fathoms' is a measure of depth. It's also called 'the deep six'."

Austen raised an eyebrow at that. "Bailey mentioned a project down here, the one your men were originally guarding. He said it was called 'Deep Six'."

"Then maybe DiCaprio just showed us one of his cards," Navarro said, as he led Austen to a pair of French doors marked *TO THE LOWER DECKS*. "He's got access to things that only M&B and the State Department know."

Navarro tapped in a security code and the doors opened with a *chuff* of compressed air. Austen stepped through and down a plush carpeted stairway. Dim lightning came from faux gold candelabra mounted on each wall.

"You and I wondered if DiCaprio worked for State," Austen considered. "Maybe he's a mole someone planted at Motte & Bailey?"

"I don't know," Navarro admitted, as he followed her down the stairway. "But one thing worries me. '*Where still waters run six fathoms deep*' sounds an awful lot like '*still waters run deep*'. He's saying that something looks placid on the surface...but isn't. There's trouble ahead."

They descended another level before Navarro directed Austen down a corridor to the left. The carpeting came to an end beyond yet another set of doors, to be replaced by linoleum or bare steel. The lighting got harsher as they made their way towards the ship's midsection and arrived at the vessel's medical bay.

The physicians' main office was a long, deep room painted a soothing mint green. Cushy chairs for doctors or patients to recline in had been hastily dusted off and pressed into service. The ghostly scents of long-smoked cigar tobacco and antiseptics made a jarring mix, but Austen ignored it.

The office was well stocked with implements to treat small cuts and broken bones. Austen rifled through the supply cabinets and muttered a couple choice curses.

"Anything here you can use?" Navarro asked.

"Not much. Over-the-counter painkillers. Topical ointments for sunburn and yeast infections. Three shelves of anti-diarrhea pills." Austen slid open a large drawer at the end of the counter. "There's a punch bowl in here filled with foil-wrapped condoms. Someone's stashed a half-bottle of brandy next to it."

"October would appreciate that remedy. Hair of the dog that bit you and all that."

Austen closed the last cabinet with a *click*. "Where are the patients?"

"Follow me." Navarro led the way to the adjoining chamber. "This is the observation room."

Three long windows had been carved out of one wall. At the very end of the room lay a secured door, a sitting stool, and a small plastic tub. A pair of galoshes and a disposal bin sat nearby. The acrid smell of a bleach solution emanated from the tub.

"That's the best I could do for a decontamination shower," Navarro said. "Gloves, masks, and the last of the protective eyewear are on the shelf up by the door.'

Austen focused her attention on the viewing windows. An open medical ward lay on the other side, nine beds lined up against the far wall. Three of the beds were surrounded by extra IV lines providing anesthetics and liquids.

"What you've got there will have to do for now," Austen said. "I need to get a better look at what's going on in there."

"Leigh," Navarro warned. "Are you sure about this?"

She clenched her hands and found them unexpectedly damp. She focused her breathing as she felt an icy tingle of fear creep up her back. Austen had braved a microbial hot zone more than once, and had lived to tell the tale.

Sometimes, that had been down to luck and little else. Austen didn't know how contagious the disease in that room could be. The wrong move, or even a simple inhale, could mean instant infection.

"Nick, I'm not sure about this. Any of it. But this is what I do. It's what makes me who I am. I don't want to compromise that."

The big man pursed his lips for a moment. "I get it, believe me I do. But if you catch this…then we're all back at square one in stopping this thing."

"Well, whatever those black-masked people sprayed them with wasn't exactly a health tonic. In fact–"

Her mind pulled up short at that.

The M&B report had said the suspected cartel gunmen had worn black cloth covering the lower part of their faces. It wasn't a particularly good type of disguise, so why wear it in the first place?

Immediately, she flashed on the second line in DiCaprio's message.

The black masks will tell you where to start.

"Of course," she breathed. "I should have seen it before."

Austen slipped on a pair of gloves, following it up with the eye protection and face mask. Navarro went with her to the end of the compartment as she sat on the stool and slipped the galoshes over her shoes.

"Why don't you want to wait for Piper?" Navarro urged. "Let's see if she found anything to protect you from whatever's in there."

"We don't have that luxury," Austen said, in a voice muffled by the mask. She placed a gloved hand on the door handle. "But I've got a hunch that whatever's in there doesn't spread via aerosol, like influenza or the measles."

"What if you're wrong?"

She opened the door with a *clank* of metal on metal. "Then you'd better find a way to wheel another bed into this medical ward."

With that, Austen pushed on through and stepped into the beating heart of the outbreak's hot zone.

CHAPTER FOURTEEN

The lights in the medical ward cast soft circles of illumination. Bed linens, curtains, and floor tiling were all colored the same soothing shade of green as the doctor's offices outside. Aside from the beeps and whirrs of medical monitors, it was quiet. Too quiet to Austen's ears.

Coughs, groans, even sounds of pain were common among patient wards. These weren't pleasant things to hear, not by a long shot. But they told her that people were still fighting for life.

Silence meant death.

Once again, Austen's mind flashed back to an earlier expedition, one sent to fight an outbreak of Black Nile virus. She'd felt the African sun beating down on the nape of her neck like a physical force when she arrived at the field camp. The quiet of the place had revealed nothing but bodies and the stench of rotting flesh.

At least this time, she smelled nothing so terrible. Her nose picked up only the rawness of rubbing alcohol. She relaxed a jot. Certain diseases, when they reached a terminal stage, could perfume the air with the scents of strangely altered body fluids, turning sweat musky and spilled blood rancid.

Austen twisted a control knob by the door to raise the light levels a jot. A flutter of murmurs and grumbles came from the patients. She went to the nearest bed and had to suppress the urge to let out a gasp.

She'd only seen John Redhawk as a tough, wiry man with a sunburned complexion. The man in the hospital bed still looked tough. But whatever sickness burned within him had turned his florid skin tone a grayish white. He hadn't lost weight, but the individual muscles in his neck stood out like bundles of cord.

"Redhawk," she said, "It's Austen. Are you awake?"

The man blinked. The motion seemed to take a lot of effort.

"Ain't dead yet," he replied. His already harsh voice now had an extra handful of grit thrown in.

"How do you feel?"

Redhawk opened his eyes more fully to look at her. Austen noted that they looked normal enough, without the egg-yolk colored sclera of patients gripped by malarial fever.

"How do I feel? Like cold hammered shit."

"I figured as much," she said. "You know I have to ask, see if I can figure out anything."

"My men and I...we can't keep anything down except maybe water. The upchuck's got green crap in it. Even though no one's been eating their vegetables."

Austen nodded. The green was a sign of bile acid malabsorption. But that was a symptom, not a cause.

"What else? Anything you can tell me might help."

"Shooting pains in the limbs started about an hour after I touched Jansen, getting him out of the crash. But they went away later. Everything's numb now."

He raised a hand. Austen took it and examined the skin. Redhawk's fingers had taken on a strange gray-blue tinge, as if frostbitten. Yet the flesh underneath was warm.

Austen went to the little green nightstand between Redhawk and his neighbor's bed and pulled out the drawer. She took out a pen and a small pad of paper. Then she went to

74

stand by the foot of Redhawk's bed.

"Let me know if you feel this," she said, as she pulled the sheet up to expose Redhawk's bare feet. The man's toes had the same strange coloration as his fingers. She pressed the end of the capped pen against one toe, and then another. After a couple of touches, she leaned harder into the last three, making the skin blanch under the pressure.

"Ow," Redhawk said, without feeling. "Ouch. Ow."

"Not feeling much?"

"A bit on the last couple, that's it. You think it's permanent?"

Austen bit back her first reply: *I hope to God it's not.*

"Unlikely," she hedged. "Just remember, all nine of you are in good hands."

"Seven," Redhawk corrected her.

"What—"

"If you're here, then there's seven in good hands. The others are walking with the Great Spirit now." Redhawk motioned with his head towards the beds further down the ward. "Two of the three people we recovered from the crash site were badly wounded. They passed a couple hours ago. The last one, Jansen, he slipped into a coma or something."

A chill ran through Austen's body as she looked over to the beds with the extra IV bags and tubing. The heart and breath monitors had already been turned off. The occupants of the beds lay still, as if sleeping.

She heard a sudden drumming at the observation windows. Piper and October stood next to Navarro in the observation room. The younger woman held up a package of transparent face shields in triumph. Austen gave her a thumbs-up.

Navarro held up a telephone receiver and then pointed towards his left. She looked towards where he was pointing. At the far end of the ward lay a second door.

"Just take it easy for now," Austen said. She grasped Redhawk's hand, trying to be comforting.

"Ain't going anywhere," he replied curtly. "You just find out what this is and cure it, okay?"

Austen gave the man's hand one more squeeze before turning to stride down the length of the ward. In the process, she noted the uniformity of the patient's symptoms. They lay passively, quietly, as if accepting their fate.

Or as if something were slowly smothering their will to live.

She opened the door and stepped into a smaller room. A surgical table lay gleaming in the center. The shelves surrounding it were stocked with topical antiseptics, bandages, and a basic set of surgical tools.

So, this is where they'd take someone for emergency surgery, Austen thought. *At least if they weren't able to airlift someone off the ship.*

She spotted the telephone mounted on the wall across from the table. One of the yellow buttons at the base flashed urgently. She crossed the room, picked up the receiver, and tapped the button.

"Doctor Austen," Navarro said, "what's your status?"

"I'm fine," she replied. "Listen, we've already lost two of the three crash survivors. These people need medical care, and fast."

"We've asked the local health clinics, but they don't have protective gear that's any better than ours. They won't send anyone to work with something this infectious."

"It's not, and you need to tell them that. Can you put me on speakerphone out there?"

A pause. Navarro's voice sounded tinny as he said, "You're on it now."

"Whatever this bug is, it's dangerous," Austen said. "We're going to have to be careful, but we won't need biosafety suits or even HEPA filters. It's definitely not airborne."

She heard excited murmuring at the end of the line. "How can you be sure?"

"Just a hunch I got when looked at the details of the bioterror attack. Those people who carried it out had on roughly what I'm wearing. Unless they're interested in slow and painful martyrdom, they felt safe enough to spray this bug all over the crash site."

"Maybe I don't understand. If this stuff is dispersed as an

aerosol, then it's *got* to be transmitted via the air."

"That's just it," Austen insisted. "It wasn't dispersed as an aerosol – at least, not the way an airborne bioweapon is supposed to be released."

"Now I want to know too," October chimed in. "Explain. But use small words, if you please."

"If the bug here can be dispersed like an aerosol, that means it's lightweight enough to behave like the air itself," Austen explained. "You could inhale an infectious dose just by walking into a room. But our bioterrorists didn't use *atomizers*, which you can get out of something as commonplace as perfume bottles. They used *spray bottles*, which throw out relatively large droplets of liquid to stick on a given surface."

"So you don't catch this by inhaling it," Piper clarified. "You get it by touching something – a patient or a surface – that's been contaminated with the substance."

"No one's coughing right now, but it might be possible to transmit it through the air through a cough or sneeze," Austen added. "I see you found some face shields."

"That was a bit of luck," Piper said. "Someone pilfered them from a closed dental clinic."

"More than a bit of luck. Put one on and get in here."

"Me?"

"Yes, you. Everything a pathologist needs is here. Two dead bodies. A surgical room to perform a makeshift autopsy. And we've got one more thing that's more important than everything else combined."

"What's that?"

Austen's voice was matter of fact. "A desperate need to know what the hell we're dealing with here."

Piper's voice shook, but she still managed to sound determined.

"I get it. Okay, I'm coming in."

CHAPTER FIFTEEN

She heard her name being called in the darkness.

Leigh, someone said. *Leigh!*

Austen tried to blink, but her eyes refused to work right. She felt a pressure upon her chest, as if she were underwater. She heard her name. She thrashed her limbs, trying to reach the surface before her lungs burst.

"Hey, settle down," Navarro said, as he grabbed hold of her flailing hand. "Wake up, it's me."

Austen let out a gasp as she finally came awake.

She'd fallen asleep on one of the green lounge chairs in the doctor's office aboard the *Stella Maris*. Emily Piper had draped herself over one of the other chairs. The younger woman let out a snore as her two-tone hair fell partway over her face like a veil.

"I'm awake," she said groggily. "What's going on? Are the patients–"

"They're fine. Asleep and stable. We need to talk."

Austen rubbed her eyes and got up, her limbs stiff from standing most of the night. She did her best to shrug off the deep bone-weary tiredness as she followed Navarro from the medical bay back up the aft staircase.

"That was some pretty sharp guesswork earlier," Navarro said. "About how this bug spreads. Did you get that hunch from our mutual secret friend?"

"DiCaprio pointed out the right detail to me, yes."

Navarro opened a pair of doors and they stepped out on the cruise ship's foredeck. The sky was clear, and the pale orange light hinted at a bright and marvelous dawn. They continued further forward until they arrived at a cavernous dining room overlooking the ship's broad bow.

Austen couldn't help but gape at the wide-open space. Tables and chairs for three-quarters of the room had been packed away. Dust covers lay draped over the unused dining booths that lined the edges. A rectangular area laid out for ballroom dancing had been covered with a transparent protective cover.

A dozen remaining tables and a long serving bar had been moved next to the windows. Austen's mouth watered as she and Navarro walked down the line, scooping up breakfast items and pouring steaming cups of coffee. She only took a token amount of eggs and bacon, reserving the rest of her king-sized plate for glistening chunks of grapefruit, pineapple, and papaya.

Navarro led them over to an empty table. He decided to remain quiet for a bit and ate his breakfast while Austen gobbled down her food with relish. Their seat gave them a view of Hoogeveen's U-shaped harbor. The city sprawled out along one arm of the 'U', while the other half remained choked with jungle and abandoned dock pilings.

"The last time we worked together," Austen remarked, "we were eating boiled sheep's head in a Soviet-era blockhouse. Now, we get tropical fruit on a cruise ship. Things are looking up."

A group of men at the next table were dressed in the white-and-blue uniforms of the cruise line. They stood up abruptly once they recognized Austen. Their leader, a man with a nattily trimmed goatee, threw her a venomous look as he pulled on his captain's hat and strode off.

"Good thing the skeleton crew they kept on included a couple of the cooks." Navarro nodded towards where the last of the ship's officers were exiting the dining area. "By the way, that fellow who just left was Captain Rosella."

"I know. Believe me, I know."

"He looked as mad as a wet hen."

"I suppose I can't blame him." Austen said. She punctuated her words with long sips of dark coffee as she went on. "Piper and I completed our two autopsies last night. October was able to get us some body bags, but we still had to get the corpses into cold storage before serious decomposition and rigor set in. So, we commandeered the walk-in freezer amidships."

Navarro raised an eyebrow. "Maybe he was worried about what would find its way into the food."

She came close to snorting into her coffee. "No worries, this particular freezer had been empty for a long time. Captain Rosella was aghast at the idea more than anything else. Poor man almost had a stroke when he saw us laying out the bodies."

"Did the autopsies tell you anything?"

A shake of the head. "Not much. We saw traces of peripheral vasoconstriction in both bodies – the narrowing of blood vessels in the fingers and toes. That's causing the grayish skin tones and lack of feeling in Redhawk and the other survivors. As to what killed them, everything points to the wounds they got in the crash, not by any illness."

Navarro looked grim. "Tell it to me straight, then. Is Redhawk going to make it? Are any of his men going to walk out of that medical ward?"

She pushed back from the table and let out a breath before speaking.

"I don't know, Nick."

"They've got a chance, right? I mean, I was able to get some nurses in from the Church of St. Agnes…"

"Believe me, that helps. They're getting properly hydrated now, along with regular doses of tetracycline and glyceryl trinitrate. One's a general antibiotic and the other's a vasodilator. I'm hoping that these can slow or stop the progression of symptoms. But that's it. I've never seen anything work this fast on the human body."

"Not even *Nostocales*?"

"Not even that. We took lots of samples, and we can test them as soon as M&B flies in the equipment we need. October said he'd set up a secure satellite feed on the foredeck so we can confer with Ted Preble in London. But in the end…I still don't know what we're dealing with. I don't know if I can save your friend, Redhawk."

Navarro looked away and worked his jaw for a moment. "How about you? How are you holding up?"

She gave him a wry look. "Why would you care? You did what Piper would call a 'ghosting' on me after our dinner in D.C."

"That dinner…I didn't think we were on a date. Not exactly."

"It's still damned impolite, Nick. It seemed out of character for you."

He hung his head. "I don't know if that's true, Leigh. This job of mine takes me away to God-knows-where. It does it quickly, and for unknown lengths of time. I've said goodbye to so many people over the years…"

"Yes?"

"It hurts. I'd never admit this to anyone else, but it does hurt. So, I guess you could say that I avoid it. I'm sorry I disappointed you. I guess I'm still what you'd call a slow learner."

"I'm sorry too, then," Austen said with a sigh. "I should have understood what working for M&B requires of you. And we still have something in common, you know."

"What might that be?"

"Well, I *did* drop everything to come down here when you called. That proves I'm still a slow learner too."

Navarro looked up at her. A hopeful grin blossomed on his face.

"You're something else, you know that?" he said. "And

now that you and I are done refueling, we need to get a move on."

"We do? Where to?"

"The provincial governor's *palacio*. Mayor-Governor Daan de Murken is going to be your last, best shot at convincing anyone down here to call in the WHO."

"All right," Austen said, as she put the cup aside and got to her feet. "That's definitely at the top of our to-do list. Just let me stop by the medical bay and tell Piper what I need done."

"You might want to pick up another set of gloves and face mask."

"Another set? Why, is the Governor sick?"

"No," allowed Navarro. "But trust me on this one: you're going to feel like you need to wash your hands after dealing with him."

Michael Angel

CHAPTER SIXTEEN

Surinamese Rainforest
Suriname – Guyana Border Zone

Erich Zann was a little happier than before.

His collar still stuck to the back of his neck, among other things. But that mild irritation was forgotten as he pushed back from his office desk. He stared out the window at the mist that still hung heavily about the compound.

It formed banks of fog as thick as soup. It sank everything into a mucky well of moisture. It turned even the brightest sunshine into the murkiness of light cast through a prison window.

Zann knew about prisons all too well.

He'd thought himself above the law when he'd moved on from enforcing drug deals to making them. The stacks of euros in his briefcases became taller, and the bills had more zeroes at the end. He got wealthy. He got sloppy.

Someone finally decided it was his time to go. INTERPOL pulled off one of its biggest raids in a decade, planning it all while his eyes were on some other prize. Another stack of bills. Another line of blow. Another top-flight pair of call girls fresh from Central Europe, Ukraine, Thailand, or whatever options his loins desired for the night.

They spent twelve armored cars, a thousand round of ammunition, and seven lives in his capture. A deal was made by someone in the shadows. The national security apparatus of the EU sent him in chains to a castle that used to house the torture victims of the mad Carpathian kings.

They tried to bribe him. Then they beat him. And when he'd refused to give up any more information than his name, his birthday, and what orifice the prison boss could shove his questions into, they'd thrown him into solitary confinement.

Zann didn't remember how long he'd ended up in the stinking confines of his closet-sized hell. He knew that they cut his daily rations back to almost nothing. He knew that his bulked-out fighting body had shrunk from hunger. He recalled once wrapping one hand around the opposite wrist. His middle finger and thumb touched quite easily.

But the main thing he remembered was that one day. A gray day like now, only punctuated by the sounds of screams and gunfire. A piercing light as the door to his cell opened. A hand extended out of the light and pulled him back into the world.

Something moved out in the mist.

He looked down into the courtyard with a wicked smirk. Doctor Tiwari was busy with his twice-daily duties. The snaps and growls of the creatures at the far gate were now expected; they had learned when feeding time was upon them.

Somewhere, Tiwari had located a set of elastic bungee cords. He'd used these to jam shut the lid on the barrel of wet food. Then, instead of lugging the container across the yard and back, the diminutive doctor simply pushed the barrel on its side and rolled it to its destination.

Once there, he removed the cords and grabbed a garden spade from the wall mount next to the gate. It was a simple matter to shovel the compound's offal to the animals after that.

It was a clever system. Too clever by half.

Zann wouldn't take the bungee cords away, of course. That would be counter-productive. He didn't like to stifle his people's passion for innovation.

But he made a note to himself to have the spade taken away. Until Tiwari figured out another workaround, it would be amusing to watch the fastidious doctor handle half-rotten gristle and organ meat with his bare hands.

The intercom system installed in his desk lit up with a green glow and an accompanying chime. He debated taking the call for a moment before pressing the answer button.

"What is it?"

One of his functionaries in the monitor room downstairs spoke crisply in return.

"Mister Zann, we have an update from Hoogeveen City."

"Go on."

"*Eindstreep One* has retrieved the epidemiologist from the *Stella Maris*. His personnel carrier has now been spotted arriving at the governor's *palacio*."

"Interesting." Zann steepled his fingers and looked out into the grayness. "I didn't expect Navarro to stay so close to that side of things."

"Shall we escalate?"

"One moment."

Zann reached across his desk and skimmed one of his older reports. The customs people at the airport had noted the arrival of the two medical personnel. He considered.

"They actually managed to stop a bullet," Zann said, with grudging admiration. "But they can't be everywhere at once."

"Sir?"

"We're going to escalate, yes. *Eindstreep One* must be kept busy. But we also want him kept separate from the rest of the problem. And to do that, we're also going to *amplify*."

Zann rattled off a series of orders. Then he cut the connection, sat back, and watched Tiwari feed the howling mass of beasts far below.

Michael Angel

CHAPTER SEVENTEEN

Republic of Suriname
Hoogeveen City
Palacio of the Provincial Mayor-Governor

To Austen's eyes, the *palacio* of Provincial Mayor-Governor Murken could have served as the backdrop for any one of a dozen movies set in a seedy, tropical backwater town. The weathered adobe-red walls cried out for a coat of paint, the grounds could have used a trim, and the floor layout inside cast everything in shadows.

The Governor's personal office was no different. Amenities like a minibar and a big-screen television only served to highlight the old, worn furniture. Sunlight and humidity filtered in through half-closed wooden shutters. Ceiling fans circulated air scented with hibiscus, burnt tobacco, and stale sweat.

Daan de Murken didn't seem to mind the heat, even though droplets of perspiration beaded his forehead, threatening to run down one of his two jowly cheeks. His dun-colored suit did little to hide his rotund build, which simply sloped down and out into a kettle-sized pot belly. And yet the man's eyes were calculating, predatory. A pencil-thin mustache perched above his upper lip like a greasy falcon.

The Governor greeted Austen and Navarro cordially, inviting them to sit before his hacienda-sized teakwood desk. He even offered them a spot of tea before listening to Austen explain what the mystery disease could do to the people of Hoogeveen.

And yet her heart still sank as the man finally spoke.

"Miss Austen," Murken said. "Are you seriously asking me to contact the WHO for you? When it's so obviously premature at this point and time?"

"I'm not asking you," she said carefully. "I'm telling you. This is a massive threat to the health of your country's citizens."

"How, exactly?"

Austen took a deep breath to steady herself. "Like I said not two minutes ago, we are dealing with a virus or bacteria that infects and sickens people with unheard-of speed."

Murken held up a stubby-fingered hand.

"Let me stop you right there, *Mis een Dokter*. I am not ignorant of public health concerns. Let me ask you: how many people around the world die of the common flu, each year?"

Austen blinked. She wasn't expecting this tack from the slovenly-looking Governor.

"It depends," she said. "A quarter-million. More than half-a-million in a bad year."

That got a look of surprise from Navarro. "Are you serious? We have the vaccine for that one, don't we?"

"There's many different strains of the flu virus," Austen replied. "They mutate over time and replace the older strains. That's why flu kills around eighty thousand people in the United States annually."

"That figure is lower here in Suriname," Murken put in. "But it must be in the thousands. Yet the WHO is never called. How many people have died from this 'mystery bug' of yours to date?"

Austen paused.

"Not as many," she gritted. "Yet."

"That is the operative word, isn't it? You would have me shut down the airport. You would have me chase away my cruise ships. That would risk crashing my country's economy. And that in turn would cause riots. Riots and deaths, yes. All because you don't know what is making a handful of people sick."

"Governor–"

"After all," Murken said, waving aside Austen's objection, "it's not like they're visiting Goblintown or anything. Here in Hoogeveen we are fun, we are sun, and we are not about chasing people away from our Keti Koti festival."

Austen had been about to ask what Goblintown meant, but the word *festival* sent a shiver through her.

"Wait, what's the Keti Koti–"

"That's a Sranan Creole phrase meaning *the chains are cut*," Navarro informed her. "The day slavery was outlawed in this country. It's as important to Suriname as the Fourth of July is to people in the United States."

"Those ships you saw at the docks will be joined by twice as many more," Murken said happily, "All for the biggest festival of the year! I do hope that you shall stay long enough to attend."

Austen swallowed, hard. She kept her voice as steady and as even as she could.

"Governor Murken," she said. "You're looking at exposing thousands of people to...whatever I'm trying to chase down. Then, after your festival, they'll disperse all over the Caribbean.

"From there, most will hop on an international jet to God-knows-how-many countries all over the world. You're creating the perfect tinder box for this to turn into an explosive pandemic. That's where disease erupts simultaneously across the globe. If that happens, *nobody* will have the resources to stop it!"

The mustache atop Murken's lip quivered as if ready to take flight. "You are what we call a *natte deken*, Miss Austen. A wet blanket. I'll pass on your information to the people in the capital, but that's all I can do."

"You need to contact the WHO *now*, Governor. You need to get those cruise liners out of Hoogeveen harbor now, and bar anyone new from coming in. And you damn sure can't hold a festival in the face of a threat like this!"

Navarro moved to put himself in between the two, but Austen angrily shook him off.

"Because if you don't," she concluded grimly, "you're looking at a catastrophe, one that will cost thousands or even millions of lives!"

Murken merely raised an eyebrow at that.

"Mister Navarro," he said, "I appreciate that you have brought a most delightful looking woman to my office. Explain to me why you chose one who tends towards hysteria."

"In the time I've known her," Navarro said carefully, "Doctor Austen's been correct about every threat to the well-being of...of humanity as a whole."

"Indeed. Is she aware of your role here? About the project you protect on account of my good graces and your own State Department?"

"Governor—"

"While I receive some welcome payments in cash from your people, I can't say that Deep Six is meant to advance the health of 'humanity as a whole'."

"Sir, I realize—"

"You are not paid to realize," Murken snapped. "You are not paid to, as we say, 'stir the pot'. You are paid to keep the lawless elements in this city away from your charges. And that is all. *Begrijpen?*"

"Yes," he said tightly. "I understand."

"Good. Leave me, for I have work to do."

Austen managed to restrain herself until a pair of guards showed her and Navarro out of the room. She restrained herself as they were escorted to their waiting armored truck. In fact, she remained quiet until the driver pulled up to the same tiki-hut styled parking spot.

She looked out the truck's window at the festival plaza with a haunted expression.

It was empty of tourists for now, but construction personnel worked feverishly to prepare the area for larger crowds. Forklifts moved tree boxes and planters. Tiling was being repainted, sound systems tested, and a score of wooden stalls were going up to serve food and drinks.

"And so, the preparations for the festival go on," Austen finally said. "I suppose that I could have tried to be more convincing."

Navarro shrugged. "I'm not sure you could have done any better. That whole meeting was classic Daan de Murken. He's the type of man to start looking around for an umbrella only when it begins pouring rain."

"What are we going to do, Nick?"

A cell phone's ring echoed in the truck's passenger compartment. Both Navarro and Austen went for their phones. Navarro came up with the lit screen.

"Navarro," he said. A pause as he listened. "Okay, that's the first bit of good news I've had all day. I'm heading your way."

"That sounded encouraging," Austen said, after he hung up.

"I asked M&B for people to comb through the footage from Redhawk's drones. Looks like they finally found something. I've got to head back to the forward operations base."

A second ring punctuated their conversation. This time it was Austen's phone. She thumbed the button to put it on speaker.

Piper's voice came on the line. She sounded near panic. In the background, Austen heard a bone-chilling cacophony of monitor alarms and human screams.

"Austen, it's Piper! We're seeing spikes in blood pressure and heart rates over 100bpm! They're going to tip over into arrhythmia any minute!"

Oh, dear God! Austen thought. "How many of the patients are affected?"

"Uh, it looks like *all* of them."

"On my way!" She snapped the connection closed. "Nick, I've got to go."

If Navarro replied, his words were lost in the *bang* of the door as she threw it open. Austen fairly leapt out of the vehicle. She ran towards the *Stella Maris,* racing against the scant time her patients had left.

CHAPTER EIGHTEEN

Austen heard men crying out as she ran down the long corridor below decks. She didn't make out coherent words, and she definitely heard a scream or two thrown in for good measure. But something else chilled the blood in her veins.

The sound of high-pitched, maniacal *laughing.*

She pushed her way through the medical bay doors. Then she dashed over to the observation windows. It took a couple seconds for her to absorb all she saw.

Save for Redhawk, the patients thrashed spasmodically in their beds as if jolted by electric current. One man sat up straight and let out that horrific laugh again as he stared emptily at the ceiling. A stream of blood dripped from his lower lip.

Others babbled incoherently. One screamed and cringed from an unknown assailant, eyes darting feverishly from side to side. The monitoring equipment she and Piper had installed just last night added to the din. Each unit *dinged* frantically, signaling irregular heartbeats and increasing blood pressure.

Piper and two of the nurses from St. Agnes wrestled with yet another of Redhawk's squad members. The man's spasmodic movements were still too strong for the pair of nurses to hold his arm steady. The young woman jabbed the man's arm twice, missing the vein both times. Finally, on the third try she managed to hit her target. The man's struggles slowed.

Austen tore herself away from the sight. She threw on a pair of gloves, followed them up with a rain poncho, full-sized dental face shield, and a pair of galoshes sloshed through the bleach solution. The smell of rubbing alcohol mixed with bleach greeted her as she pushed her way into the ward itself.

"Talk to me," Austen said, as she joined the three women. "What's the medication and dose?"

"Diazepam," Piper replied. "Five milligrams."

"Make it twelve for the next one." Austen moved to the man who continued to let out horrific gales of laughter.

"That's a high dose!"

"Not when you've got patients as densely muscled as these men. And we need to knock them out in a hurry."

As if to prove her point, the two nurses barely managed to hang on to the man's arm as he flailed about. Piper located the correct pre-loaded dosage and shoved the syringe towards Austen.

"Here, you do the injection!"

Austen took it and uncapped the needle. As the two nurses struggled to hold the man's limb down at his side, she leaned her full bodyweight against his arm, bracing it against the side of the bed. She slammed the syringe home and thumbed the plunger.

The man let out a gasp and a shudder as he went limp.

God help me, Austen thought. *That's only two down, six more to go.*

One of the nurses cried out and pointed to the comatose patient, the one Redhawk had called Jansen. "Doctor, *kijk daar!* It is horrible!"

Jansen's blue eyes were open, though the pupils were contracted to pinpricks. He'd turned his head to the side at an unnaturally angle. He slammed his forehead against the metal side rails again and again with a *CLANK* and a growing spray of blood.

Piper moved in to restrain the man's head, along with the nurses. Austen paused a moment as she observed the continued movement from the other beds. What had changed internally or externally to trigger these seizures?

As if in answer, Jansen's blood glinted off of the side rail, making her look up. The room was significantly brighter than before.

Austen thought back to the first time she'd entered the ward. Her hand had twisted a control knob by the door to raise the light levels a jot. That had gotten a flutter of murmurs and grumbles came from the patients.

She blinked. *Could it be that simple?*

Ignoring the pandemonium that continued around her, Austen ran back to the entry door. She touched the light adjustment knob and turned it so that the lights dimmed.

The screaming from the unmedicated patients ceased, to be replaced by exhausted moans. Piper looked up as Austen rejoined her. The young woman's hands shook, and her eyes had gone wet.

"We're too late for him," she whispered.

Jansen lay still once more, his eyes staring into oblivion. The monitor at the head of his bed buzzed as it displayed flat lines across the entire screen. Blood dripped from his mouth and both nostrils, but the drip had no pressure behind it. The pump had stopped.

One of the nurses moved to close Jansen's eyes.

"I don't know what happened..." Piper said, in a broken voice. "How did you get them to stop?"

"Educated guess," Austen admitted. "I saw something like this when I increased the light level before. Only it wasn't anything so severe."

Piper let out a gasp. "We just turned the lights up so that we could examine Jansen, he was showing signs of renewed internal bleeding. I...did we..."

Austen shook her head.

"Don't blame yourself. It's a dark path that you don't want

to go down, believe me. I've never seen anything like this in all my years. How would you have known?"

"The light…triggered a seizure?"

"No, it triggered some form of delirium. A photosensitive delirium. Come on, I want the rest of the patients sedated before anything else happens. And we need to figure out some kind of restraint system."

Piper, Austen, and the nurses spent the next half-hour administering sedatives and attending to minor scrapes and cuts. The laughing patient had bitten his lower lip, requiring a cold compress.

Finally, they came to Redhawk's bed. He looked up at them, his eyes weary.

"Don't need a shot," he said, in a tired voice. "Ain't gone loco yet."

"Not yet," Austen agreed. "But please, take the injection for me. We don't want you to hurt yourself."

"Just a minute." Redhawk raised a shaky hand. "The lights…they made things worse."

"How? Did they burn you somehow?"

"No, not really. Good thing, too. Apaches would make damn lousy vampires. But the last couple of hours…I've been seeing and hearing things. Strange things."

"Like what?"

Redhawk thought for a moment. "Bursts of sound out of nowhere, distorted visions. It comes and goes. That got worse when the light got turned on."

"You think the others are seeing similar things?"

"I heard McCall talking to his Dad, and his father's been dead for years. Mason's having recurring nightmares of being chased and eaten by wolves. And Ojeda, the one who bit his lip…he's been acting like he's on one bad cosmic trip. So, maybe you better give my arm a jab."

"Stay strong," Austen said, as she injected him with the sedative. "We'll figure this out."

Redhawk nodded and closed his eyes. Austen motioned for Piper to join her by the door.

"This is bad. It's like they're overdosing on adrenaline. And these are men who've been in active combat multiple times. They're used to dealing with adrenal surges, channeling that 'flight or fight' mechanism." Austen tapped her fist on the wall in frustration. "Any idea when we're going to be able to test those samples?"

"Oh!" Piper exclaimed. "With all this craziness going on, I didn't get a chance to tell you. M&B got the equipment we needed in on an early flight."

"And they didn't get shot up at the airport? That's a stroke of luck right there."

"Your friend, the one who looks like a grizzly bear walking around on two legs? He brought the equipment to the business center on the main deck and hooked it up."

"Bless you, October," Austen breathed. "Were you able to run any of our samples?"

"I set all of them up for automatic analysis. If everything worked properly, then we'll have data to look at. And if October was able to get the satellite dish installed, then the results should've been sent to Ted in London as well."

Austen looked up. Her eyes looked hopeful for the first time today.

"All right, come on," she said, as she opened the door to exit the ward. "I want to do an autopsy on Jansen, but I'm betting this data is more important. And we've *got* to find out what we're dealing with before we lose any more of our patients."

Michael Angel

CHAPTER NINETEEN

———— ⌘ ————

Motte & Bailey's FOB, or 'forward operations base' looked like a decrepit set of warehouses slapped together inside a half-abandoned industrial park. That was part of an intentional strategy called 'security through obscurity'. Only a careful eye would spot protective berms made of innocuous looking gravel piles or stacks of welded scrap metal.

Work inside was kept away from prying eyes as much as possible. But there were still telltale signs of activity. Vehicles rumbled in and out, kicking up plumes of dust. Lazy-seeming guards looked suspiciously in shape. Antennas and dished arrays made a surreal cluster of shapes atop the roof.

Navarro's personnel carrier made it through the perimeter security checkpoint and pulled around to the rear of the building. He waited patiently as a set of electronic sniffers checked the vehicle's underside for anything magnetic, electronic, or explosive. He sat up as he noticed that the raised concrete pad atop the roof sat empty.

He frowned for a moment before speaking to the driver.

"Sims, you still on duty for the rest of the afternoon?"

"Officially, until five," the young man said. "Unofficially, I'm there if you need me."

"I might." The sniffers let out a *bleep* and the door to the motor pool retracted up with a rattle of blast-resistant plates. "Do me a favor. Get this beast refueled. Then keep it warmed up and ready to roll."

"We expecting trouble?"

"Not sure, but someone's got Abbott and Costello up and running again."

Navarro got out and made his way deeper into the building. He passed a row of fully stocked supply shelves set up as impromptu walls separating work from sleeping areas. Like in many active FOBs, his ears registered the sounds of mechanics working in the motor pool, the *whirr* of forklifts moving crates, and the distant hum of the air filtration units. The smells of hot metal, drying laundry, spent gunpowder, and grilling meat were familiar and welcome to him.

He made his way past several of the weapons lockers over to an interior set of rooms made from a double-wide trailer. It wouldn't have looked out of place in a down-and-out mobile home park, save for the multiple cables that punctured the walls and roof to deliver data and power to the MIC, or main information center.

The blue-green glow of monitors greeted him as he entered. A half-dozen men and women worked at separate screens, headsets in place and fingers jabbing at keyboards. Another man he didn't recognize stood in the rear conference room, staring at the main monitor screen. He rapped on the doorframe to announce his arrival.

"I'm Nicholas Navarro," he said, as he walked in and extended his hand. "I got a message that you're my interim Drone Surveillance specialist."

The man turned and beamed a smile that gleamed white against dark skin. He was tall and wiry, without a spare ounce of body fat. Tightly curled hair sat high atop a domed forehead. While he wore the standard M&B gray combat fatigues, he also sported a lapel badge in the shape of a Masai shield with crossed spears.

His words carried the lilt of an accent that wasn't too far

removed from Ted Preble's.

"I have that privilege. Samuel Wanjiru, at your service." He took the proffered hand and shook it firmly. Navarro's surprise at his voice must have shown, as he added, "Niles Bailey just hired me away from the Nairobi branch of Kenyan Intel. We use drones to keep poachers away from the more valuable animals."

"You and John Redhawk, my prior drone expert, will have a lot to talk about."

"Indeed," Wanjiru agreed. "I take it that you noticed Abbot and Costello are up and running again?"

"I didn't see them on the roof pad, so I assumed you put them back out on patrol."

"I have them at high altitude in reconnaissance mode. Two of the analysts in the main MIC are monitoring them, but I doubt they'll be doing much. The AI programs installed on those drones are top-flight."

"That's not surprising. These are Redhawk's pride and joy."

"It's a good thing, too. I was able to focus on what you really needed: video forensics analysis."

Navarro nodded. "You found something in the drone footage?"

"I believe I have, yes. Let me show you." Wanjiru turned back to his keyboard and tapped in a few commands. The monitor switched to a view of green rectangles punctuated by a blob and streak of bright orange. "These rectangles are low-rise buildings, as seen by Costello's thermal imaging system. Specifically, this shot is from the launch event spotted by you and Redhawk."

Launch event, Navarro thought sourly. *What a great euphemism for an event that snuffed out multiple lives.*

Wanjiru pointed first at the blob, and then the streak. "Here we have the emergence of the backblast cone, the area of hot gas vented by the firing of the missile. And here is the missile itself. I'd assumed that this was a variant of the FIM-92 Stinger."

"I agree, the Stinger would be the ideal weapon to take

down a bird from a tactical position. It's just that the attack came as such a shock. The cartels haven't used anti-aircraft missiles before."

"Well, whatever they are using…it is strange. Let me show you what I mean by taking you back about twenty seconds before the missile was fired."

A few more taps on the keyboard, and the display shifted so that the building was canted at a slightly different angle. The area that had been obscured by the blob now showed an orange blur next to a small yellow cylinder. Two specks of orange glinted from floors above and below the cylinder.

"Let me guess," Navarro said, as he jabbed a finger at the screen. "Two spotters, spread out to help the shooter get range and direction to the target. The firing platform is here, and the yellowish cylinder is the actual tube holding the missile."

"It seems my work is half-done already. Yet, it is that last detail which caught my attention. The yellow indicates relatively high heat compared to the background. That's not right."

"How do you mean?"

"To fire a missile, a coolant unit is placed into the grip stock no more than sixty seconds before firing. The unit injects liquid argon, which cools the targeting unit. Otherwise, it's impossible for a heat-seeking missile like the Stinger to home in on a hot engine or rotor unit."

"They shouldn't have been able to launch," Navarro murmured to himself. "Curiouser and curiouser."

"Lewis Carroll would agree, yes. Now, let's move to one second before firing." A press of the keys, and the image shifted again. This time, a huge vertical orange streak painted the guts of the building. "This is the backblast. Notice how it extends far into the building."

"That's impossible! There aren't any rooms in that structure that deep."

"Our mystery weapon wasn't fired from inside a room," Wanjiru corrected him. "It was fired from inside a *stairwell*. And notice the length of the blast itself. It's abnormally large."

Navarro considered. In his mind, he saw the missile's launch burning a white-hot arc across the sky. Something about that image made him stop and think twice.

"Were you able to locate the building itself?"

"It's a five-story low rise residential building at 120 East Gondastraat. It's in the part of the city M&B has designated as the Red Zone. I hear the locals have nicknamed it *Goblintown*."

"With good reason. It's a free-fire zone for the cartel's people. No one wants to be caught out there when it starts getting dark. But that still gives us a window of time we can use."

Wanjiru raised an eyebrow in surprise. "A window of time to do what?"

"To clear up this mystery," Navarro declared, "And maybe to figure out who targeted that bird once and for all."

Michael Angel

CHAPTER TWENTY

The secure personnel carrier jolted as it rolled over patches of broken asphalt. It jostled the people in the back, making one of the men grab hold of a door handle to steady himself. Sims threw a worried glance back as he heard a muttered curse.

"Sorry about that," he called. "We just crossed into Goblintown. There's potholes out here bigger than our tires."

"That's because they gave up on road repairs in this part of the city," Navarro observed. "Just keep clear of the worst ones. We break an axle out here, then we're going to have a rotten day."

"Roger that."

Navarro turned back to face the four men who shared the space in the rear of the truck. A printed schematic of the target building and neighboring structures lay clipped to a makeshift display table. Each of the M&B men carried the standard-issue M4 carbine and nothing else, which made them less than happy.

The first objection came from Hagen, which he expected. The barrel-chested redhead's favorite combat toy was the M32 MGL, a revolver-type multiple grenade launcher. His buddy Campbell was a virtual twin in looks and attitude. He nodded along, backing up his friend's words.

"Lieutenant," Hagen complained, "I don't see why we can't bring a grenade launcher to this party. If we're going inside, then we need to clean out rooms or flush people out. Best tool for the job."

Navarro shook his head. "I'm not a Lieutenant, not since I left the Corps. But the drone intel is showing a few infrared hits inside our target, and they're not moving much."

Kimura rubbed his sparse black goatee as he spoke up next.

"Could be bad guys," he pointed out, as he adjusted his helmet headset along with the others. "Pulling guard duty, acting as sentinels for an internal room."

"Unlikely. The building's abandoned, and none of the cartel people have claimed it as a base of operations. That means we're looking at a couple of squatters, maybe even a sleeping family. We're not going to cause any collateral damage if we can help it."

The final question came from Reyes. Again, Navarro had expected this. M&B had recruited the wiry-bodied expert from the U.S. Army's Sniper school, where he'd taught courses on the M110 rifle.

"*Jefe*, we've got three other low-rises on this block. Excellent places to set up and snipe you as soon as you stick your head up. Let me take up a spot in the building across the street, I should be able to counter–"

"Normally, I'd agree," Navarro interrupted. "But I'm counting on us getting in and out before anyone knows we're even there. In any case, I'm going to need your skills inside with me."

Reyes patted the phone he carried at his hip. "If I knew my photography skills would be in such demand, I'd have hung out with my uncle Hector some more. He does stuff like this for the cops in LA."

"We're coming up to the target area!" Sims called from up front.

Navarro let out a breath, set his hand on the sliding door's handle, and spoke once more to his squad. "Campbell, Hagen,

Kimura, I want you to set up a four-man perimeter with Sims around this vehicle. Reyes, you're with me."

He got a chorus of assents and nods.

"Watch your back, gentlemen," Navarro added. "Doctor Austen's trying to figure out why Redhawk's men are sick. But the only thing you can pick up out here is sudden-onset lead poisoning."

The gallows humor earned him a couple of grim chuckles. Sims pulled the truck to a stop by the side of the road. A *shunk* as the door slid back and the five men got out.

Navarro quickly scanned up and down the length of the street. It lay deserted and quiet, save for the distant background noise of traffic from elsewhere in the city. The setting sun turned the crumbling concrete walls of the buildings blood red and the broken asphalt oil-slick black.

Sims got out and unslung his M4. The other three men assigned to perimeter duty fanned out as Navarro had instructed, quickly taking positions to watch the street as well as the doorways of the nearby buildings.

"Let's go," Navarro said to Reyes.

The two men jogged up a set of steps towards the target building. To Navarro's eyes, it looked like it had been originally designed as an upscale apartment complex. The glass-paneled French doors were gone, and their boots crunched over the shattered remains. A wide, open foyer had been turned into a mass of long-dead fern planters and ripped-out mailboxes.

Navarro toggled his headset. "Wanjiru, talk to me."

The man's Kenyan lilt echoed in his ear. "I've put Costello into a surveillance orbit around your block. Aside from those low-level IR readings, there's been no new activity in your area."

"Hope it stays that way."

Reyes took point, making his way to the stairwell door. He cautiously pushed it open with the barrel of his weapon. The smell of stale urine spilled out of the interior, and the floor was carpeted with used needles.

"*Putos adictos*," he muttered. "It's clear."

Navarro went in first. He carefully scanned the cramped space and the winding stairs leading on up. High above, the sunlight streamed in from a crack or window in the outer wall.

"Yeah, that's where we're going," he murmured.

Floor by floor, Navarro made his way up. Reyes covered the rear, glancing apprehensively below for anyone emerging out of the gloom. A rush of warm air spiraled in from above, carrying the nose-tickling scents of fractured concrete and over-ripe tropical fruit.

They'd reached the fourth-floor landing when two new scents reached Navarro's nose. He halted abruptly. Reyes, who was still scanning below, bumped into him.

"What's the problem?" he whispered.

"I'm smelling the remains of propellant," Navarro answered. "Up ahead is where they launched the rocket to take down the bird."

"Is that a problem?"

"No, but the smell of rice cooking is. Someone's up here."

Suddenly, the door to the landing creaked open. Navarro's weapon came around with lethal speed. His finger went to the trigger—

—and he came within a millisecond of shooting a woman with ragged clothes and wide, frightened eyes. Her mouth opened as if to let out a shriek.

"*Stilte, stilte,*" he said quickly, remembering some of the Dutch words he'd memorized. "*Niet kartel.*"

"*Niet?*" She eyed them warily, even as Navarro lowered his weapon. Behind her, in the hallway off the staircase, lay two small children, barely old enough to be toddlers. A little nest of scrounged clothes, canned goods, and a pot of rice had been stashed further inside.

Navarro looked up towards the next turn of the stairs. Sunlight poured in from up an irregular opening in the outer wall. A long, purplish burn mark had engraved itself into the side of the stairwell. Further up, he spotted circular pits that had been drilled or punched directly into the concrete.

"Reyes, you're up," he said. "See if you can get some

pictures of those long burn marks, maybe those circular bits punched into the wall."

"On it." Reyes shouldered his way past Navarro. He gave a little wave and smile to the toddlers as he passed the doorway. They only stared back at the strange-looking man.

"*Niet veilig. Gaan, gaan,*" Navarro said to the woman. *Not safe. Go, go.*

In response, she held out a hand in supplication. "*Helpen?*"

He dug into a pocket as Reyes began snapping away. Navarro came up with a couple of crumpled Surinamese bills and chemical test strips. He pressed the bills into the woman's palm. They'd used many of the strips yesterday when testing for chemical residues on the downed helicopter.

Navarro knelt by the closest burn mark., He tore open one of the remaining strips and did a quick swab of the wall. He packaged up the sample, dropping it into his pocket.

"What do you think this is?" Reyes asked.

Navarro moved up to the next turn of the stairs, where the light poured in. Reyes handed him a badly scorched chunk of metal the rough size and shape of a pack of quarters. He was about to reply when Wanjiru's voice sounded in his ear again.

"I've got visual on the two of you," he said. "That crack in the wall is larger than I thought."

Navarro squinted against the sunset. He was just able to make out the gull-winged drone. It flew high above, almost invisible against a skirl of cloud.

"Any new thermal readings?" he asked.

"No..." Wanjiru's voice hesitated. "I may have a calibration issue with this drone. Your forehead is showing a slight rise in temperature. Likely from your being out in the sun."

Navarro frowned. *I haven't been up in the sun, though. Reyes has. That means...*

On instinct, Navarro dropped to his knees.

With a *crack*, the sniper's bullet smashed into the concrete where his face had been a second ago.

Navarro half-walked, half-slid backwards down the stairs. Reyes poked the barrel of his weapon outside and let loose a blind spray of fire up towards the neighboring building. The *rat-tat-tat* of his M4 thundered in the confines of the stairwell.

The children let out a wail as the mother dove back inside and slammed the stairwell door with a *bang*. Navarro toggled his headset back to the squad's frequency.

"We're taking fire up here," he announced, trying to sound calmer than he felt. "We've got snipers in the adjoining building, and they're using laser rangefinders."

"Copy, we hear and see your outbound fire," Hagen responded. "Do you need assistance?"

Reyes put in one more burst from his M4 before diving past the opening, trying his best to keep low. A second *crack* whistled past as he did so. He let out a cry as he tumbled down the last couple of steps.

Navarro went to the man's aid, pulling him upright and searching for the wound. "Where are you hit?"

"Ricochet," Reyes panted. He raised an arm, grimacing as he did so. "Took it on the body armor above the elbow. *Mierda*, this stings!"

"We'll check it back at base. Can you walk?"

"Hell yes, I just want out of this shooting gallery!"

Navarro spoke into his headset again. "We're okay. Coming to you now."

They men hurried down, taking the stairs two at a time. Navarro's headset chimed, and he heard Wanjiru's voice again.

"I have multiple heat signatures approaching your building from east and west. Men on foot. Likely not the local constabulary."

"Hagen, you catch that?" Navarro asked. "Someone just pulled the fire alarm."

"Roger that. We're on it."

Navarro and Reyes emerged into the foyer to the sound of gunfire echoing like a familiar drum beat along Goblintown's streets. On the far side of the personnel carrier, Hagen and Campbell kept up murderous arcs of suppressive fire. Kimura and Sims kept watch over the relatively quiet near side.

Kimura slid open the side door so that he and Reyes could

pile in. Sims slipped back into the driver's seat. The truck's engine turned over with a welcome grumble.

Navarro ran around to the far side of the truck, unslinging his M4 and providing cover fire as his last two men got on board. Then he followed suit, sliding the door closed behind him.

His skin crawled as bullets began whining off the outer plate. Yet more rounds of rifle fire rattled the truck, this time from the opposite side.

"Get going!" he shouted to the driver.

Sims didn't need any more encouragement. He gunned the engine with a roar, swung the vehicle around, and headed out of Goblintown's rickety streets as quickly as possible.

I hope this was worth it, Navarro thought, as the truck jounced its way back towards the Green Zone. *Hell, I hope Leigh's already figured this whole damned thing out.*

CHAPTER TWENTY-ONE

The cruise ship's business center turned out to be a well-appointed lounge equipped with a dozen or so workstations, two dozen printers, and even a couple dust-covered fax machines. How much business actually got done when the ship was up and running was questionable. The arms of the workstation chairs had built-in holders for drinks.

Austen walked in, followed closely by Piper. She spotted a desk that had been pushed out from the wall. A mug sat atop the desk, a little wisp of steam curling up from it. She headed that way and caught the scent of a strong-smelling earthy beverage mixed with berries.

"October?" she called.

The desk vibrated as something went *thump*. October got up from behind the desk, his bushy eyebrows coated with dust. He winced and rubbed the top of his head with one meaty hand.

"*Chert poberi*," he muttered. "I am missing my friend Redhawk even more now. He can fit under desks better."

"Sorry about that," Austen said, as she approached the big man. "I didn't know you were down there."

He shrugged and pushed the desk back into place.

"Is nothing. Satellite dish is hooked up now." October grabbed the mug and took a long sip. "Was what you call a 'pained in the neck', but it is done."

"We owe you one for that," Austen said, as she caught another whiff of the man's drink. "What is that, anyway?"

"This? Is tea!"

"Seems like an awfully light drink for someone who likes vodka."

October let out an ursine snort at that. "Tea is *second* national drink of Russia. Besides, this is *zavarka*, special tea. Made with herbs from my parent's dacha."

"That must be where the berry smell is coming from."

"Is good. Is very strong. Will put much hair on your chest! I will get you cup."

Austen did her best to keep a straight face upon hearing the offer.

"I'll...pass for now. Maybe later, when I need some hair on my chest."

"Leigh," Piper called, from the nearby corner of the room. "It looks like we're just getting our results now."

October and Austen joined Piper as an attached printer began spitting out sheets of paper. The big man took another slurp from his mug and looked on curiously. Austen checked the settings on the bank of medical equipment.

True to his word, Niles Bailey had provided everything Austen had asked for. Better yet, everything looked in order, from the device that did chemical analysis to one that cultivated organisms in various mediums. Green indicators flashed reassuringly and a chime sounded as results flickered onto an attached monitor.

"Your machines sound happy," October remarked.

"Wish I could say the same for myself," Austen said, as she scanned the printouts. "Damn it, I thought we had something here!"

"Is problem?"

"Yes, is problem! These samples show nothing but normal background microbes. Standard gut flora. A couple minor

116

contaminates, but that's it. Nothing out of the ordinary!"

"I'm seeing the same thing," Piper said, as she paged through the screens. "Standard Gram stain shows nothing."

"Damn it," Austen fumed. "What about Gram-negative bacteria?"

"I made sure to add a wash and a set of counterstains. That came up negative, too." Piper gave her a puzzled look. "I don't get it. All this stuff is state of the art, it even checked for signs of viral infection and came up empty."

"Some of the tiniest bugs are the hardest to spot. But there's a simpler way to see if we're dealing with a viral bug."

Austen walked around to the side of the bank of machines. The sample vials Piper had set up hung securely inside a secure biosafety cabinet. Austen peered at each vial, looking for debris settling at the bottom or floating at the top.

"I don't understand," Piper complained. "The equipment already said–"

"What works in a lab can be different than the field," Austen said abruptly. "And sometimes, the old-school ways are best. Viruses hijack a cell's internal mechanism, forcing it to pump out copies of the virus until the cell finally bursts."

"Okay, I get it so far."

"That tell-tale debris from the burst cells should be trapped inside these vials. And I'm not seeing anything. You know where that puts us?"

"Up a certain creek without a paddle, that's where."

Austen turned to October. "Can you raise Doctor Preble over the satellite dish?"

The big man gave her a gap-toothed grin. "Is no problem. I shall put on room speakers."

October went over to the next free console. He carefully typed in the commands needed to activate the dish and make the connection with London. The line picked up on the first ring.

"Ted, it's Leigh," she said, without preamble. "We sent the results from our testing over to you. Did you receive them?"

"Hang on a moment," Preble said. The clicking of a

computer keyboard sounded ghostly over the room's speakers. That was followed by an intake of breath. "Good lord, have you gone over the toxicology report yet?"

"Not yet. We were looking for direct traces of a bacterial or viral infection, but came up blank."

"Well, I'm seeing toxins. Just a trace amount. But it's one bloody magnificent brew-up, I can tell you that."

That made Austen sit up straight. "What are you seeing?"

"The blood samples are showing...*something*. Not metallic or synthetic chemicals, either. This looked like a positively nasty soup of organic alkaloids. What's more, they look similar to...oh, hell, that can't be right."

"Go on," she urged. "What do they look like?"

"Neurotransmitters. Substances that carry communications between nerve cells. I'm seeing at least two that are analogous to serotonin and epinephrine."

Piper's eyes went wide. "Serotonin can promote a feeling of well-being. The strange lassitude of the patients when we arrived...could that be connected?"

"Maybe." Austen chewed her lip for a moment. "It's can also be a vasoconstrictor. That might account for the blue-gray toes and fingertips."

"And the epinephrine. That's *adrenaline!*"

"Piper's right. You're on to something, Ted," Austen said. "We just came from sedating an entire ward of patients. A moderate increase in light triggered an intense fight-or-flight response. Anything else you can tease out of that 'soup' is going to help us figure out what's going on."

"I'll try," Preble said. "But these compounds are organic in nature. I'm going to have to take this into the university lab and run it by the experts there. It's the middle of the night over here, they won't be in until tomorrow morning at best."

Austen sat back for a moment, deep in thought. Her mind was filled with the sounds and smells of a viral epidemic. Hot African sun. Decomposing bodies.

She wasn't going to let that happen again.

Austen turned to address the others in the room. "Would

you two mind meeting me back at the medical bay? I'd like a minute or two to talk with Doctor Preble alone."

"But—" Piper objected, "If you're going to make a decision, then I deserve—"

"Now, Piper," Austen said sharply.

The younger woman glared at her, but she kept quiet. October simply nodded and led the way to the door. Austen heard a dull *thud* as Piper struck the wall with a fist on the way out.

"What is it, Leigh?" Preble asked quietly.

"We just lost one of our patients," Austen said, in a similarly soft tone. "He'd already gone comatose from an earlier injury. But whatever this bug is, it punched right through that state of unconsciousness and caused him to bash in his own skull."

"That's not possible. Not without a lethal dose of epinephrine."

"Possible or not, that's what we're damn well looking at! Those other patients I've got, including Redhawk...how long before these neurotransmitters burn through the sedatives?"

"There's no way tell for sure," Preble admitted. "But once they do, they'll either expire from heart failure or simply burst a blood vessel. In the lungs, in the brain, anywhere that's a tripwire will do."

"And here's my problem: I can't conclusively prove that this infection is lethal. And since I've got it contained, I can't even claim that it's virulent. That's a problem if I try and call the WHO over this."

"What about the local officials?"

Austen stifled a bitter laugh. "The only responsible ones died in the helicopter crash. I've been to see the Governor as well. He's a joke."

"What do you plan to do?"

"When Niles Bailey recruited me for this job, he told me that it would be helpful...if some of my patients didn't make it. Because without some proof of this disease's lethality, I wasn't going to be able to get the alarm out. I'm going to have to reclassify the three deaths related to this case. File them as victims of this bug, whatever it is."

She could practically hear Preble shaking his head. "That's a violation of our code of ethics. Don't compromise yourself. Think what this will do to your career, Leigh!"

"But this is what I do. It's what makes me who I am. I don't want to compromise *that*."

"But...you'd be ruining your reputation."

"If my reputation is the price for saving people's lives down here – for saving John Redhawk, for that matter – then isn't it worth it? Shouldn't I be willing to pay the fare?"

"I know it's a bad situation. But unless you get...I don't know, a sign from God, then you shouldn't do this."

"A sign from God? Really, Ted?"

"I'm a badly lapsed Anglican. It's just a figure of speech."

Austen heard the pounding of steps coming her way. Piper burst into the business center and skidded to a stop before her, clenching a sheaf of papers in her hand.

"It's happening," she gasped. "New. Outbreak."

The news hit Austen like a physical blow. Her knees felt weak and threatened to buckle as she spoke.

"What? Where?"

"Fifty miles to the west." Piper spread out the papers on the desk between them. "Town called Kolhorn. Then there's *another* outbreak to the east. Suburbs of the capital, in Paramaribo."

"How many? Who's on this?"

"Two dozen in each case, at least. These cities have working hospitals, at least. Trauma teams cordoned off the area in the capital, so Governor Murken must have passed on your warning, at least. Kolhorn's only got a couple doctors from *Médecins Sans Frontières* who are still trying to get a handle on that one. But the news is already spreading on local channels."

Damn it all, Austen thought. *The genie's out of the bottle.*

"Ted," Austen said wearily, "It looks like we just got our sign from God. We don't have the outbreak under control anymore. Can you contact the WHO for me on this one?"

"That'll be my first call when I hang up with you," Preble promised. "After that, I'm phoning my local bishop. I need to find out when they're holding the next service I can attend."

CHAPTER TWENTY-TWO

Daan de Murken wasn't used to being called out of bed after nine in the evening. To be precise, he wasn't used to being called after hours *at all*. So, when the heavyset Governor waddled out into his office, bleary-eyed and wearing little more than a stained silk robe over a pair of slippers, Navarro knew that he was already on thin ice.

"Governor," he said, "I've got some new information–"

In response, Murken held up a hand and extended a single index finger. The message was clear: *Wait*. Navarro kept quiet. The Governor shuffled to his office's minibar, mixed himself a vodka gimlet, and tossed it back with a sigh. He then made his way back to his desk and all but threw his bulk into his chair.

"Mister Navarro," he sighed. "It is only my respect for your people's work that has gotten me out of bed when I should be fornicating with my mistress, drunk, or asleep. Preferably, in that order. So. Whatever you show me had better be *erg belangrijk*."

Navarro took a breath and started over.

"I've got some information that should lead us to the people who shot down Hoogeveen MedFlight 3209. I saw the launch that brought down the helicopter. Something's been bothering me about it."

"Other that the deaths of the people on board?" Murken asked sardonically. He reached over his desk to grab a cigar from his humidor. "No, please go on. You have me curious now."

"I've seen anti-aircraft missiles launch from up-close before. At short range, they burn their way across the sky in a perfectly straight line. But this missile didn't. It flew in a high arc."

"Meaning what, exactly?"

"That we were looking at an entirely different kind of weapons system," Navarro said, as Murken clipped the end of his cigar and carefully lit it. "The drone footage confirmed that something suspicious was going on. So, I sent in a team to visit the launch site."

"Ah, the game's afoot!" Murken took a puff of his cigar and exhaled a fragrant cloud of smoke. "I'm sure the Goblintown locals didn't appreciate the visit."

"Things got a little lively," Navarro hedged. He set a sheaf of photos on the Governor's desk. "We found these burn marks and punches into the cement inside the building's stairwell. Also, we did a chemical analysis of the scorch residue. It's not rocket propellant. It's from a mix of nitrocellulose and nitroglycerin."

"I'm no chemist, but I'll assume that's important."

"Flight 3209 wasn't hit by a Stinger. It was taken down with a modified RPG-7. A rocket-propelled grenade."

Murken blew another puff of smoke. "And that means?"

"RPGs are cheap compared to a real anti-aircraft system. They're also a hell of a lot harder to track on the black market. That's the main reason the cartels haven't been using Stingers or the like to shoot down anyone. It brings too much attention, too much heat."

Navarro pulled the scorched chunk of metal Reyes had found out of his pocket.

"This is a bolt we found in that same stairwell," he continued. "It had been punched into a solid concrete wall to hold a modified RPG launch system, one with an extra propellant charge attached behind the warhead. There's only one exotic weapons smith around who does work like this. Johan de Diaken."

Murken sat up as he coughed on his own cigar smoke. "The *Deacon*? You think the Deacon has something to do with this?"

"I thought that would get your attention. If he's not responsible, then he should be able to tell us who is."

The Governor rubbed his chin. "Let us say that we'd want to 'speak' to him. Would our friend Geoffrey Chadwick at Deep Six object?"

"He would. However, I spoke to my own higher-ups about it. If I get your approval, then we could bring him in."

"And why would you need my approval?"

Navarro smiled thinly. "Because the Deacon upped stakes after you sentenced him to death. Our intel places him in the Grenadine Islands to the north and west of Suriname. Which happens to be run by your cousin. Perhaps you could ask him to look the other way for us?"

Murken was silent for a moment. He took another puff and then blew a perfect smoke ring. The act seemed to please him.

"Very well, I shall. Now, if you'll excuse me, I need to get back to—"

Navarro looked up at the sound of a commotion in the hallway outside. Someone shouted, *Daar niet naar binnen gaan!* just before the door burst open.

Leigh Austen strode up to the Governor's desk, her face grim.

"Sorry to keep you from your bed," she said without preamble. "But no one's getting any sleep tonight."

"You again," the man groaned. "How is it that you pick the worst times to show up?"

"Never mind that," Navarro said. "I'd like to know how you got past Murken's security guards."

"October's keeping them entertained." Austen snatched a remote off the Governor's desk and switched on the big-screen television. She thumbed through the channels until she found the local television station. "You need to see this."

The news report from Kolhorn showed camera footage of Surinamese police holding back crowds from a quarantine barrier. Shots rang out, with at least two people falling to the ground before canisters of tear gas were broken out. A second report from Paramaribo showed rows of people in hospital beds, their features slack and their fingers an unmistakable blue-gray.

Daan de Murken's jowly cheeks went pale. His voice fell to a choked sputter.

"*Godverdomme*...when did this happen? How?"

"Apparently, two incidents took place this afternoon," Austen said. "Witnesses say that men in black leggings and masks sprayed a customs house in Kolhorn and an army barracks in Paramaribo with an unknown substance. No one was killed in the initial attacks, but people are now starting to get sick."

Murken's desk phone began to ring. He seemed to shrink from it even as he picked it up.

"*Ja, Meneer de President,*" he said quietly, and the voice on the other end of the line rattled off a series of orders. Beads of sweat appeared on Murken's wide forehead as he set the phone down in its cradle.

"What you have shown me is just hitting the international news channels," he said, jabbing his finger in Austen's direction. "I have been told to follow the advice of my 'medical experts'. Since they are dead, it seems that I have no choice but to listen to you."

Austen let out a breath.

"All right. For starters, I want those cruise ships at the wharves out of here. No later than tomorrow morning, if possible."

"Couldn't these people have already been infected?" Navarro pointed out.

"It's a risk, yes. But here in Hoogeveen, it looks like we have this thing contained. So, we need get as many people out of harm's way as possible."

"My harbor people are short-staffed," Murken complained. "This will take some time."

"I've got a couple people with me that can help," Navarro said. "Let your harbor master know that we'll be performing an assisted evacuation at first light."

"Once those ships are gone, nothing else comes in or leaves," Austen added. "As for the airport…passengers on an international flight won't show symptoms before they disembark. So we need to shut it down *now*, except for one function."

"What's that?"

"Paramaribo seems to have things at a low boil, but you saw the riots in Kolhorn. If you have any short-haul aircraft, I want to fly anyone infected here to Hoogeveen. We can use vans or ambulances to bring people to the *Stella Maris*."

"We're going to need to figure out how to disinfect both aircraft and automobiles," Navarro warned. "This won't be easy."

"No, it won't. But it has to be done. You've set up the best isolation clinic between here and Paramaribo, and we're going to use it."

Murken set his half-smoked cigar aside with a sigh.

"I will make sure these things are done. What else will you need, Doctor Austen?"

"Prayer, Governor Murken," Austen said. "Any outbreak requires a lot of luck to contain it. I wouldn't object to having someone put a divine thumb on the scale in our favor."

With that, Austen turned and strode out. Navarro nodded to the Governor and followed in her wake.

CHAPTER TWENTY-THREE

Nobody got much sleep that night.

To their credit, the government officials in both Kolhorn and Paramaribo were able to enforce quarantines of affected areas in both cities. However, the butcher's bill to do it came to a half-dozen deaths and many more injuries as people attempted to flee the area. Fistfights broke out at the capital's municipal airport over seats on the last flight out of the country.

The cruise liners in Hoogeveen harbor had rounded up their passengers and were informed of what to look for should anyone fall mysteriously ill. However, the ships still lined the docks a scant hundred yards from the *Stella Maris*.

Sims drove one of M&B's personnel carriers back down to the docks in the dim light before the sun truly rose. Next to him, October gulped coffee from a spill-proof container. Navarro sat in the main passenger compartment behind the two, his attention divided between a set of maps and a long list of special equipment to be flown in that afternoon.

"October," Navarro finally said. "I'm going to have to leave you down here while I finish setting up our operation for tonight. Are you sure you can handle this?"

"Of course," October said. "Is easy like cake."

"You mean like pie."

"Pie is good too," the big man agreed. "I am liking the kind with little crumbs on top."

Navarro let that one pass. "Just see what you can do to help get these boats out of here. We can't bring patients in from the airport safely until they're gone."

Sims drove past the main wharves, turning down the last pier at the end. He pulled to a stop next to a ship that had been painted in a green-and-olive camouflage pattern. The country's red-and-green striped flag fluttered at the stern.

Navarro and October got out and looked up at the vessel. At two hundred feet long, she was roughly two-thirds the length of the *Stella Maris*. A pair of M2 Browning .50 caliber machine guns were mounted on her forward deck, but that was immaterial to Navarro. As far as he was concerned, anything that could lead the deep-drafted liners out of the docks was welcome.

He spotted a naval officer in earnest conversation with a trio of sailors at the base of the gangplank. The officer was a blond, badly sunburned man who wore a brimmed cap adorned with the Surinamese gold star. He snapped out some orders, sending the sailors off at a run, and then waved to the newcomers to join him.

"I didn't expect to see you again so soon, Navarro," the man said gruffly. "And if I did, it was going to be back at another of Murken's all-night parties."

"I thought so too. This world works in funny ways." Navarro indicated his companion with a nod. "Captain Henriks, this is October Shtormovoy. He's a good friend of mine from many missions back. And, unbeknownst to me before now, he's also a qualified harbor pilot."

"You don't say?" Henriks appraised October with a jaundiced eye. "We need a pilot. Hell, we need a harbor tug, but the *verdoemde* thing is in drydock. And our old harbor pilot hit the bottle one too many times, so he fell overboard one night and drowned. Can you handle the job, Mister

Shtormovoy?"

"I was pilot for Vysotsk harbor. Big place. Almost as big as this one," October said proudly. "I can do job. Can also handle drink better."

"Then welcome aboard the *Nieuw Amsterdam*."

"I'll leave you both to your tasks," Navarro said, as he turned to leave. "In the meantime, I've got more places to be."

"Nicholas," October said, as he put a hand on Navarro's shoulder. "I see what maps you have on table. You have dangerous job ahead. Be careful. Try to not get shot."

Navarro simply nodded knowingly. He turned and jogged back over to the where Sims had kept the armored truck idling.

* * *

Over at Hoogeveen's airport, the sunrise made Austen squint. She ignored it as much as possible while she supervised the unloading of a dozen patients from the recently arrived cargo plane. From there, the patients got a seat on one of the three working ambulances left in Hoogeveen.

She wouldn't go so far as to call the airport 'busy', but it was a beehive of activity compared to when she and Piper had arrived. Three companies from the Surinamese army had set up around the airport perimeter to provide security. The apathetic customs agent had been replaced by a diminutive, eager-to-help airport manager who kept her apprised as to which flights would arrive with patients from Kolhorn or medical supplies from Paramaribo.

"*Geweldig*," the manager said, as she made a series of checkmarks on her clipboard. "That's the last one in for the next couple of hours, so far as I know."

"Thanks, and keep me posted of any changes," Austen said.

The manager retreated to the relative coolness of the terminal while Austen waved her sterilization teams to move up into place. These were a group of six soldiers she'd wrangled from a dour Surinamese colonel.

Each team consisted of three people. One controlled and monitored a pump connecting a hose to an industrial-sized tank of bleach solution. Another helped hold and manage the writhing hose, preventing it from kinking. The final member stayed at the business end of the hose, directing a stream of disinfectant from the nozzle to coat the inside of planes or other vehicles.

Her method was primitive as hell, and it couldn't have been put into action unless Governor Murken had done some quick bureaucratic work. He'd let Austen commandeer hoses and pumps from the local fire department. Then, she'd been guaranteed bleach from every chemical supply shop, dry cleaners, and laundromat in the city.

It smelled awful. Even at a distance, even wearing goggles and respiratory masks, the men could only bear the spraying for a minute or two at a time. But it did work. In the concentrations used, even hard-to-kill microorganisms like spores of *clostridioides difficile* would shrivel and die.

The hiss of the hoses stopped. A gush of foamy gray suds washed back out of the cargo bay and coated the runway pavement. The sterilization teams backed off as the fumes filled the air.

Austen looked up as a familiar armored truck pulled to a stop at the edge of the runway. The side door slid open and Navarro got out. He attempted a smile as he approached, but to her eyes it looked brittle and fake.

"Doctor Austen, I've got some news for you. I don't think you'll like some of it. In fact, I don't think you'll like any of it."

She sighed. "I knew this day was starting off too smoothly. What is it?"

"I just dropped October off with the Surinamese equivalent of the Coast Guard. It's going to be a few more hours before all the cruise liners cast off and clear that harbor."

Austen bit back a curse. "I've got patients already loaded in those ambulances. Where are we going to put them?"

"They're not in critical condition, so they'll just have to wait," Navarro said reluctantly. "But I'd at least move the vehicles into the shade cast by the terminal building, keep things more comfortable."

"I'll make sure that gets done. What other news do you

have that I won't like?"

"There's a Cessna Skymaster arriving from Caracas in the next hour. Should be taxiing over to the far runway. Just leave it be."

She stared at him. "Last night, I made it clear: Nothing is to leave or come in."

"You also said that we had things contained here in Hoogeveen. I'm not bringing anything in. That plane's dropping off me and a four-man squad where we can pick up a boat for our new mission."

"A new mission? We've got our hands full here with our patients!"

"Our hands are full, but they're your patients," he corrected her. "My men aren't doctors by trade. I'm trying to figure out who shot down that helicopter just so they could spray-bomb the people inside with that mystery microbe. You're doing your part, Leigh. You need to let me do mine."

Austen didn't like it, but she finally nodded. "All right. Can you at least tell me what you're doing?"

"I'm heading out to do a snatch-and-grab of a man called 'The Deacon'. He's a former drug cartel leader who went into making and selling illegal weapons. I've got a hunch that he can lead us to whomever took out that Red Cross flight."

She looked away for a moment. "Is this going to be dangerous?"

"No more than the usual."

Austen still didn't meet his eyes. "Dangerous, then."

"Does that bother you?"

"A bit." She finally turned back to him. "I was hoping I could still stay mad at you for ghosting me, that's all."

Navarro began to say something, but he thought better of it. Instead, he cleared his throat and answered her unspoken question.

"I'll be careful. Damned careful."

"I know you will, Nick."

He gave her a sidelong look. "You still don't seem all that happy about this."

"Happy?" She gave him a wry grin. "If you can avoid being killed, then we'll be getting help to fight bioterrorists from a former drug kingpin and gun-runner. What's there not to like?"

Try as he might, Navarro couldn't come up an answer for that.

CHAPTER TWENTY-FOUR

Commonwealth of the Grenadines
Île San Espérer
Southeast Caribbean

The evening star twinkled above the rapidly purpling ocean horizon as the powerboat's motor chugged to a stop. The low-profile cabin cruiser lay quietly in the lee of a palm-fringed island, rocking on the swells. From the outside, the cabin cruiser looked set up for a day of sportfishing.

Inside, four of the five men geared up for the night ahead. They each slipped on a camouflage-patterned wetsuit with a horizontal front zip and a hood. The hood contained pockets to house both an earpiece and microphone.

Navarro switched on his system and toggled it to switch between different circuits.

"Wanjiru, do you read me?" he asked.

The man's voice was faint, but audible. "I read you."

"Are Abbott and Costello up and flying?"

"They're orbiting the Deacon's island at an altitude of one thousand meters. However, I shall be able to bring them down nearly to treetop level once dusk is further advanced into night.

135

They should be able to use their payloads effectively then."

"Sounds good." Navarro toggled the switch to jump to the squad's circuit.

"Everyone hear me loud and clear?" A chorus of assents sounded in the cabin as well as Navarro's ear. "Okay, our friend Mister Diaken owns this entire island. He's paranoid enough to have lookout posts on the east and west shoreline. From there, it's a forty-degree incline up the island's main hill and up towards his three-story mansion. The place is open, with lots of wraparound balconies. We don't know how many bodyguards he has inside."

Reyes' voice chimed in from his position up above on the powerboat's bridge.

"There's at least three bodyguards on duty, I can see that much."

"Say again? Were you able to pick them out?"

"The sun's down. I count three separate cigarette flares. One on the ground, two on the second story balcony. *Idiotas.* Didn't even need the night vision binoculars to spot them."

Navarro smiled grimly. "Sounds like our quarry's guards have gotten sloppy. All the better. Any questions?"

"We're going to have problems finding cover when crossing those beaches," Campbell said. "Or when heading up that slope."

"The drones will be helping us there. Just wait for my word to move ahead."

"Any chance I can swap out the beanbag loads in our shotguns?" Hagen asked, in a sardonic voice. "We really doing this while trying *not* to kill anyone?"

"We're hoping to get the Deacon to work with us," Navarro reminded him. "Intel says that the Deacon staffs his private island mostly with relatives. If we happen to kill his favorite cousin, then we can kiss cooperation goodbye."

"Can't say I like it. The bodyguards on that island won't be playing beanbag."

"You still have your shaped charges?" Navarro asked. Hagen tapped a pocket at his wetsuit's waist in answer. "Good.

If we have to blow something up, maybe that'll keep you satisfied. Anything else?"

Navarro got nothing but shaking heads in response.

"All right. Kimura and I will be taking the eastern beach. Campbell and Hagen, you have the western one. Reyes is here for pickup or in case everything goes to hell. Good luck, don't lose your weapons cases, and try not to get shot."

Campbell and Hagen were the first to disembark. They sat on the swim platform at the stern as they slipped on dive fins and a full-face snorkeling mask. Staying close to the surface allowed the men to avoid lugging a bulky air tank, while relying on the darkness to keep from being spotted.

"You two watch out for sharks," Kimura joked. "You both owe me from that last round of Texas hold 'em."

"Like hell we do," Campbell replied. "And if I see any sharks, I'm sending them *your* way."

Once the men entered the water, Navarro handed them their weapons. Each man's gear came wrapped in a waterproof rucksack. With a quiet splash, the two disappeared.

Navarro and Kimura took their places on the swim platform. When their masks and fins were in place, they slipped into the dark water. Navarro felt the weight of the rucksack on his back diminish as his nose filled with the tang of brine against rubber. The ocean surrounding him was the temperature of bath water.

The two men swam towards their destination, checking their distance and direction with the help of a dimly lit GPS tracker mounted on their wrists. As Navarro's eyes grew more accustomed to the low light, he made out dim flashes of light in the water. Bioluminescent plankton outlined their movements with a blue-green shimmer.

That same luminescence made it easy to spot the crash of waves as they rolled onto a small sandy beach. The lookout post was a simple veranda with a view of the ocean. Navarro swam parallel to the shore until he found a rock he could climb on to with a view of the lookout post. Kimura was able to find a similar spot nearby to pull himself out of the water.

Two men occupied the open-air porch. Navarro could hear them talking about something, though he couldn't make out the words over the open surf. One stood, cradling an assault rifle in the crook of his arm while leaning against one of the veranda's support beams. The other reclined in a beach chair, puffing away on a cigarette.

Navarro slowly removed his mask and fins. Then he shifted his rucksack around to where he could unzip it. He took out a snub-nosed weapon made of gray plastic with a dull green finish. The power switch had been painted over to hide its light, but he was still able to find it by feel.

Navarro toggled the microphone at his throat and spoke under his breath.

"East Beach team is ready to rock. Report in, West Beach."

He got nothing but the sound of static.

"Report in, West Beach team."

Navarro forced his nerves to remain calm as he tried a couple more times. This was no time to get the jitters. When there was no response, he switched circuits.

"Wanjiru, this is Navarro. We're in place. Can't contact the West Beach team."

"Hang on, I'm bringing in our drones down low enough to take a look-see." Another minute went by with nothing more than the splash of waves and the rough sound of laughter from the lookouts. "Okay, I've spotted their thermal signatures. Looks like they had to fight a stronger current than we anticipated. They're drawing into position in the next minute or two."

"Good. Activate the jammers. We don't want any calls for help going out."

"On it."

Three hundred meters above the island, Abbot and Costello continued their near-silent orbit as they continued to descend. A shoebox-sized piece of hardware came to life aboard each drone's midsection and extended a set of four antennas. Save for the specially shielded M&B equipment, everything from telephone to WIFI signals ran up against a wall of static.

Kimura drew Navarro's attention with a hand gesture. He pointed to his mouth, and then towards the two guards. Navarro looked around the rock and saw where the reclining guard had just thrown away his cigarette butt. He stretched his arms as if preparing to get back up.

"Tell West Beach to move as soon as they're in position," Navarro said to Wanjiru. "We're moving in now."

Michael Angel

CHAPTER TWENTY-FIVE

Navarro closed the circuit and gestured to Kimura. The two men flicked the power switch on their weapons and steadied them atop their respective rocks. Even through his wetsuit, Navarro could feel the weapon growing warm under his fingers.

Motte & Bailey's contracts for riot control had required them to add more non-lethal ordinance to their arsenal. Navarro had procured a pair of beam weapons built around diode-pumped solid-state lasers. Because they produced temporary blindness, everyone trained on the things called them Dazzlers.

He squeezed his eyes shut for a second as he pulled the trigger. A barely-there *foomph!* echoed in his ear. It was followed by a duplicate whisper from Kimura's weapon.

The results on the receiving end were significantly more dramatic.

The reclining man rolled out of his chair with a cry as he clapped his hands to his eyes. The other guard screamed and fell a step or two back as if physically struck. Navarro leapt up from his hiding spot and dashed up the beach, Kimura in hot pursuit.

Even blind, the standing guard sensed someone approaching. He brought his weapon up just before Navarro hit him dead center in the face with the heel of his palm.

The man's head snapped back. He sank to the ground, unconscious. His rifle landed with a clatter on the veranda's tile. Navarro whirled, ready to help Kimura, but he'd already disabled his target.

"Zip ties," Navarro said. The two unconscious men's wrists and ankles were quickly bound. "Let's see what's happening on West Beach."

Suddenly, the single *crash* of a shotgun sounded over Navarro's headset. His hand went to his communications gear. He heard a *grunt*, followed by panting. Finally, Hagen's voice came in clearly.

"West Beach secure. No casualties. Took both guards out with beanbag rounds. Securing them now."

Navarro looked over to Kimura as the two shucked their wetsuits off. "Sounds like you'll still be able to collect on that round of Texas hold 'em."

His companion flashed a smile and gave him a thumbs-up.

"Anyone hear you?" Navarro asked Hagen.

"Doesn't look like it. Timed the shotgun with the incoming breakers."

"All right, let's move on to the next part of the plan. Ditch the wetsuits and head up to the base of the open slope. Then wait for Abbot and Costello to drop in."

"Roger that."

The semi-darkness of dusk now gave way to true night. Navarro and his men had to pick their way through the blackness, aided only by wan moonlight. They were kept on track by their wrist-mounted GPS units and the occasional bit of advice gleaned from Wanjiru's drone cameras.

Finally, Navarro peered up towards the Deacon's palatial house from the shelter of an entire hedge's worth of night blooming jasmine. The bare slope up ahead would be a perfect killing ground for anyone crossing it. But only so long as they were seen.

"Let's raise the curtain," Navarro said to Wanjiru.

In response, the orbiting drones descended to treetop level. The insectile whine of propellers drew the guard's attention skyward. Which was just what everyone wanted.

Abbott and Costello ignited the packages of incendiary pyrotechnics strapped to their bellies. Everything from magnesium flares to standard-issue Roman candle fireworks boiled out from the drones' steel fuselages, turning night into day.

"Go, go!" Navarro urged, as he charged up the hill.

Exposed like this, he felt the skin on his back crawl. He did his best to put it out of mind. The drone's fireworks were simply for display. It attracted attention and would ruin any viewer's night vision for a minute or so. But it wasn't a blindness-inducing dazzle-weapon.

He came across the first bodyguard standing and smoking outside one of the mansion's side doors. The man didn't spot Navarro, at least not immediately. But he let out a cry of alarm as Hagen and Campbell emerged from the tree line on his right, charging across the open ground at a full tilt.

"*Halte!*" he cried. His hand dropped the still-smoking cigarette and went to a holstered pistol on his hip.

"Hey!" Navarro shouted, as he drew close.

His target whirled about to face him. A flick of a switch, and the man received a blinding blast of laser light. He screamed and fell back a step as he drew his gun.

Navarro dove forward into a running tackle. He drove his shoulder into the man's midsection just as the gun went off into the air. The sound exploded close to one of his ears, sending a jab of pain into his skull.

Blinded and winded, the bodyguard put up little resistance as Navarro got up and kicked the gun away. Kimura arrived and rolled the man over on his belly. He put a knee in the man's back and then zip-tied him into submission.

"Wait here," Navarro ordered. "In case anyone tries to ambush us from the rear."

Kimura nodded. A double set of *BOOMS* thundered from

overhead as a pair of shotguns went off. Panting, Navarro made his way around the curving side of the house, where he'd lost sight of his other two men. He came out into a well-manicured garden of date palms and more fragrant hedges of night jasmine.

The garden lights shone upon a broad set of stairs leading to the second story. He heard a metallic *SHUNK*, followed by the sound of Hagen cursing. Navarro cautiously made his way up the steps until he had a clear view of the second story landing.

Two more bodyguards lay to one side, unconscious and bleeding. Campbell had bound their wrists and ankles and was busy attending to their wounds. Hagen stood next to the mansion's outer wall. The regular wooden door lay off to one side, broken off its hinges. A flat plate of steel hung in its place.

"That thing slid into place before we could jam it," Hagen complained, as he slapped a pair of shaped charges into place on the left side of the barrier. "This model's pretty good, but it's got a weakness by the sliding mechanism."

"Trade you my Dazzler for the shotgun," Navarro said. "You blow it, I'll take point. What do you have besides beanbags to clear the room?"

"Fiocchi shells."

"That should do." Navarro nodded, as the two men traded weapons. He loaded the shotgun with the 12-gauge rubber buckshot pellets as Hagen prepped the charge detonators. "You and Campbell, follow me."

Hagen moved to a safe distance off to one side. He held up a trio of fingers. Then two. Then the index finger alone. Navarro tensed himself for the rush.

A *click* from the detonator, followed by a teeth-rattling *BWAM!*

The door flew halfway open as the explosion ripped through the hinges and flung it to one side. Navarro charged through the opening, heart pounding and lungs tingling from the smell of burnt plastique. He peered through the mist of explosive residue at a lushly appointed living room.

A burly man emerged from an interior room, weapon in hand. Navarro pivoted and let loose with the shotgun. There was a scream as the rubber buckshot knocked the figure down. Hagen and Campbell followed, their eyes scanning for more trouble.

Navarro saw more movement from the inside room. A flash and chime from a wall panel next to the light switch. He dove forward, jamming his shotgun into the doorway before a second steel barrier could slide closed. The metal security door resounded with a *pang* as it slammed against the weapon's barrel and then retracted.

Safety feature, he noted. *Made it easier for me, at least.*

He slipped through the doorway just as his companions let out shouts of warning. Navarro didn't listen. Rather, he focused his attention on the surroundings and the man sitting before him.

Pictures of firearms and shelves of books lined the interior room. An ornately carved wooden desk in the shape of a half-moon sat at the center. Behind the desk sat a man Navarro recognized from photos as their quarry.

The Deacon's features were strong and defined, as if carved out of granite. His hair was dark, while his eyes gleamed preternaturally light gray. His eyebrows were as thick as October's but impeccably groomed. What's more, they did not raise in surprise or concern as Navarro approached him, shotgun in hand.

"Johan de Diaken," Navarro announced, "You're coming with us. We need to talk."

The Deacon leaned back slightly in his chair and looked appraisingly at Navarro. His voice carried the same trace accent as Governor Murken's.

"Very well, I shall go with you," he said, with a tiny shrug. "You know, you could have just asked."

Michael Angel

CHAPTER TWENTY-SIX

Surinamese Rainforest
Suriname – Guyana Border Zone

The mist was still there, hanging over the compound like a malign presence.

But now, shafts of sunlight carved paths through the murk. They stabbed through to the twisted remains of the jungle floor. And that wasn't all.

Erich Zann stood on the catwalk outside his office and gazed out over the rainforest below. A warm breeze ruffled his close-cropped hair. The formerly verdant greenery had taken on the smell of corruption. The stink of a freshly drained sump.

But what really irked him was that the beasts had gotten loud again.

For the first time in days, weeks perhaps, the damned things had been *quiet*. His ears no longer throbbed with the distant sound of howls, snarls, or teeth gnashing. Yet today things had been stirred up again. Stirred up like the greasy residue from the bottom of a noxious pot.

Behind him, Zann's guards slid open the door from his

office. They all but pushed the diminutive Doctor Tiwari outside. Zann gestured for the man to come join him.

Tiwari pushed his square-rimmed glasses back atop the bridge of his nose. His fingers and palms had taken on an edge of callus. His frame had lost a little weight from the extra physical effort he'd been putting into feeding his charges. He walked timidly to stand next to his boss and captor.

"I suppose you know why I asked for you," Zann said.

Tiwari didn't have to guess. "The noise."

"Well, in part. But let's start there. You had them quiet only a little while ago. Tell me what happened, so that I can figure out if you need to be punished again."

"We've observed increased passivity if those infected are allowed to progress along the path of the disease," Tiwari said. "Doing nothing is simply the best option. Long periods of torpidity follow if there are no other stimuli to rile them up."

"So you did...nothing." Zann rapped his fingers on the catwalk's steel balustrade. "Then explain why they are restless again."

"The breaks in the mist. Apparently, as their condition progresses, so does their photophobia. Sunlight acts as a stimulant, possibly a negative one. Certainly, it is more powerful than I could have imagined."

The doctor's voice died as he felt Zann's rough hand rest atop the nape of his neck.

"All the best equipment we could get for you," Zann mused. He felt one of the smaller man's vertebrae at the base of his skull between thumb and forefinger and toyed with the idea of snapping it. "And all you came up with is 'do nothing'. Why did we ever agree to hire someone like you in the first place?"

Tiwari waited until Zann removed the hand from his neck before speaking.

"About my 'hiring'," the doctor said carefully. "I was told that I could return home, and with a full bank account, after a certain period of time. That period has passed, and I've tried my best to do all that you asked."

148

"Tried, yes. Succeeded, no."

"I need to return home!" Tiwari said, with more force. "My wife doesn't even know where I am…when I left, she was expecting. You're depriving me of seeing the child being born, of being part of–"

"I feel touched, Doctor. You've confided a very loving and paternal urge to me, and I appreciate that." Zann's voice dropped a notch. A single, angry notch. "But let me be plain. I don't give a stinking shit about your expanding brood, or your being there to watch your wife birth one of your whelps."

"But–"

"Run along, Doctor. If necessary, you are going to be a guest here long enough for your wife to find another husband to warm her bed."

Two of Zann's guards approached. One escorted Tiwari back inside. The other remained where they stood. Zann threw the man an annoyed glance.

"Well? What is it?"

"We just received this message," came the reply.

Zann snatched the proffered paper from the guard's hand, scanning it with a frown. Zann then read through it a second time, to make sure that he understood its import.

"So, that's the way they're playing this," he said to himself. "Not what I expected, but I can still make use of it."

"Sir?"

"The Deacon's been captured," Zann said. "Fine. Send the next team out. Brief them thoroughly. Make sure that they know what to do."

CHAPTER TWENTY-SEVEN

Republic of Suriname
Hoogeveen City

Austen woke to the sound of grumbling engines, honking horns, and people chanting *Open de stad! Open de stad!*

She sat up with a start. It took a moment for her to remember where she'd ended up.

Groggily, she rubbed her eyes and looked around. She was in the passenger seat of an M&B personnel transport, heading towards the Governor's palace. The up-armored truck had slowed as it approached a crowd of people surrounding the building.

Inwardly, she groaned.

What in God's name are you people protesting? She thought. *Don't you know that there's an epidemic going on? One that could explode into a pandemic at any time?*

Austen had spent most of the day directing incoming planes, supervising their decontamination, and sending ambulances down to the Hoogeveen dockside. From there, Piper was able to handle the transfer of patients to the makeshift wardrooms aboard the *Stella Maris*.

Finally, as the hot sun slid towards the western horizon, a weather-beaten Lockheed L-100 touched down on the runway. Austen felt about battered as the aircraft looked, but her mood improved when the cargo ramp slid down and disgorged a team from the WHO.

Austen now had a team of six doctors and eight more nurses at hand. Just as critically, they'd brought along crates of desperately needed medical supplies. She sent the entire lot down to the cruise ship via ambulance and a commandeered cargo truck.

The help had arrived just in time. Piper had been about to break out plastic trash bags for use as barrier protection and door seals. Now they'd have proper gear to wear and enough monitoring equipment to keep patients alive.

With no more planes due in, Austen retreated to the nearly deserted airport terminal. She'd found an employee breakroom with a communal food area. After a quick search, she promptly pillaged it for hot water and a pre-packaged cup of dehydrated noodle soup. The soup made a poor-but-palatable dinner and got her back on her feet.

From there, Austen had hitched a ride back to the *Stella Maris* on the Surinamese army equivalent of a Humvee. She spent the next hours ensuring that the newly arrived patients were medically stabilized, put under varying degrees of sedation, and secured from spreading the disease beyond their respective wards.

Only after midnight, when her hands shook from fatigue, did she let the WHO personnel escort her and Piper back to the doctor's office for some dreamless sleep. That had lasted until dawn, when Navarro had sent Sims to pick her up and bring her to the Governor's palacio.

The young man's normally smiling face had taken on a deep scowl as he leaned on the truck's horn. He alternated between gunning the motor and letting it idle as he inched forward through the angry crowd. Austen noticed signs in English and Dutch: *Festival Anders Niets! Open Now! Keti Koti Nu!*

Finally, a couple policemen managed to corral the

protestors and clear the palacio's driveway for a moment. Sims revved the engine and lumbered through the gap. He pulled up to the doors and screeched to a stop.

"We're here, Doctor Austen," he said. "Sorry to wake you up back there. Things were getting a little crazy."

"No problem," she said, after a yawn. "As far as I'm concerned, everything's been a little crazy in this country since I got here."

Austen opened the door and stepped down. She made her way past a pair of the palacio's guards and went inside. The interior was as shabby and shadowy as she remembered, but at least it was cooler than outside.

She heard her name called. Navarro stepped out of one of the side corridors and fell into step with her. He held a cup of coffee in each hand.

"Perfect timing, I just found where they hid the machine," he said, passing the cup over to her. "Are you all right, Leigh? You look tired."

"Do I now?" They came up to the waiting area in front of the elevator. She took a long, grateful sip from her cup. "Been working all night. We're up to a hundred and twenty patients spread across four different medical wards."

"I thought the WHO finally sent you some help."

She nodded as he reached out to press the 'up' button. "They did, and I'm grateful. But that's still around thirty patients per doctor. I feel like a dab of butter that's been spread over too way much bread."

"Any progress towards a cure?"

"We still don't know what the hell is *causing* the disease," Austen said, between sips of coffee. "We're buying time with sedatives, tetracycline, and glyceryl. We can't turn the lights down much more. Redhawk's ward is almost pitch black as it is."

Navarro drained his coffee before answering. "I could always give you a pair of my night vision goggles."

"Don't tempt me. Speaking of which, what happened last night?"

The big man shrugged. "Not much. I took a swim. Did a little cardio afterwards."

She stared at him for a moment before cracking up. "You know what I mean! Did you manage to pick up this 'Deacon' character?"

"I did. Surinamese security is bringing him in to speak to the Governor. Figured that you and I should be there too."

A *ping*, and the elevator door opened. They got in and selected the top floor for the Presidential suite. Austen waited until the door closed and the elevator began ascending before speaking again.

"Is that the reason for these crowds? That's practically a riot going on outside."

"People are angry. They want the port open for the Keti Koti festival. It's practically the only way some of these people can support their families."

"Son of a…" Austen bit her tongue. "This thing isn't contained, not by a long shot. We're still getting cases in from Kolhorn and Paramaribo, and that's from the area outside of quarantine!"

"They don't see any sick people walking around. People make assumptions."

"People are just plain stupid, that's the problem," Austen grumbled, between sips of coffee. "Sorry. I sound negative, but I'm just frustrated."

"Don't apologize to me," Navarro said. "M&B's sent me places in the midst of a civil war or uprising. I've seen people killing each other for years over things like which end of an egg a person cracks open first."

She let out a snort that October would've been proud of. "That's from *Gulliver's Travels*. Don't worry, I still haven't told anyone you like to read the classics."

Navarro grimaced. The expression made the scarred side of his face look as if he were wincing in pain. "You get what I mean, though. Trivial things. People can be stupid. Aggressively stupid, sometimes."

"We sound like a couple of misanthropes," she remarked.

"People who don't like people."

"Yeah? Then why do you and I keep doing the jobs we chose?"

Austen and Navarro traded a glance.

"Slow learners," they said together.

Another *ping*, and the doors opened. They stepped out of the elevator, only to come face-to-face with a man sporting thinning hair, the start of a middle-age gut, and a gray suit. He had the expression of someone who'd just eaten a bucket of lemons.

"There you are, Navarro!" he snapped. "I've just given Governor Murken an earful about your reckless disregard for the facts on the ground!"

"If I disregard anything, I don't do it recklessly," Navarro replied, with a perfect poker face. "This is Doctor Leigh Austen. She's been leading the fight against this recent bioterror attack. Doctor Austen, this is Geoffrey Chadwick. He's in charge of Deep Six, which—"

"—is something that's rather above your pay grade," Chadwick finished.

"Nice to meet you too," Austen murmured, but the man ignored her.

"You've cut the number of our guards in half, Navarro. Explain."

"We're stretched thin due to the outbreak," was the weary reply. "If that concerns you, then perhaps your people could cut back your activities?"

"We've got our orders and deadlines too! This is expressly against the terms of our contract!"

"No, it isn't," Navarro said. His voice was patient, but Austen noted that his fists were clenched. "If you actually read Motte & Bailey's contract, the lead contractor on the ground – which would be me – has the right to alter force levels based on major disturbances and developments. I'd say that an outbreak of an unknown disease counts."

Chadwick's face turned an angry shade of red.

"I'm holding you responsible for all of this!" he said, in a voice just below a shout. "I'm taking this to Niles Bailey. Hell, I'll take this to State. I've got connections! You just wait, I'll make sure you never forget this!"

With that, the man stormed off.

"Nice fellow," Austen remarked. "Looks like he's suffering from a bad case of the stupids."

Navarro just let out a breath. He absently rubbed the scar that wended down the side of his face with a finger.

"Come on," he said to Austen. "Now we've got real fish to fry."

With that, Navarro turned and led the way down the hall towards Governor Murken's office.

CHAPTER TWENTY-EIGHT

Daan de Murken paced back and forth before his office desk, peppering the man cuffed to the chair in front of him with questions.

"Who did you build that weapons system for, eh? Who purchased it? How did they pay you? You're going to tell us, one way or another!"

For his part, Johan de Diaken appeared supremely unmoved. Even as Austen and Navarro joined them, his expression of disinterest did not change a jot.

"Like I would tell you," the Deacon said, without heat. "Go weep."

"You seem so *onbewogen*, so stoic for now," Murken said ominously. "But that is easy when you are sitting here in a nice chair. There are chairs in the basement that are not as comfortable. Chairs that draw blood. Remember, Suriname never signed on to any Swiss Convention regarding the rights of prisoners."

Navarro cleared his throat to announce their arrival. "Governor Murken, this man is in my custody."

"Of course," Murken's greasy mustache twitched. "But that is only because I allow it for now."

The Governor began to turn away. His brow twitched. Murken suddenly spun on his heel and delivered a punch to the side of the Deacon's face.

The *thwap!* of knuckle on skin made Austen wince. The Deacon's chair rocked to one side with the force of the blow. Navarro stepped forward to place himself between the two men.

"Enough," he said quietly.

Murken squinted hatefully at the M&B man. Then, as if thinking better of it, he strode out of the room. Navarro let out a breath. He sat on the edge of Murken's desk and faced the Deacon. A deep red mark marred the man's chiseled cheekbone.

"You're getting a shiner from that," Navarro observed.

The Deacon shrugged. "I've had worse. Have you looked into a mirror, my friend? That's some cut you got on the side of your face. How did you acquire it?"

Navarro's facial scar twitched even as it was mentioned. "Not your business. I need the same information that Murken wanted. I don't want to resort to flaying your skin to get it."

"Surely not. You only managed to put my uncle and two of my nephews into the hospital. Rubber bullets break bone and damage organs too, after all. I also hear that their blindness is just wearing off."

It was Navarro's turn to shrug. "You're a tough man to reach. And you have a reputation."

"You are certainly playing to it." The Deacon let out a theatrical sigh as he looked over to Austen. "So. I take it that you are the one they brought in to seduce me into giving away my secrets? I suppose you could convince me if you show enough enthusiasm to make the mattress springs squeak. Normally, I prefer my women younger, but you seem lithe enough at least."

Austen looked over to Navarro. "Can I have a turn belting him?"

"This is Doctor Leigh Austen," Navarro said. "She's been leading the fight against the bioterror outbreak. Be nice to her, or you'll regret it."

"I'm already regretting it," the Deacon admitted, as he looked Austen over again. "You are not a girl from the streets, I can see that now. I apologize, Doctor Austen. I have a talent for rubbing people the wrong way."

"You certainly rub Murken the wrong way," Austen agreed. "Why?"

"During my rise to the head of the Waalwijk Cartel, I had to do some unpleasant things. I did not want to, of course. But if you injure a man, the hurt should be so severe that his vengeance need not be feared."

"Machiavelli," Austen noted. "That's almost verbatim from *The Prince*. Color me impressed. You're a reader. Is that why they call you 'The Deacon'?"

"A fine guess, Doctor. For that, you may call me Johan. But no, 'Deacon' is a play on my family name."

"I see."

"Mind you, I was known to get up on the proverbial soapbox every now and then to encourage my men." He tilted his head towards her and gave her a roguish smile. "Had we met under different circumstances, I could quote more than Niccolò to you. I would read you books of the finest poetry instead. Pablo Neruda, perhaps. Or is Roberto Bolaño more to your liking?"

Austen smiled back automatically, almost against her will.

"I'd rather you tell me what unpleasant things you did, Johan."

"Oh, these things…most were to my competition. Others were to the police force or military people who persisted in causing me trouble."

Navarro made a short bark of a laugh. "That's a very polite way of putting it."

"I'm a polite person, Mister Navarro."

"Really?" He leaned forward to focus his dark eyes on the Deacon's light ones. "I've met people like you before. Charming on the outside, stone cold on the inside. Your ways are so polished, like the skin of an apple. But beneath it all, the core's rotten."

"A few courses in psychology doesn't qualify you to judge me."

"I don't need to crack a book to know you." Navarro looked over to Austen. "Our friend here killed more than eighty people in his rise to power. He personally executed ten of them. Five with his personal firearm. Three with knives. And the last two were the only undercover policemen Governor Murken ever managed to get inside his organization. Johan here strangled them to death with a length of piano wire."

The Deacon didn't flinch. "Are we so different, then? Mister Navarro, I don't think you become the head contractor of a for-hire military outfit by reading Shakespeare or holding tea parties."

"You're a criminal psychopath. What would you care?"

"Call me what you wish. I read people just as well as you. And I can tell that you and the lovely Doctor here have a connection. A spark, if you will."

Austen let out a gasp. Navarro had to will himself not to look in her direction.

"That's neither–"

"Oh, I beg to differ, *soldaat*. Does she know your past? Does she know how many people you've killed? And what do you do it for? Some filthy dollar bills to put in your pocket?"

Austen sensed an opportunity. She stepped forward into the room's brighter light before Navarro had a chance to respond.

"What do *you* do it for, then, Johan?" she asked.

"Me? Once, when I ran a quarter million pounds of white powder and brown *skag*, I did it for money. For power. But I gave it up. I left it all behind and retreated to my island of solitude. I did it for what's in my wallet. It is there, on Murken's desk."

Navarro's brows furrowed, but he picked up the wallet and opened it. Wordlessly, he handed it over to Austen. Inside a flap of plastic protective casing lay the picture of an attractive woman in her thirties with her arms around a little blonde girl with light gray eyes. From what Austen could tell, the girl could have gone to grade school anywhere in Virginia.

"They want for nothing. But they live in the States, safe from me and my business," the Deacon said. "It is like an *echtscheiden*, what you call a 'separation' or 'divorce'. We find a place between my island and their home to meet once, twice a year. That is all the risk I can bear to expose them to."

Austen stared at the picture a moment longer.

"You may not move drugs anymore," she said. "But you still make and sell weapons."

The Deacon nodded sadly. "You cannot understand, not truly. You grew up in a place that is like heaven to people like me. It is easy to be saintly in heaven. But here, in my country, we know that it is not heaven. We have no saints. Only people who do what it takes to survive."

Navarro scowled. "That's a load of horse–"

"Wait a minute," Austen said, and she came over to look down at Deacon's bruised face. "Even on your island, you must get television. The local stations here in Hoogeveen. Do you know about the sickness sweeping your country?"

"I've heard about it. The word is that you get the 'lazies', and then you get the 'crazies'."

"It slows you down, yes. Then, it drives those who get it insane. I've already had one patient bash his brains in on a bed railing. And here's the kicker: so far, everyone exposed to this bug comes down with it. One hundred percent. The lethal exposure for this thing is up there with measles and smallpox."

The Deacon gave her a look. "You think it will spread, Doctor?"

"Yes." She made sure the man saw her eyes as she spoke. "It will spread. Eventually, even to the United States. Even heaven won't be able to keep it out."

The man put his head down. His strong jaw worked back and forth. Navarro watched in silence.

"I believe you," Austen said. "I believe that you did the best you could to make a living while providing for your family.

Now, help me. Help them. Before the sickness comes."

The Deacon was quiet a few moments longer.

Finally, he exhaled and raised his head. The corners of his eyes glistened with moisture.

"All right," he finally said. "I will help. What do you wish to know?"

CHAPTER TWENTY-NINE

Leigh Austen had worked in several makeshift medical wards before now, but she'd never been in one that had a full-blown chandelier. A veritable forest of crystal prisms hanging overhead gleamed softly in the dim light. It occurred to her that she had no idea how they'd ever disinfect the ornamental light fixture.

Still, she had bigger fish to fry right now. She adjusted her face mask as she walked through what had been the forward ballroom on the *Stella Maris*. The row of makeshift hospital beds stretched out before her like a never-ending nightmare.

Doctors and nurses in mint-green gowns went about tending to their patients, though they practically moved in slow motion. She couldn't blame them. The lights had been kept so low that it was difficult to read charts and give medication.

She was just completing her de-gowning procedure outside the ballroom when she heard two people arguing. She hurried to step through the tub of bleach solution and safely bin her gloves as she tried to make out the voices. One was an older male, the other a woman.

Austen walked out into the hallway in time to see Piper arguing with a goateed man wearing a blue and white captain's uniform. Italian curse words flew back and forth. From what she could tell, the young woman was giving as good as she got to Captain Rosella.

"This is my ship," he declared. "Not a beggar's hospital. You people have ruined her, you must leave! *Esci!*"

"I don't care if this is your ship," Piper shot back. "Those are my patients down there, and they're not going anywhere, *uomo pazzo!*"

"*Ridicolo, piccola ragazza!*" Rosella spat in reply. "I go to complain at the harbor master's office! He send me a pilot to kick you off and let me leave! *Proprio così!*"

The captain pushed his way past Austen and stomped off. She watched the man go. Her lips curled in amusement.

"I wish our Captain the best of luck," she said to Piper. "From what I've heard, the harbor pilot had one too many bottles of rum and keel-hauled himself. There isn't anyone qualified to lead this ship out of the harbor, let alone throw us off."

"Thank God for small favors," Piper said, as she brushed back her shock of brown and pink hair. "That guy's got a serious attitude problem."

"It must be tough seeing your pride and joy turned into a floating hospital. Still, it seems like you could throw a little Italian back at him. Good job."

"Thanks," Piper said, as she held up her phone. "Finally, one of my language apps came in handy. By the way, I must've been asleep when you left this morning. Did your guy friend manage to get this drug dealer or arms trafficker on our side?"

Austen's cheeks colored. "Navarro brought him in. I did my best to convince him to help us. And Nick's not my 'guy friend'. He's just my friend…who, ah, happens to…be a guy."

Piper's eye roll spoke volumes. "Uh-huh. Yeah, whatever."

Just then, a chime came from Austen's phone. She breathed a sigh of relief.

Thank you, Lord, for getting me out of that awkward moment.

"Austen here," she said, as she answered the call.

"Leigh," came a crisp British voice, "It's Ted. I've got some information for you on those organic compounds, and it's quite strange. Are you anywhere close to a monitor?"

"Hang on, we can get one up and running in a minute," Austen muted the phone and gestured to Piper. "Let's go."

The two women hurried upstairs and into the business center. Piper opened her email on the computer monitor next to the sample testing equipment they'd set up in a corner. It took her only a moment to locate the message attachment that had just arrived.

Austen took her phone off mute and tapped the speakerphone button. "You're on, Ted."

"It took a while to tease out and isolate several of the compounds from the data you sent me," Preble began. "It's a right stew of things. Aside from the molecules that look like neurotransmitters, there's a host of alkaloids too. Ephedrine, chelerythrine, even quinine. It's like nothing anyone's ever seen before."

"Isn't...isn't chelerythrine an antibacterial agent?" Piper ventured. "Maybe that's an indicator that we're dealing with a virus. I wouldn't expect any species of bacteria to be churning that substance out, not unless it had a death wish."

"Good point," Austen acknowledged. "It's normally produced by plant cells. So is quinine, for that matter of fact. Perhaps we're looking at a virus common to the plants?"

"Not to rain on one's parade," Preble said, "But ephedrine is a muscle-cell stimulant. One that is only found in animals."

Austen began to pace. She couldn't help herself. "So this has parts of both. It must have some sort of dual-machinery in its cells, something! Hell, every time we take a step forward, we go back one!"

"That's impossible, Leigh. There's no way this bug could churn out organic molecules that mimic those found in both plants and animals!"

"*Should* be impossible," Austen corrected him. "We may be looking at something that's new. Something that jumped species."

"Species, yes. But jumping entire *kingdoms*? That's just plain rubbish. There's a reason that we humans don't worry about catching Dutch elm disease, or corn leaf blight. Our cells have completely different structures."

"I don't know, Ted. Maybe we're looking at a new mutation from deep within the rainforest. But something's changed the rules here."

Austen stopped as she heard a hammering at the door. She looked up to see another man in a blue and white naval outfit. One of Rosella's crewmen shouted through the glass at them.

"*Baia medica! Persone stanno morendo!*"

The man then ran off in a panic.

She turned to Piper. "The hell? What did he say?"

The younger woman's face went pale.

"He said that people were 'dying' in the medical bay."

"Damn it!" Austen cursed. "Ted, we've got to end this, we have an emergency!"

"Understood," Preble said. "Finger and toes crossed."

She broke the connection. This time Piper led the way back downstairs. Austen's stomach twisted itself into a knot as she realized something. The trouble was in the medical bay. That meant someone in Redhawk's squad was in trouble.

This time, Austen didn't hear male laughter as she and Piper ran down the lower corridor towards the medical bay.

This time she heard the skin-rippling howl of a wolf.

The two women pushed their way through the doors and skidded to a stop before the observation window. The other side had been plunged into near-blackness. But even in the dim light, they could see things.

Horrible things.

They'd been forced to swap out the plastic restraints on Mason, Redhawk's second in command, for steel cuffs. These rattled like ghostly chains as the man strained against them. The muscles in his neck stood out like steel cords as the man let out another frenzied *howl*.

The other patients babbled incoherently, pulling against their own restraints until joints creaked. Monitors at the head of each bed flashed scarlet red as the indicators for rapid heartbeats and vessel-bursting blood pressure topped out. One patient's shoulder made the gristly sound of a drumstick being ripped from a fresh cooked turkey as he dislocated it.

"Oh, God! Oh, God!" Piper breathed, as she and Austen ran over to the gowning area.

Her hands shook as she groped for a pair of gloves. One of the shaped pieces of nitrile dropped to the floor. Without thinking, she went to pick it up.

Austen grabbed her wrist, stopping her. Piper looked up at her, eyes wild.

"Take. Your. Time." Austen said. "You can't help anyone if you don't gown up properly. Either you bring a new bug inside, or you catch what they have."

"Gotcha." The young woman swallowed. She took a breath and started over.

Once they'd both gowned, the two pushed their way inside. The trio of nurses in the room struggled to hold one of the patients still before he ripped out his IV line. An empty bedpan went flying and ended up on the floor with a clatter as they tightened the restraints.

Alone amidst the chaos, John Redhawk lay quietly. His hands drummed out a phantom beat even as his hands were balled into fists. His eyes were closed, and his lips moved in a silent chant.

"Diazepam," Austen said, as she pulled a syringe out and loaded it. "Twenty milligrams."

"Jesus," Piper breathed, as she took the needle. "That's close to lethal—"

"Not much choice." Austen grabbed a couple more syringes out and loaded them. "We've got to get this administered!"

Piper ducked a swing made by one partially restrained patient. The man's face contorted into a fearful grimace, and he screamed at her like a banshee. That look faded away to confusion as soon as she jammed the needle into the catheter and pressed the plunger. Another five seconds, and the man slumped back.

Austen managed to get two more patients sedated with the help of the nurses. She then turned to the howling Mason, syringe in hand. But she never got a chance to inject him. The man's eyes simply rolled back in his head as she drew close. Then he flopped back onto the bed in a pool of his own sweat.

The monitors went into a droning *buzz* as he flatlined.

"He's gone into cardiac arrest!" Austen shouted. "Defibrillator! *Now!*"

CHAPTER THIRTY

The men gathered around the conference table inside Motte & Bailey's FOB pored over a Hoogeveen city map and a detailed building diagram. Navarro looked over the small group appraisingly. The four men he'd taken to Île San Espérer were poker-faced over the new assignment. Sims, on the other hand, looked eager to fight. Even October looked happy to be there.

I suppose I can't blame him, Navarro thought. *He's been stuck shepherding boats out of the harbor for the last couple of days.*

"Great," Hagen groused. "Another raid into Goblintown. What happens if we run into the friendly local neighborhood resistance again?"

"I've got a second squad ready to go in," Navarro tapped a spot at the edge of the Red Zone. "They're at most five minutes away."

"Are we sure that we shouldn't just go in with more men?"

"I'm being told that it's best if we go in with a light footprint."

Hagen raised a ginger eyebrow. "By who?"

"Our new best friend, Johan de Diaken. He'll be joining us as well." Navarro held up a hand as the men began murmuring.

"Remember, he knows this area and the building interior better than any of us. He's already waiting for us in the personnel carrier."

"We're not giving him a gun or anything, are we?" Reyes asked.

"Not unless our collective IQ drops to room temperature, no. He's going to remain in partial restraints, and he's got a locator cuff on his ankle. If the Deacon tries to make a break for it, he won't be getting very far. And he won't be doing that."

October's jaw worked as the big man chewed that over. "*Ty dolzhno byt' shutish'!* How are we being so sure of this?"

"Because he's facing the death penalty for his crimes here in Suriname. Governor Murken would dearly love to execute the Deacon, but we've worked out a deal for him. He'll be getting a partial pardon in exchange for his help tracking down the bioterrorists."

Now Wanjiru looked surprised. "How 'partial' might this pardon be?"

"A reduction in sentence from execution to exile-in-perpetuity. I'd say he's got plenty of incentive to behave. Any other questions before I bring the Deacon in?"

There were a couple more murmurs, but no arguments. Navarro nodded to Sims, who left the room. A minute later, the young soldier returned, guiding his charge by the arm.

The Deacon arrived wearing wrist and ankle shackles joined by a six-inch chain. An electronic monitor hung below his right ankle cuff. Wraparound dark glasses restricted his vision. Yet the man appeared unbowed and unfazed. He only blinked, teary-eyed, as Sims removed his glasses.

"None of this was necessary," he complained. "Especially the glasses. It's not like I'm planning to revisit this hidey-hole anytime soon."

Navarro shrugged. "We like our workspace privacy as much as you do, Johan. Now, I need you to tell my men what you shared with me and Doctor Austen earlier."

"Very well." The Deacon wiped his eyes with his sleeve and

then looked around the room as he spoke. "Six months ago, I received a request from the Zielverkop cartel to come up with a 'kit' of sorts that they could use to extend the lethal range of a rocket-propelled grenade. This would effectively turn them into short-range anti-aircraft missiles. The contract they offered was extremely lucrative. So, I created the kit for them. Apparently, my invention worked as promised."

"Why this cartel?" Kimura asked. "And why did they need this hardware?"

"I don't ask questions when enough cash is pushed at me. However, I can offer an educated guess."

"Let's hear it."

"This cartel isn't involved with massive shipments of raw coca. They're what we call *oud pachters*. You would call them people from the hill country. Ones with 'red necks'."

The Deacon paused as he heard a couple snorts at that, and then continued.

"The Zielverkop ship refined cocaine and gold dust directly out of the jungle. You can only get into some of these places by helicopter. My guess is that they're having problems with someone else moving in on their operations. Shooting the competition down would be an easy way to maintain their monopoly."

"We don't know everything that the Surinamese government is doing in the jungle zone," Navarro added. "Or even our own employers. If one of them is getting too close to this cartel's operations, that may be why they resorted to bioterrorism."

"You think the bug that Redhawk's guys picked up is from the jungle?" Reyes asked. "It seems like they figured out a way to harness it, put it to use."

"The best way is to locate their headquarters and ask them ourselves," Navarro said. "And our friend here has an idea how to find it."

"I don't know where the Zielverkop make their home," the Deacon said. "But I've dealt with their *gewisselaar*, their money man, many times over the years. I know where he's based, and where he keeps all the records of the cartel. That is the building you have diagrammed on this table."

Wanjiru spoke up next. "I suspect that this money-man can erase all the records with a magnet, should we get too close."

"Not so! This man was old when I first joined this deadly game. Now, he is ancient. And he has a quirk of the old: he only trusts what he commits to paper. Even if we don't find him, we'll have his records."

"That's too rich a target for us to pass up," Navarro agreed. "Our objective is the *gewisselaar*, or failing that, his stash of records. We'll be rolling up to this end of the Suikerstraat. The Zielverkop stronghold is inside an abandoned sugar plant. Drone surveillance shows no IR signatures or movement outside the building. We expect significant passive security measures to be in place instead."

"We have drone support during mission?" October asked.

"I'll have both of our drones up," Wanjiru said. "They'll have the enhanced IR sensors and jammers we used in the Grenadines. But no fireworks, alas."

"We've got three entries or exits out of this building," Navarro continued, as he pointed to the map. "Hagen and Campbell will take and hold the western side of the building, here. Reyes and Kimura, you'll be watching the gate at the north end. October and I will be escorting the Deacon in through the main loading bays on the south side."

"We still doing the 'non-lethal weapons' crap?" Hagen asked.

"You're authorized to blow up as much stuff as you want," Navarro reassured him. "October and I are aiming for a capture, so we'll be the only ones using dazzlers this time."

October crossed his arms and grumbled sullenly. "Everyone is to be having fun but me."

The meeting broke up on that note.

Navarro and his squad were still in the process of gearing up in the back of the armored truck as Sims drove out the base's side gate. With two extra people in the rear cabin, the space got crowded. The Deacon watched silently as October and Navarro prepped their laser-diode based weapons, checking both charging levels and sights.

"If that weapon is non-lethal," the Deacon finally said, "might I have one to defend myself? If we should run into trouble?"

The back of the truck went quiet, save for the grumbling of the motor. Navarro glanced back at him with a skeptically raised eyebrow that said: *You have to be effing kidding me.*

The former drug capo saw the look and sensed the sudden change in mood inside the vehicle. Hagen frowned. Then he racked his shotgun with a loud, meaningful *CHA-CHACK.*

"No harm in asking," the Deacon said, quickly dropping the subject.

Twenty minutes later, Sims pulled the personnel carrier over to the side of the pothole-riddled street. He kept the motor running as he slid into the shade behind a burned-out square of apartments two blocks from their destination.

Navarro glanced around through the windows as he toggled the circuit on his headset. Goblintown wasn't a great place to sightsee in the best of times. But this section, with its crumbled streets and burnt hulks of old buildings, looked post-apocalyptic in its squalor.

"Wanjiru, this is Navarro. Give me an update."

The reply was prompt. "I have Abbott and Costello in a holding orbit five hundred meters above the target. Nothing, ah, 'kinetic' for half-a-dozen blocks in all directions."

"So far, so good."

"Abbott has detected a working automatic camera system covering all three entryways. Costello's IR sensors have located an electrical line that's emitting heat right outside the western gate. Likely a power source for an alarm system."

"Roger that." Navarro nodded to Sims. The younger man stepped on the gas again. "Wanjiru, activate the drones' electronic jammers. I don't want the cameras to be transmitting our movements."

The Zielverkop stronghold was a large rectangle of loose brick, rusty roll-up doors, and tattered roofing held together by globs of old tar and zinc strips. Even under the hot tropical sun, it had a chilly, forbidding look. Navarro spotted a swivel-camera above the gate, but it had frozen in place thanks to the drone jamming.

Sims pulled over and Kimura threw open the side door so that he and his teammate could step out. Reyes carried an insulated wire-cutter the shape and length of a set of tree pruning shears. He brought it to bear on the power line, parting it with a *snip*. Meanwhile, the personnel carrier lumbered on towards its next stop.

"Lights are out," Reyes reported. "I'm tracing the wire back. Looks like the juice went to an electrified fence and the entry doorplates. Nasty."

Sims hit the brakes on the second stop. Campbell and Hagen got out and headed for their designated spot. Navarro spotted Campbell's upraised thumb as soon as they performed their initial sweep.

"South gate," he said. "Make it quick. Whoever's inside would have to be blind not to know that something's up."

The truck kicked up dust as it slewed around the corner of the building. It slid to a stop in the middle of a wide driveway. Ahead lay a double-wide roll-up door for trucks and a smaller entryway next to it.

October slid open the door this time. He steadied the Deacon as the man got out with one hand while cradling his Dazzler in the other. Navarro adjusted the chest plate on his body armor, swung his leg out—

—and froze as he heard a triple-tone chime come from the inside of the vehicle.

"That's our emergency line," Sims said, surprised. "I thought that it was only for us calling out. Not in."

"We can get calls in," Navarro said, as he flipped open the lid on the vehicle's center console. The lights on the handset flashed red and green. "But only if it's a November Charlie level situation."

October leaned back into the truck. "Nicholas, we must move, now!"

He's right, Navarro though. *Even the most brain-dead cartel gunman would know that something was up as soon as the cameras went dead and the electricity shut off.*

But he knew Motte & Bailey protocol. He'd even used a November Charlie signal to get Leigh Austen down to Suriname before the sun set. You *never* ignored that call sign.

Navarro made his decision as the phone's triple chime went off yet again.

Michael Angel

CHAPTER THIRTY-ONE

The nurses wheeled in a defibrillation unit that had been brought in on the plane from the WHO. Austen started the charging process. Just as the machine began to hum, she heard another sound that filled her with dread.

Ojeda, the patient who'd dislocated his shoulder without so much as noticing, stopped his straining. He flopped back on his bed, feet twitching spasmodically. The droning *buzz* of a second flatline filled the room.

Austen stared, speechless. *This can't be happening.*

"Piper, take over!"

The younger woman stepped in to pick up the defibrillator pads. Austen ran past the beds filled with unconscious patients and climbed astride the motionless Ojeda. She positioned her gloved hands on his breastbone, lined up her shoulders, and began performing CPR.

"Clear!" Piper announced. The nurses drew back as the defibrillator activated with its signature *SNAP!* sound. Mason's body twitched. The monitor lines stayed flat.

Austen counted to thirty as she did chest compressions. She bent forward to give Ojeda the required two rescue breaths, but stopped short. Her mind raced as she realized that she couldn't put her mouth on his with a facemask between them.

Not to mention that mouth-on-mouth would lead to a catastrophic exposure, she thought. *But how am I going to get him to breathe?*

"Clear!" Piper shouted again. A second *SNAP!* "Damn it, come on!"

Austen got off Ojeda's prone torso, rummaged in a nearby cabinet, and came up with bag valve mask, complete with a squeezable resuscitation unit. She slapped the mask over the man's face and began manually pumping air through the face tube. Once she completed that task, Austen returned to a set of chest compressions.

She dimly heard a third 'Clear!' and yet another *SNAP!*

Austen lost track of time as she focused on keeping up the pace of the CPR. Ojeda's eyes remained rolled back in his head, and his entire body had gone slack. A bulge of fluid puffed up on his shoulder where the joint had popped out of its socket.

Sweat popped out on her forehead as she kept on. She felt light-headed, dizzy. She pressed on, swapping the squeezes of the mask with the pumps on the breastbone.

"That's enough, Leigh!" Piper finally said, as she brought the defibrillator over. "Let me try."

She almost fell off the side of the bed. Wobbly-kneed, Austen groped her way to a nearby chair. Closing her eyes, she focused on her own breathing, forcing her lungs to get more oxygen, even constrained by her own safety mask. Eventually, the light-headedness faded away.

Austen heard her name called again. She opened her eyes.

Piper slumped in the chair next to her. Helplessly, she gestured towards the patient beds. Both Mason and Ojeda's monitors were quiet. Someone had disconnected the machines' speakers.

But the screens showed nothing but flat lines.

"I tried," Piper said plaintively. "I never got a single blip out of either of them."

"We both tried," Austen said, her voice hoarse. She put a gloved hand on Piper's gowned shoulder. The gesture felt so inadequate. "Don't forget that. We did all we could."

Piper said nothing for a moment.

"I'm so tired," she finally said. "I'm sorry. I don't know how you do it."

"You just do."

The younger woman groaned. "I was being serious."

"So was I. You work through the pain and you learn from it."

Piper looked at her for a moment with scared eyes.

"Yes, you can do this," Austen said firmly. "Go on and get something to eat, something to drink. There's an open dining area past the foredeck. And if you bump into Captain Rosella again, give him a right hook for me."

Piper tried to laugh at that. She stumbled out as if in a daze. Austen looked over the now-quiet ward. She realized that she still had one more dose of sedatives to give.

She got up, loaded a syringe, and walked to Redhawk's bed. He opened his eyes, which looked haunted and weary beyond belief.

"You didn't find a cure yet, did you?" he asked. She shook her head. "Shit. I figured as much."

"Redhawk, this is important," Austen said. "You heard what was happening to your men. They were crying out, straining against their restraints in anger or fear. You're not showing the same symptoms."

"Who said I wasn't?" Before she could ask, he added, "I mean, I'm seeing and hearing things too. I've been talking with tribal elders from a time when they wore sabretooth cat skins. I've been taking rides into space. I've even watched this wardroom melt around me like warm taffy. But...it's not unfamiliar."

"It's *not*? How?"

Redhawk thought for a moment. "Back at the Rez, we had ceremonies when I was growing up. Religious ones. Used certain substances to see things. Right now, it feels like I'm on them."

She nodded, understanding. "Hallucinogens."

"Yup. Peyote. Mushrooms. Things from my culture. It's a matter of discipline, remembering the tribal wisdom. Knowing that you're on a trip helps." Redhawk's already stern face took on a grimmer cast. "But whatever's going on is getting worse. I can feel it in the back of my head, like an undertow. If I let up for a minute, it'll pounce."

"I'll got diazepam here," she said, as she held up the syringe. "It'll help you sleep."

"Good. And I got one more request." The man's eyes locked on hers. "If you can't figure out how to cure this…whatever it is, I want you to give me another dose of sedative. One that lets me sleep. Permanently."

She gave him a concerned look. "You don't know what you're asking for."

"Like hell I don't. I mean it. An Apache is not a man, not if his mind and spirit are lost."

Austen tried to answer him but found that she couldn't speak. She simply nodded as she injected the sedative. Redhawk's eyes finally closed, and a snore drifted up from his lips.

Something in back of Austen's mind nagged at her. Something that Redhawk had said before she'd sedated him. She gave final instructions to the nurses and then de-gowned as quickly as possible before making her way back to the business center.

Knowing that you're on a trip helps.

Things from my culture.

Peyote. Mushrooms.

Peyote was a plant. A spineless cactus with cells that contained psychoactive alkaloids. The mushrooms used by Redhawk's tribe were likely from the genus *Psilocybe*, a polyphyletic group of fungi that threw off various psychedelic compounds.

That stopped her.

Her brain went through part of her last conversation with Ted Preble.

She'd speculated that the organism was a 'jumper'.

Something that had made the unlikely leap between species. Ted had dismissed the idea.

Jumping entire kingdoms? That's just plain rubbish...There's no way this bug could churn out organic molecules that mimic those found in both plants and animals.

But there *were* lifeforms that could do much the same thing. Another 'kingdom', another classification into which living organisms were divided. Many could break down or even colonize plants and animals, and to do that they needed to be able to manufacture similar compounds.

The answer came to her in a thunderclap of insight: They were dealing with a new kind of pathogenic *fungus*. One that threw off alkaloids into the bloodstream.

She got up and went over to the biosafety cabinet, where they'd stored their samples. The question now became one of location. They'd only detected the hallucinogenic substances in the bloodstream, not the pathogen itself.

Where would it be hiding?

Austen cycled through the samples of blood and tissue until she got to the tiny patches of skin they'd collected. She moved a sample into a separate biosafe glovebox so that she could slide it under a microscope.

She found what she was looking for almost immediately. Long, branching filaments wrapped themselves around the cells in the upper layers of the epidermis. These were classic structures of fungal growth called *hyphae*.

"There you are," Austen murmured to herself, as she grabbed tools to isolate the sample. "And you're placed right where you can drip those alkaloids into the bloodstream – or be spread by touch."

She took photos of what she saw with the glovebox's built-in camera. Then she portioned the sample to grow in multiple types of medium. Finally, she returned to the monitor and fed both the chemical samples and her pictures into a database of fungal pathogens.

The computer let out a blip as it displayed the closest match. Austen sat back and let out a breath as if someone had hit her in the gut. For a moment, all she could do was stare at the image that came up.

The monitor glowed with the rough white and black lines of a medieval woodcut. The artist's jagged strokes depicted a skeletal figure shrouded in a dark, hooded robe. One bony hand clasped a pole. At the end of the pole gleamed a wicked curved blade.

A *scythe*.

CHAPTER THIRTY-TWO

"Sims, take point," Navarro said, as he handed over his laser weapon. "You are to follow October's orders to the letter."

"With pleasure. I'm tired of only doing the driving." The young man beamed as he took the Dazzler, exited the vehicle, and came around the other side.

October kept the Deacon between him and Sims as they headed up to the entryway. He kicked the door open, scanned the dim interior, and waved for them to follow. Navarro tore his eyes away and picked up the phone.

"Nicholas Navarro here," he said respectfully. "What do you need, Mister Bailey?"

"What I need is your goddamned obedience," came a familiar growl. "Before I have you shit-canned from this cut-rate mercenary outfit."

Navarro felt as if someone had slammed him in the gut with a sledgehammer.

The voice on the other end of the line wasn't Niles Bailey.

It was Geoffrey Chadwick.

For a moment, Navarro couldn't speak. When he did, his voice teetered between surprise and sudden anger.

"Chadwick? What the *hell* are you doing? How did you get this number?"

"I told you, Navarro," Chadwick said smugly, "I've got connections. Now you're going to listen to what I want, and you're going to listen good."

Navarro bit back several streams of curses. His hands trembled as he held himself back. But before he could do anything more, his headset came to life.

"…is dead," October said, his voice crackling through a sea of static. "I see records only."

A chill ran through Navarro's veins. He lowered the headset to pay better attention.

"Say again, October?"

"Inside big records room. Money-man is dead on floor. Wait."

The line crackled with static once more.

Then it exploded with the *rat-tat* of machine-gun fire.

"*Oy, blyat!* People are shooting at us!"

Ice water ran through Navarro's veins. "Get out of there! Go hot!"

"*Khorosho, ponyal.* Get down, *pridurok!*"

By 'going hot', Navarro gave October permission to ditch the Dazzler and go to lethal weapons. Immediately, the thunder over the headset doubled as the sound of service pistols being fired joined the blast of noise. He switched over to the squad circuit.

"All squads, move into the building. October's taking fire."

"We heard it," Hagen complained. "Our entryway's been bricked up. So are the windows!"

"Same here," Reyes chimed in, from the opposite side of the building. "We've got a fire door welded inside the main entry. This wasn't on the schematics."

This can't be co-incidence, Navarro realized. *This was a trap.*

He heard a buzzing sound. Amazed, he looked to where he held the phone in his hand. Chadwick's angry voice buzzed from it like an annoying mosquito.

Navarro slammed the receiver back into its cradle.

"Wanjiru," he said, "Any movement heading our way?"

"Nothing yet. The drones are picking up vibrations emanating from the building. Now...oh, my. That can't be good."

"What is it?"

"I'm seeing a serious IR bloom in the interior."

Navarro heard a deep rumble come from inside the building. With a *BOOM*, a section of the roof exploded upwards, throwing slugs of hot tar out like blobs of lava from a volcano. Smoke billowed into the sky, along with the continued sounds of gunfire.

"All right," Wanjiru said, "Now I'm starting to see movement heading towards the building."

Navarro switched circuits once more. "All squads, retreat to the south side of the building and form a perimeter. Be alert for hostiles approaching from outside."

"From outside?" Reyes asked. "What about October?"

"I'm heading in to get him."

Navarro slipped into the driver's seat and cranked the ignition. He floored the accelerator as soon as the engine grumbled to life. The truck's rear wheels spun and smoked for a moment on the rough asphalt.

The big vehicle rumbled forward, gaining speed as it caught traction. Navarro steered it directly at the metal roll-up door. He belted himself in as the steel surface loomed up ahead like a gray stone cliff. He squinted and bent over the steering wheel as if leaning into a strong wind.

With a *BWAM!* the armored vehicle punched through the thin metal door without so much as scratching the ballistic glass. Navarro caught a glimpse of a long, empty loading bay that ended in a four-foot high concrete barrier. He slammed on the brakes and yanked the wheel around to the left.

The wheels locked up and the heavy truck slid across the smooth cement floor at a diagonal. A crunch, and the passenger side corner of the front bumper crumpled under the impact. Navarro's breath whistled out of his chest as the seatbelt kept him from being flung out of his seat.

He ignored the pain seared across his chest and lap as he unsnapped the belt and got out of the vehicle. Sweat poured down his face as he felt a sticky, furnace-like heat hit him. He took a breath and smelled the acrid scent of burning sweetener and plastic.

Navarro made his way around to the passenger side. The tire there had been jammed against the concrete barrier, but it hadn't burst. He slid the side door open and grabbed an M4 from the personnel carrier's weapons locker.

Smoke came from the open doorway leading from the loading bay deeper into the building. The cloudy mass lit up as someone let loose with a burst of small arms fire. He brought his carbine up and readied himself to fire until he made out October's bulky silhouette.

"Over here!" Navarro called.

There was a *click*, then a *clatter* as someone threw away an empty weapon. October emerged from the smoke just as flames began to lick around the edges of the doorway. Panting, the big man half-ran, half-staggered as he dragged two people behind him, one in each hand.

"Come on! I've got you covered!"

He glimpsed movement from inside. That was followed by a burst of gunfire as October reached the side door. Bullets ricocheted off the side of the vehicle.

Navarro grimaced as he let loose with a fearsome arc of fire from his carbine. He cut down two men who stumbled into the loading dock. They were both clad in black and carried assault rifles.

The first tumbled off the end of the loading platform in a heap and lay still. The second spun around and back to slump against the burning doorframe. The flames caught on the dead man's shirt and began licking at the flesh on his face.

Navarro didn't waste time staring at the gruesome spectacle. Without taking his eyes off the burning doorway, he called out to October.

"You wounded?"

"No. Just smoked like can of fish." The big Russian shoved

his two burdens into the truck and then crawled inside next to them. He let out a sad groan. "*Sevodnya bylo plokho.*"

Navarro retreated from his position and made his way back to the driver's seat. Shards of burning acoustic tiling began raining down around the truck as he shifted it into reverse. He coughed and had to squint through the smoke as he swung around to back out of the loading bay.

A second explosion rocked the building as they shot out into the sunlight. Clangs and booms buffeted the cab as structural beams began to collapse inside. Navarro brought them to a stop as he spotted his two groups jogging up to meet the battered vehicle.

He turned to look in the back. The Deacon sat up and let out a pained groan, but he looked unhurt. October's face was stained with soot. He sat on a floor that had been slicked with blood, hands pressed to Sim's shoulders as if he could wake him.

The young man lay motionless. The entry hole of a bullet wound creased the bridge of his nose. The exit wound had blown out the back of his head. Gore still dripped out the larger of the two holes.

"There were many men," October finally said. "*Poshlo vse k chertu,* they waited for us! They shoot us, we shoot back. Sims got hit. I threw grenade. Did not think old sugar burned so well."

"Not just the sugar," the Deacon said dejectedly. "The paper. It's all gone now. All of it's just so much kindling!"

Stunned, Navarro slumped back in his seat as his four troopers clambered aboard. His eyes went to the building as flames leapt high into the air. The burning sugar, hot tar, and melting zinc mixed to form a choking, acrid smell.

All he could do was stare as the only lead he had went up in smoke.

Michael Angel

CHAPTER THIRTY-THREE

Austen looked up from where she'd just administered medication to the last of her patients. A tall, broad-shouldered man had just entered the medical ward. The barely-fitting protective gear stretched tight around his upper torso.

"Nick," she called, as he came to join her. "What are you doing here?"

"I wanted to see John," he said simply. Austen looked Navarro over more closely. Even through the face shield, his eyes looked tired. Sullen. "You didn't leave word about him or anyone else getting better. So I wanted to see him one more time. Just in case."

In normal times, Austen knew that she'd have assured him that John Redhawk of the Salt River Apaches would pull through.

But these weren't normal times anymore.

"Come on, I'll take you to him," she said. "When we walk in, take a moment to let your eyes adjust."

She led Navarro over to the next ward. Once they closed the door behind them, the light level plunged dramatically. Navarro smelled nothing but antiseptic solution and rubbing alcohol as he stood and waited for his pupils to expand.

His mind went back to a long-ago day, when he'd visited his aunt's musty-smelling basement. The only light had come through tiny, taped-over windows that had been installed at ground level. A notion occurred to him.

"Have you thought about simply giving the patients wraparound sunglasses?"

"We tried that already. This disease makes the patients' entire skin react to light. It's not as intense a reaction, but it's enough to send them into convulsions."

"So much for that thought, then." Navarro waited a moment longer and added, "Okay. I can see well enough for now. Where to?"

"All the way at the end." Austen guided him through the gloom. "There's a stool you can sit on next to the bed."

He found it and sat down with a creak. He squinted at his friend's dim profile. Still, it was heartening enough to see the man's hawk-like nose, as well as the rise and fall of his chest.

"Can he hear me?" Navarro asked.

"He's been very heavily sedated," Austen replied. "It's...well, it's doubtful."

"But it's possible."

She paused. "Anything is possible. Talk to him, Nick."

Navarro let out a breath. He glanced around at the other beds, watching the low and rhythmic beat of the monitors. Redhawk's stern face was at peace. For that alone, he felt grateful.

"John, we got a lead on tracking down the bastards who put you in this bed," he began. "We're working with what the policy wonks in Washington call an 'unstable asset'. We picked up a former drug capo and present-day weapons smith and gun runner who calls himself 'The Deacon'. He agreed to help us, and that's as much thanks to Leigh here as anything else."

Austen looked down and smiled to herself as Navarro went on.

"The Deacon told us that he'd sold the weapons system that shot down that helicopter to a bunch of smugglers, the Zielverkop cartel. We didn't know where to find them, but he had an idea. There's a location in Goblintown where their moneyman did his business – and even kept all the cartel's records. We went in to capture the guy, or failing that, to grab his record stash."

Navarro fell silent for a moment before continuing. But now, his voice began to falter in spots.

"John...it was a rough day. If you had been there, you'd have said, 'Rough day, my ass. That whole mission fuckin' just went ass-up.' And it was. Right as we went in, I got a phone call. One of those calls you get from someone who thinks their office is down the hall from the Almighty. I thought it was Niles Bailey. It wasn't."

Austen glanced over to Navarro in surprise. He nodded.

"It was Geoffrey Chadwick. I got him off the line, but before I could do that, the mission had to proceed. I sent in the new kid, Sims. He went in with October at his side. But it was a trap, a goddamn trap. October was able to drag Sims out. But the kid..."

Navarro looked over to Austen and shook his head.

"Sims is going home first class. He might not appreciate it, but his parents will. I hope. As for the objective...the money man was dead when they got there. And in the fighting to extract October, the rest of the damned place went up like it had been doused in gasoline. So we're back to square one on that front."

He took another breath as he got to his feet. He rested a gloved hand on Redhawk's arm, right above where he'd been restrained to the hospital bed.

"Keep fighting, my friend. Even if I failed, I know that Leigh won't let you down. I know that you've got as much faith in her as I do."

Inwardly, Austen cringed. Redhawk had asked her, in so many words, to put him out of his misery if no cure was forthcoming. But Navarro kept on talking.

"She'll do whatever it takes to get you back to us. Besides, you still need to tell me what October did with all the vodka you gave him for winning the contest. The one about how I got my scar."

He turned and nodded to her. Austen took them back into the main ward, where the brighter light dazzled their eyes for a moment. She then followed him out to the gowning area, where they removed their protective gear in silence.

Navarro sank into one of the plush green seats in the former doctor's office. He rubbed his eyes and looked around. Then he stifled a yawn before he spoke again.

"Must've been a rougher day that I thought. Sun's not quite down yet and already I want a nap. Where'd Emily Piper go off to?"

"She's aft, setting up a new patient ward. We're closing on three hundred patients now. Every time we think we're at an end, we get another dozen in from Paramaribo, or Kolhorn."

"Jesus."

"But there's a little bit more hope now, I think. We finally figured out what we're dealing with – a formerly unknown type of fungus. It entwines itself into the epidermis and bleeds toxins into the bloodstream."

Navarro sat up. "That's something, anyway. But…a *fungus*? You mean like ringworm, or athlete's foot?"

She shook her head. "Those are just irritating. Most fungal diseases aren't a joke. They kill more than a million people a year, and blind half as many. This one's a killer, too. It's a plant-based fungus that somehow learned to parasitize humans. It's related to *Claviceps purpurea*, the fungus that causes ergotism."

"I'm not familiar with that one. Ergotism, that is."

"It's what you get when the body ingests these alkaloids, and it was much better known in the Middle Ages. *Claviceps* grows on overly wet rye and related grains. The burning sensations in the limbs, the strange lassitude, the convulsions, even the hallucinations are classic symptoms.

"Some historians think that community-wide ergot poisoning led to the accusations of witchcraft at the Salem Witch Trials. But that's not the worst of it. Ergot can infect an entire crop over dozens of square miles. So, entire villages in the Middle Ages would eat contaminated grain and die *en masse*. For that reason, the disease was simply called the Reaper's Scythe."

"What does that mean for Redhawk's survival?"

"I don't know, I can't. At least I have something to try now. The WHO sent us some wide-spectrum antifungal medications, which I just gave to Redhawk and his squad. Amphotericin and micafungin. But these take a while to work. Up to twenty-four hours. All I can do is keep my patients sedated and stable while we see if the medication works."

Navarro nodded. He cocked his head as he looked at her again.

"That's all good news. Yet you look about as happy as I feel right now."

Austen sank into the seat next to him. Her voice took on a dejected tone.

"I lost two of Redhawk's men. Your men. Mason and Ojeda went into cardiac arrest, and we couldn't revive them. I'm sorry, Nick. I failed."

"I'm sure you did your best," he said. Navarro put his hands over his eyes. "I...it's been a long day, Leigh. I never allowed myself to cry over the men I lost on that last mission with you to Ozrabek. Sims getting hit...that got to me more than I thought it would."

"Maybe you feel like it should have been you?" she suggested gently. "I mean, because you had to stay back. To take that call."

"Maybe." He lowered his hands and looked over to her. "You shouldn't say that you failed Ojeda, or Mason. The way I see it, you're the one who's figured out how to keep John and the rest of his men alive."

"I wish I could see it that way." Austen sighed. "I've been the one telling Piper to move on, to just 'get through it'. And here I am, trying to figure out how to face failure on my own."

Navarro grimaced at that. "I'm no philosopher, Leigh. All I know is that you have to work through whatever pain life hands you. No one ever gets much choice in the matter. But if you can do it, you end up stronger for it. One of my teachers called it 'building character on the cheap'."

She laughed at that. "I guess I've had my character-building moments as well. I've always just wanted to help people. That's what made me who I am, at least."

"Sometimes," Navarro said softly, "I reckon that my scar made me who I am."

When Austen spoke again, she picked her words delicately, carefully.

"I remember there was a contest among your men. About that scar. Whoever got you to spill the beans on how you really got it would win the prize. If you don't want to talk about it, I understand. But if October already won...perhaps you'll share that story with me?"

"Technically, the honor goes to the Colonel Chelovik, but October overheard me talking to him. The scar was a gift of sorts. From my father."

"Your father?"

"He gave me this scar with the edge of a broken bottle. He came home drunk, which he did all too often. He started beating my mother." Navarro let out a breath. "I tried to stop him. He turned on me, and we fought. I was seven. I lost."

A look of sorrow crossed Austen's face. "Oh, Nick. I'm sorry—"

Navarro shook his head. "It's all right. My father was one tough son-of-a-bitch. And the local neighborhood bully. He'd go down to the local dive bars specifically to get drunk and start fights. The town we lived in was small. Everyone knew each other. And everyone in town...they just plain hated him.

"My second grade teacher was married to this one guy my old man put in the hospital. She told me that someday, my father would meet someone bigger and a hell of a lot meaner than him. And when he did, he'd never be seen again on this side of God's green earth. And you know what?"

"What?"

"She was right. Many years later, he disappeared and was never seen or heard from again."

Navarro stood up. The sadness in his face had been replaced by a newfound determination. As if the story about his past had drained the despair away. And replaced it with something else.

Austen realized that she'd been holding her breath.

"What happened to your father?" she finally asked.

He gave her a smile. One that both thrilled her as a woman and chilled her to the bone.

"I got bigger," he said simply. "And a hell of a lot meaner."

With that, Navarro turned and left the room.

Michael Angel

CHAPTER THIRTY-FOUR

Hoogeveen City
Downtown Boat Docks

The purple twilight gave way to a light breeze. The breeze brought mist. It blurred the outline of Hoogeveen City as if to hide its derelict face from the world. The droplets were warm and sticky, the way they often were in the topics, and they clung to the banks of the small river that trickled its way through the city's guts.

A rhythmic *chug-chug-chug* came from upriver. The shape of a small motorboat materialized from the mist and headed towards the city's boat docks. The two-stroke outboard engine sputtered out as it approached, leaving the vessel to drift its way the last few yards until the prow banged into one of the wooden pilings with a *thump*.

The dockmaster looked up from his newspaper at the sound. He raked his fingers through a mop of gray hair, set the paper down, and left his shack of an office. He limped down to where the river's current pressed the side of the little boat against the dock frame.

"*Wat is hier aan de hand?*" he grumbled, as he fished a

flashlight out of his pocket and flicked it on.

His beam fell upon a grey-skinned arm that stretched out from the boat. A skeletal hand at the end scrabbled around like a drunken spider on the dock's wooden boards. Filthy fingernails dug into the wood as it finally found purchase.

The dockmaster took a step back in horror. His flashlight swept across a worn, dirty face that contorted in agony as the light hit it. A scream rose from the thing in the boat, one echoed by the dockmaster as he ran, blubbering, from the dockyard.

Slowly, with breath hissing from tortured lungs, the being in the boat crawled up onto the dock planks. The figure resolved itself into the haggard frame of a man wearing a makeshift shawl or cloak. It shambled more than walked down the length of the dock and headed into the city.

Waving like a drunk, the figure did its best to avoid bright lights. It was helped by the fact that half of Hoogeveen's lampposts were permanently out. Either they'd shorted out from neglect, or they'd been broken by everything from thrown rocks to random gunfire.

The man reached up and pulled the stained hood down lower over his face as he made his way into the city. Images and sounds jangled in his brain. His eyes watered as they tried to make out a half-lit street sign.

The upper half of the sign bore white squiggles on it. He ignored it. Text was almost beyond his comprehension now, as was most abstract thought. But the lower half grabbed his attention.

A white stencil in the shape of a house had been stenciled on the placard. Inside the house shape lay a scarlet cross. Below these symbols, the sign-maker had helpfully added an arrow pointing to the right.

The figure turned that way. He passed a few people, who didn't spare a second glance. Beggars were unfortunate and all too common in this part of Hoogeveen, so they didn't attract much attention. Still, to ease the pounding in his brain, he moved down a dark alley that paralleled the brighter boulevard.

Now cloaked in darkness, the figure felt the absence of light the way a healthy person would embrace an air-conditioned room after being in the scorching sun. He moved more surely now, ignoring the ripe smells of garbage and leaking sewage.

He heard the sounds of voices. Voices that didn't sound like the demonic shrieking inside his head. He made out rough laughter and chanting as he drew near to the end of the alleyway. He squinted against the light of a fire someone had lit in an empty trash barrel.

A crowd of people stood on the sidewalk and in the middle of the road, blocking the evening traffic. They carried signs in English and Dutch: *Open de stad! Murken Coward! Festival Anders Niets! Open Now! Keti Koti Nu!*

He blinked, trying to understand what was happening. He recognized the place now – the square in front of the Mayor-Governor's *palacio*. But it never had this many people in front of it.

But it didn't matter. The sign said that help was this way, and he had to get help.

He took two shaky steps out into the plaza, trying to keep his eyes down.

Someone laughed and threw the dregs of their bottle of liquor into the trash barrel. The glass shattered as it landed next to the fire inside. The remaining droplets of alcohol flared up into a sudden burst of light.

The man let out a cry of pain and fell to his knees. His hood felt back in a heap of cloth on his shoulders as his shins hit the pavement.

The people closest to him turned and saw the horrific gray of his skin. They let out everything from screams to yelps of alarm. Panic rippled through the crowd at the speed of sound.

"Epidemie!"

"Run, get away!"

"De ziekte is hier!"

Signs were dropped or thrown away as people fled. In mere seconds, the crowded square was empty save for a few confused *palacio* guards and policemen. One of these approached the man, calling out to him.

"Are you hurt? *Alles goed met je?*"

But it was too much to stay upright. The world slid to one side as the figure slumped to the still-warm pavement.

"Stay back," one of the other officers warned. He put his hand on his partner's shoulder, restraining him. "*Die is ziek.*"

The alarm was passed up the chain of command. The mist grew thicker as time passed and the police put up a protective cordon at a respectful distance. The fallen man didn't so much as stir until the wail of an ambulance's siren drew near.

Two men dressed head to toe in protective clothing got out and wheeled a stretcher over. A press of the wrist turned up a faint pulse. They loaded him onto the stretcher and headed off to the harbor wharves.

The gray-skinned man blinked as his consciousness returned with a stab of pain. He felt himself being wheeled up a ramp at a sharp angle. The smell of the sea tickled his nostrils. His last lucid thought was that he must be on a boat of some kind. Then his eyelids simply got too heavy, and they closed again.

Emily Piper met the orderlies as they maneuvered the stretcher into the newest makeshift ward they'd opened aboard the *Stella Maris*. She'd just donned a new set of protective gear to help bring in the latest patients. She grabbed her clipboard and blinked as she read the intake form.

"Oh my God!" she exclaimed. "This guy's from here in Hoogeveen?"

"*Het lijkt zo,*" came the orderly's reply. "They picked him up downtown. At the palacio's square."

"Dammit! I was sure that we'd contained the sickness in this city!"

But her anger was stilled as she looked over the man's strangely weathered appearance. She checked his skin, looked in his eyes, and cringed at the horrific state of his fingernails. She even examined the dark green splotches that stained the knees and elbows of the man's tattered clothes.

Piper frowned in confusion.

Those are grass and plant stains, she thought. *You didn't get those by wandering around downtown Hoogeveen. Who the hell are you, anyway?*

She spotted a glint of metal at the man's wrist. It was a tarnished silvery bracelet that made a dull *clink* as she turned it over. A rectangular faceplate glinted back at her, along with three lines of text.

JAIME D. LUCAS
CHLOE 717-555-0108 MOTHER
PENECILLIN ALLERGY

Michael Angel

CHAPTER THIRTY-FIVE

Navarro craned his neck to look through the observation room's windows. Austen, Piper, and two nurses attended to the latest patient to arrive on the *Stella Maris*. The emaciated man lying in the hospital bed looked like rag doll that a pair of Dobermans had chosen as a chew toy.

If he squinted, he could make out the man's ashen-gray skin. A wave of tremors ran along the man's limbs as he was injected with sedatives and anti-fungal medication. The man's badly chapped lips moved, and Austen bent closer to make out the words.

She had a triumphant smile on her face later, as she de-gowned.

"I got your message," Navarro said. "And from the looks of things, I'd say that you just learned something important."

"I'd say that I learned a couple of important things," Austen replied, as she tossed her gloves into a secure bin and stepped out of the gowning area. "Piper found a penicillin allergy tag on this guy's wrist when he was first brought in. His name's Jamie Lucas, and he's an American who originally arrived in Suriname with the Peace Corps."

"The Peace Corps?" Navarro frowned. "There's nothing in

the M&B files on the Corps doing projects in Suriname."

"That's because they pulled out of Suriname a couple of years ago. But Lucas here decided to stick around. I ran his name through the databases I could connect to on the satellite link and came up with a couple of rather interesting hits."

"Let's hear them."

"Our ill friend here had been suspended from the Corps for repeatedly abandoning his posts. Turns out that he preferred panning for gold dust in the local rivers over digging drainage canals to help local villagers."

That made Navarro's ears perk up.

"The Deacon said something about that. The Zielverkop cartel specialized in taking gems and gold dust out of the jungle, from places you could only get to by helicopter."

"Well, Lucas didn't show up back in Hoogeveen by helicopter. He arrived by boat from upcountry, in Suriname's rainforest belt, and he's been dealing with this same strange fungal disease for at least five or six days."

"Are you sure about that? Because that pre-dates the bioterror attack on the Red Cross people and Redhawk's men."

"Oh, I'm sure. In fact, I'm betting that Lucas encountered this form of *Claviceps* in its natural environment."

Navarro chewed that one over. "So this new disease is out there in nature?"

"It must be. Contrary to popular belief, diseases aren't created in some madman's laboratory. The microbes that exist out in nature are deadly enough on their own. What bioterrorists do is weaponize the bug, by taking it out of its natural habitat and helping it spread."

"You think that we can backtrack along Lucas' path, find out where this bug came from?"

"Yes, I think we've got enough evidence."

Now Navarro's face broke out into a grin that mirrored Austen's own.

"Come with me," he said. "Let's double-check what you have, because this also might be what I need to find the Zielverkop cartel's base."

* * *

A thin sliver of moon was all that illuminated the Motte & Bailey forward operations base. A strategic blackout of the base had been called, in case anyone outside of M&B cared to do some snooping. In the meantime, technicians pulled double shifts preparing helicopters and amassing gear while the MIC was cleared for Navarro's briefing.

Navarro's squad members took up the center of a long row of seats. Several of them wore expressions of sullen anger over one of their number's recent death. Two of the M&B troopers, Farris and Grimes, looked happier to have been called up.

Emily Piper sat at the end of the row. She did her best to look around October's bulk in order to catch a glimpse of the Deacon. The former drug capo had been seated on the opposite end, and his expression was gloomiest of all.

Samuel Wanjiru sat off to one side, tapping commands at a keyboard. Austen spoke quietly to him over his shoulder. Several maps winked into existence on monitors projected onto a larger screen on the room's back wall. Navarro walked up to the front. He started the briefing without any formal introduction, but the room went deathly quiet as soon as he began to speak.

"All right, let's start with the most important stuff right away: Redhawk, Dale, Kenzie, and McCall are still in critical condition. But we've got some good news. Doctor Austen's figured out how to keep them from getting any worse, and she may have a way to prevent the spread of this bug."

All eyes went to Austen as she stepped up in turn.

"If you haven't heard, Hoogeveen City had a couple of serious scares last night. The demonstrations outside the Governor's *palacio* broke up over fears of an outbreak. Also, the city dockmaster ran into the main police station, convinced that they were about to be overrun by vampires or zombies. And believe it or not, those two reports turned out to be connected."

Austen got a wave of deep-throated chuckles from the assembled men. She waited until it died down before continuing.

"Both reports were the result of this man arriving in Hoogeveen City." On cue, Wanjiru tapped a key. Photos of a gangly-looking young man appeared on screen. "Jaime Lucas, former member of the Peace Corps and current critical care patient aboard the *Stella Maris*. As best as we can tell, he left Hoogeveen around three weeks ago in the company of some up-country gold panners."

Now even the Deacon began to pay attention.

"While in the Surinamese outback, Lucas encountered and is now host to a parasitic plant fungus related to *Claviceps purpurea*. That's rye ergot fungus, or the 'Reaper's Scythe'. It's spread by touch, or by touching a contaminated item. It grows at an unheard-of pace on the skin and drips hallucinogenic alkaloids into your system until you end up harming yourself, or the heart goes into cardiac arrest."

"Worst damn case of jock itch I've ever heard of," Hagen muttered. October shushed him with a guttural *tishina*!

"We don't know what happened to his fellow gold hunters, but Lucas managed to make it back to the expedition's boat and pilot it downriver. Based on his path from the docks, he was trying to get to the city's Red Cross facility. Since he had no idea that the doctors staffing it were killed on Hoogeveen MedFlight 3209, it's a safe bet that he's been isolated or travelling down the river for the last three or four days."

"But Redhawk and his guys were incapacitated in hours," Kimura objected. "How did this Lucas character make it all the way back without succumbing?"

"Partly because he only traveled at night. I could only make out some of his speech. From what I could tell, he hid in the underbrush by the riverbanks during the day. But the real solution came from our resident tropical disease specialist, Emily Piper."

Austen nodded to Piper. The young woman blushed as she stood up to address the room.

"Uh, yeah. Jaime Lucas had a bracelet showing that he had a penicillin allergy. He also had a subcutaneous drug implant under his arm. The implant fed low doses of a medication called co-trimoxazole into his bloodstream to fight a chronic infection he was dealing with. Apparently, this stuff also prevents the growth and spread of the fungus."

"Once Piper informed me, I gave our patients doses of co-trimoxazole," Austen said, as Piper sat back down. "It's not a full cure, but it stops the pathogen in its tracks. Redhawk's men won't get any worse, and if you already have this drug in your system, it can't get a foothold on your skin, either. That's good, because we're going to be heading upstream and into the jungle."

That caused a stir amongst the assembled contractors. Again, she waited for it to crest and then pass before going on.

"We've got a good idea where the bug originated," she announced. "That's where we're going to find the headquarters of the Zielverkop cartel. And that's where we can stop this madness once and for all."

Michael Angel

CHAPTER THIRTY-SIX

Austen thought her announcement about the jungle would get a reaction out of her audience. But her statement about finding and ending the Zielverkop cartel got the men talking enthusiastically amongst themselves. Navarro stepped up next to her, motioning for his people to settle down.

"I got a question," Reyes said. "That river flowing through Hoogeveen is split among a dozen branches once you start following it upstream. This Lucas guy could have come from anywhere within a hundred miles of jungle."

As if to emphasize the point, Wanjiru tapped the keys to zoom in on the map of central-western Suriname. Rivers wound like tangles of blue string against verdant green.

"Lucas was on long-term doses of co-trimoxazole ever since he contracted a specific type of *cystoisosporiasis*." Austen explained. "That's an intestinal disease caused by a protozoan parasite known as *Cystoisospora certis*. As it happens, that parasite is endemic to the waters along the upper reaches of the Kutari River. Wanjiru thinks we can narrow that range even further."

"This is an area close to the Suriname's border with Guyana," Wanjiru said. "It's from satellite data taken two years ago."

A *click*, and the monitor displayed a small jungle valley on the screen. The Kutari and three smaller rivers converged there and plunged over the side to make a series of waterfalls. Rainbow-sheened glints could be seen against the landscape.

The Deacon sat up with a creak of his seat.

"I know that area," he announced.

All eyes turned to him. He ignored the collection of semi-hostile stares.

"At least, I know some of it. My men and I explored the southern end many years ago, when I was considering the spot for a remote base. The terrain's *ruig*, tough to cross. Dense jungle. Confusing place."

"Even that knowledge could be useful," Wanjiru said. "Because we have another problem. One that's going to force us to go in on foot. Look at this shot of the same area, from three months ago."

Another *click*, and the valley vanished under a gray haze.

"This part of Suriname is old-growth rainforest, so you'd expect to see it clouded over around fifty percent of the time. However, every single shot of this area in the past year has been socked in with this same mist. It's dense enough to rule out helicopter landings. Something's happened to change the climate in that valley."

"Whatever the reason for that," Navarro declared, "we're going to have to deal with it. This cartel's been using it to run us ragged. It's pulled more and more of our resources from our original mission in this country. Only Doctor Austen and her people have kept this from turning into a full-blown catastrophe. So that means we can't give the enemy any more time to implement their plans. We're taking the initiative away from them."

"What do you have in mind?" October asked. "*Vozmozhno*, I am thinking of something using much explosives."

"I like the way you're thinking, big guy. I want to get to that river valley and put boots on the ground at first light tomorrow." Navarro looked soberly around the room. "A couple days ago, I explained the difference between what we do, and what mercenaries do to Emily Piper. We're paid to protect, not just to fight. But I also told her that we try to do the right thing, and to shoot back when needed.

"Here, we're going in to root out a bunch of bioterrorists. The first ones South America's ever seen. If that's not the right thing to do, then I don't know what is. But I'm asking for volunteers only. Doctor Austen can keep you from getting sick, but that's not going to stop a bullet. We don't know what they have down there, period. So, if you want to sit this one out, go right ahead. No one's going to say anything if you do."

Navarro paused. There was an uneasy silence. But nobody got up to leave.

"Okay, then," he said. "Go gear up. Prep for the heat, prep for the wet, and above all, get loaded for bear. Meet back at the MIC at 0530. We'll have the assignments ready."

There was a bustle as the meeting broke up. The M&B troopers filed through the doorway and disappeared into the FOB's steel-lined warren of living quarters and armory cabinets. Wanjiru nodded towards Navarro and followed suit.

"You, come with me," October said to the Deacon. Together, the two left out a side door. In the meantime, Austen motioned to Piper. The young woman stepped up to join her and Navarro.

"I need you to remain on board this ship," Austen told the younger woman bluntly. "Coordinate the bulk shipment of co-trimoxazole into Suriname with the WHO."

"What?" Piper gulped. "You're kidding me, right? I'm heading out with you and the rest of the group!"

Austen shook her head. "It's too dangerous. You did not sign up for something like this."

"But I'm…I'm part of this whole big thing now! I've proven myself!"

"You proved yourself in a medical setting. A field hospital setting. Not in the depths of a rainforest, especially one crawling with god-knows-what under all that fog."

"But *you're* going! Do you even know how to fire a gun?"

"She knows," Navarro assured her. "Trust me, I know."

Piper glared at him. "Keep out of this, you...you leatherhead!"

"Marines are leather*necks*," Navarro said evenly. "Doctor Austen's words on the matter are final. And so are mine. You're on the bench this time, kid."

Piper's cheeks turned bright red. Then she turned on her heel and all but stomped off. Navarro gave Austen an appraising look.

"You're thinking of Amy Zhao, aren't you?" Navarro observed. "Another bright young woman who didn't flinch at going into the danger zone."

"Sometimes I think you know me too well," she sighed. "I'm glad Colonel Chelovik and his crew were taken care of, for many reasons. But what that man did to Amy Zhao tops the list."

"Me too."

Austen paused for a moment. She looked around the room to make sure they were alone before continuing.

"Speaking of knowing things too well," she said, "I needed to speak to you about something that's got me worried. Jaime Lucas' brain was pretty far gone by the time we got him into a low-light ward. He said a lot of strange things. Probably just the ravings of a man driven half-mad by this strain of *Claviceps*."

"I'm listening," Navarro assured her.

"He spoke about beams of light. About teeth and claws and fangs coming out of the dark. Out of the mist." She looked up towards the screen, that showed the same fogbound valley. "And strangest of all, he said one thing several times. And...it's got me spooked."

A concerned look crossed Navarro's face.

"What was it, Leigh?"

"He said, 'I heard the beat of the jungle's dark heart'. He said it like he was terrified of it. Nick, that's just what DiCaprio said to watch out for. *Beware the beat of the jungle's dark heart.* How would he even know about something like this?"

Navarro leaned up against one of the work desks and

rubbed his chin. "Deep down, I always reckoned that DiCaprio was someone deeply embedded in the State Department. Maybe CIA, or NSA. But this…this is starting to feel like something supernatural at work. It's got the hairs on the back of my neck doing a jig, I'll tell you that much."

"I'll just have to ask him straight," Austen declared. "When I get back to the States…I'll ask him how he knows the things he knows."

"Go ahead, but I think I can predict the reply."

"You do? What do you think he'll say?"

A snort of a laugh escaped Navarro's mouth. "Does Macy's tell Gimbel's?"

Austen frowned. "I don't understand."

"It's a line from an old Christmas movie. It means that you don't give out information freely. Especially when competitors might be listening."

"Actually, you bring up a good point," Austen admitted. "What DiCaprio knows is the kind of information that could land him – or her – in jail. Or worse."

"It may also be why he puts things in riddles. We still don't know what he means about saving people from the 'burning star'. But I do know one thing so far."

"That being?"

"This DiCaprio's been in our corner all the way." He got up and motioned towards the door. "Come on. Help an old leather-head plan out how we're going to get through this pathogen-infested jungle."

Michael Angel

CHAPTER THIRTY-SEVEN

Austen rested her hand in one of the ceiling-mounted hanging straps as the helicopter made a gentle turn. She leaned into it as her nose filled with the scents of the rainforest below. Loamy soil and exotic flowers made a heady mix. She breathed it in as her hair, which she'd turned into an auburn-colored French braid, flapped across her back in the slipstream.

Navarro and Campbell had positioned themselves on either side of her. Both men scanned the ground below with critical eyes. Kimura and the Deacon sat on the bench seat opposite them. The last two troopers in Navarro's squad, Farris and Grimes, sat in the rear seats.

A second helicopter followed them at a safe distance. The glare of early-morning sunlight made Austen squint, but she made out October's imposing bulk in the passenger compartment. She spotted a pair of wide-winged silver glints high above and behind the second helicopter. Wanjiru was making sure that M&B's two drones did their best to keep pace.

Navarro's voice sounded in her ear over the headset. "Okay, the pilot's spotted a clearing up ahead. It's on the small side, so grab hold of something."

Austen wrapped her hand more securely around the strap. The helicopter dropped steeply and went into a sharp bank. Her stomach did its best to tie itself into a knot in response.

Suddenly, the smell of greenery, flowers, and wet dirt redoubled in intensity. The jungle canopy flashed by and before she knew it, the helicopter's skids touched down with a *bump*. The M&B men around her grabbed their weapons.

"Let's go," Navarro called. "Someone else needs this clearing!"

Austen adjusted her backpack and followed the men out the aircraft's side door. Her boots made a *squish* as they touched the muddy earth. The group made it to the cover of the tree line and the helicopter lifted off.

"Secure the perimeter," Navarro ordered, and his three men disappeared into the underbrush.

Austen looked around. Kapok and brazil nut trees reared up a hundred feet overhead, like the pillars of a dim green cathedral. Their trunks were festooned with vines and dotted with orchids the color of clotted cream. Heat and moisture hung in the air, immediately dotting her forehead with sweat.

Those beads of sweat felt sticky and smelled unnervingly like lemon furniture polish. That stemmed in part from the multiple layers of chemical repellents slathered over her skin. It was also a side-effect of the co-trimoxazole everyone had taken prior to takeoff.

"October said he had a talk with you," Navarro said, nodding towards the Deacon's feet. The man still wore his wrist shackles, but the big Russian had removed the anklet cuffs and electronic tracker. "Apparently, he's a softer touch than me."

"I didn't convince him of anything," the Deacon shot back. "He's a very logical man. There's nothing out here to track an ankle bracelet. Also, where am I supposed to run off to when we're surrounded by a hundred miles of rainforest?"

Navarro's reply was drowned out as the second helicopter came in. October stepped out first, followed by Hagen and Reyes. Wanjiru brought up the rear. The man held a wireless drone controller unit in his hands, his own carbine slung across his back.

As soon as he made it clear, October waved to the pilot. The second aircraft lifted off disappeared above the thick canopy. The *thwap-thwap* of the two helicopters' rotors faded away in seconds.

Austen's unsettled stomach decided on one more flip-flop as a thought occurred to her.

Now we're truly on our own.

Navarro called his men together before speaking to the Deacon again.

"All right, our satellite data says that our objective lies due north of us. But you've actually been over this ground before. Any advice for us?"

The Deacon looked around for a moment. His jaw moved as if chewing the question over. Finally, he pointed towards a slight rise in the distance. The chain linking his wrist cuffs jangled as he did so.

"*Laten we eens kijken,*" he said. "If you go due north, there is a stream, an offshoot of the Kutari that does not show on the maps. It turns into an impassable swamp. We should be able to avoid it by angling to the west."

"All right, lead the way. Team Alpha, you're with me. October?"

"What is it, Nicholas?" October asked.

"You've got Team Bravo. Follow us at one hundred yards. Wanjiru, what's our drone coverage look like?"

The man ran a hand through his tightly coiled hair before answering. "Irksome."

That stopped Navarro. "That's not good. Operating without any air recon makes me nervous. The infrared sensors should be able to see through mist."

"If it is *cold* mist, yes. The IR sensors are having problems making out anything because this is an extremely warm and humid environment." Wanjiru adjusted a few dials on his drone controller before adding, "I must warn you that the drones are not handling as well after the addition you requested to their airframes."

"Can't be helped. That addition is going to be our edge today."

"Very well."

The two groups set out into the forest, their boots making slight crunching noises as they stepped through the damp leaf litter. The Deacon remained out front, though two of Navarro's men followed close behind. Austen shifted her pack's straps and fell in line as they moved out.

To her surprise, they made good time at first. Under the old-growth rainforest canopy, comparatively little light reached the forest floor. The underbrush consisted of low-lying ferns and mosses.

Whenever they came across an old stump or length of fallen timber, the wood had been shot through with fungal blooms and scallop-edged tree mushrooms. It reminded Austen of the strands of *Claviceps* fungus entwining themselves among her patients' skin cells. She shivered as she shoved the image out of her mind.

A little later, the group crested the rise. The back slope was much steeper, and clouds of ground fog rose from below. A trickle of water burbled from somewhere off to the right, beyond tangles of hanging vines.

"Bravo team," Navarro reported, "When you reach the top of the rise, angle your path further to the west. The Deacon's memory is proving to be accurate so far."

"*Kopiya*, Team Alpha," October replied.

"Wanjiru, anything to report?"

"I have Abbott and Costello in low-altitude orbit overhead. They're not sensing anything out of the ordinary on the IR band."

"Copy. Sing out if that changes."

They descended the steep slope in a switchback pattern. Clouds of insects rose from the grove of ferns that clustered at the bottom. Austen found herself slapping at the mosquitoes that braved even the worst of their repellant, and one of the troopers murmured some choice curses.

Once past that irritation, the ground leveled out and the vegetation began to change to a mixture of oil-palms and sickly looking grasses. Tangled vines draped from the tree limbs high above or rose from the ground in ankle-snagging coils.

But what came next made Austen stop in her tracks as a ripple of fear ran its way down her spine.

Michael Angel

CHAPTER THIRTY-EIGHT

"Hold up," Austen said. "Am I seeing things? Or is it actually getting *darker*?"

"You're not seeing things," Navarro grimly agreed. "It's not even noon, so it's not like we're about to run out of sunlight."

Sure enough, the already wan light that filtered through the trees had started to dim even further. As the group watched, tendrils of mist emanated from the forest before them, as if reaching out hungrily to the approaching travelers.

"There's something up ahead I need to see." Austen shifted her pack to one shoulder and jogged past the Deacon. She moved further up the trail even as the surprised men hurried to keep up with her.

By the time Navarro reached her, Austen had pulled a sample kit out of her pack. She knelt by the base of one of the big trees, scraping a shiny residue off a vine that entwined itself around the trunk. The scraggly-looking vine and its few stunted leaves looked strangely gray, as if the green of the chlorophyll had been blanched out.

"What did you find?" he asked, though deep in his gut, he knew the answer.

She sealed a plastic packet and stuck it back into her pack.

"I can't be one-hundred percent sure, but I'm betting the slime on those leaves is our *Claviceps* offshoot in its native habitat."

Both the M&B men and the Deacon looked around uneasily at that. More and more of the plants in their path had that same sickly shine to their leaves. Avoiding their touch would soon become impossible.

Navarro lowered his voice. "Leigh, if we're in any danger, now's the time to let me know."

"The medication I gave us should keep us safe," she said. Navarro flicked his eyes towards the men in his team. Austen stood up and repeated herself so that everyone could hear her. "That medication we took, that should keep us safe, even if you touch something with that fungus on it."

I hope to God that's right, she thought to herself. *I don't know how long the protection will last.*

"There's something else up ahead," Navarro said, pointing. "I'm seeing a rock wall."

They approached it cautiously. Sure enough, a mass of moss-covered granite jutted out of the mist towards them like blunt-tipped arrow. The Deacon went up, touched the stone with one hand, and then looked to either side of the wedge shape.

"I don't recognize this, sorry. But either path should take us directly into the valley."

"Okay," Navarro nodded. "Hold up."

They waited a few minutes until the second team came up from behind. Wanjiru was so focused on his controller that he almost ran into the trooper in front of him. October frowned as he came up to Navarro.

"*Chto za cherf?* What do we stop for?"

"We've got a fork in the road ahead. The Deacon's not sure which way to take. So we'll split up. Take your team down the fork to the left. We'll take the right."

October thought it over. "I am not liking this. Yet maybe both come out at the same place, *da?*"

"That's what the Deacon thinks."

Navarro motioned for his men to follow him. In a few

moments, October's group disappeared as well down the other path. Perhaps twenty or thirty minutes had passed before Navarro heard a *crackle* from his headset. He tapped the circuit with a finger.

"Come again? Whoever that was, repeat."

"This is Wanjiru." The man's voice was tinny over the static, but clear enough. "I'm getting some strange readings from up ahead of you. It's not individual blips, like from a group of people. More like a warm mass. Perhaps it's just an eddy of especially hot mist."

"Thanks for the heads-up. We'll take precautions."

Navarro glanced about as he broke the connection. A mist had wafted out of the trees ahead and settled around them in a dense gray mass. He motioned for Campbell, Farris, and Kimura to move to the front together. He brought the Deacon back to stand next to him and Austen. Grimes faded back a few more paces to provide a rear guard.

They'd taken no more than a dozen steps when Kimura stopped. He bent down to pick up something shiny and metallic from the forest litter. He held it up, puzzled, and then handed it over to his team leader.

Navarro turned the object over his hands, trying to figure out what it had once been. The mass had been cylindrical at one point, but it had been mashed flat. Only the dish-shaped reflector at one end clued him in that he was holding the battered remains of a flashlight.

"Any ideas?" Navarro asked the Deacon.

But the man only shrugged. "Not many people go this deep into Neverland. Everything you bring, you bring it on your back. Whoever left this keepsake here, I don't think they ever—"

"Wait!" Austen hissed. "Listen!"

The darkened rainforest around them was silent as they strained their ears. No birds sang, no insects buzzed, nothing scurried in the underbrush. The quiet made the sound clear when they finally heard it.

A deep, gut-churning *throb* in the distance.

It came again. Then again. Another. There was an edge to the sound that raised gooseflesh on the nape of Austen's neck.

"What the hell is that?" Navarro breathed.

Beware the beat of the jungle's dark heart, she thought frantically.

There was a stir from the dense, fog-like bank ahead of them. A ripple, running slowly along a wide section. Hints of something within.

"Give me something to defend myself!" the Deacon pleaded. "Please!"

Navarro shushed the man. "Quiet!"

Suddenly, in the distance there was a *pop*, as if from a rifle or a comically large bottle of champagne. A white point of light appeared ahead of them, arcing up into the sky.

"Signal flare!" Campbell exclaimed.

With a *paf!* it burst. The explosion was followed by a sizzle like bacon thrown onto a hot griddle. A dazzling shower of sparks and light drifted down from overhead. Howls and snarls rose ahead of Navarro's squad in a hellish chorus.

"Go hot!" Navarro snapped. "Fire at will!"

Demonic shapes bounded or leapt out of the mist towards them, claws outstretched, fangs glistening. Navarro heard one of his troopers mutter a prayer to God.

Amen to whatever you said, he thought, as he brought his M4 to bear.

His answer to the creatures' roars was the thunder of gunpowder and jacketed bullets.

CHAPTER THIRTY-NINE

Time slowed to a crawl for a few vital seconds in Austen's world. Seconds in which the entire swath of mist before her erupted into motion. She caught snippets of the action within her field of vision as her brain tried to play catch-up and make sense of the chaos.

A mass of yellow and black and gray creatures charged at them.

The glint of wet fangs in motion. The thump of paws and thud of small hooves.

A blur of motion as Navarro and his men brought the barrels of their carbines up.

The sound of snarls and grunts were drowned out by the sustained *bratatatatat* of the squad's weapons firing on full automatic.

Austen stared, her eyes refusing to believe what the M&B men were up against.

A veritable wall of fauna from deep within the rainforest charged towards them. She made out the yellow-black patterns of predatory jungle cats. Rows and rows of earth-colored pigs, hulking tapirs, and bristly-maned peccaries.

It didn't matter that many of these species avoided humans

like the plague. It didn't matter if they were nocturnal. It didn't even matter if they normally preyed upon each other. They charged forward into the hail of gunfire without even flinching.

The blast of weapons knocked most of the animals down with one shot. Still, several made it within striking distance of their little group. The first trooper went down as a three hundred-pound wild boar shrugged off the bullets in its chest and refused to drop.

The boar swung its snout in a vicious arc. Farris screamed as the animal's tusk, a razor-sharp dagger as long as a man's index finger, slammed into his thigh. The jagged tooth tore a gash all the way down his leg, practically unzipping skin from muscle.

The man's eyes rolled back into his skull as his opened femoral artery painted the surrounding vegetation with red. The smell of gunpowder, the iron tang of blood, and the stink of freshly eviscerated guts filled the jungle clearing.

Navarro pulled out his service pistol and fired it at point-blank range into the boar's skull, dropping it. He stepped into Farris's position without a spare second to switch back to his carbine.

"Son of a bitch!" he said, over and over. "Son of a *bitch*!"

The man to Navarro's right went down next. Austen heard a series of vicious, high-pitched snarls as Campbell's head rocked back. Blood fountained from a slashed neck. A pair of jaguars, their mottled hides flecked with fungal growths, ripped and tore at the man as they overbore him.

Navarro stepped back and pivoted, firing off a long burst from his weapon. The impact of his bullets flung one of the big cats away, leaving it twitching in the underbrush.

Another of the large jungle pigs emerged from the underbrush and charged. Tusks flashed by Navarro's leg, making him dance back another step. He emptied his magazine into the animal at point-blank range.

Meanwhile, the second jaguar finished ripping out Campbell's throat. With a snarl, it looked up at Austen with iridescent feline eyes. She watched in horror as blood dripped in red rivulets from the cat's canine teeth. The chaos and thunder of animal bellows and weapons firing vanished from her awareness as the predator sized her up.

She didn't dare turn her back on the creature. Austen slipped the backpack from her shoulders. She backed up a step, then two.

The big cat leapt at her.

Austen cried out and swung the pack at the creature. A *smack*, and the jaguar rolled as the weight knocked it to one side.

It shook its head and leapt at her again.

She desperately held up the backpack as the cat bowled her over, with the pack the only thing between the two. Claws sank in and tore at the pack's outer shell of fabric, shredding it.

The animal's hot, stinking breath filled her nose. It snapped at her, coming within an inch of her face. It opened its muzzle again, but only a strained cough came out. The animal's weight lifted off her for a second.

She rolled to one side. Breathing hard, she got into a crouch. For a split second, it looked like the jaguar was trying to stand on its two hind feet.

Then she saw the chain links that wrapped across the cat's throat like a garotte.

The big cat thrashed desperately and fell to one side. The Deacon fell with it, keeping the chain securing his wrist cuffs tight against the animal's windpipe. The former drug capo pressed the animal to the earth by pressing a knee to its flank and putting his entire bodyweight atop it.

A final yowl as the cat tried to swipe at him with its claws. There was a spine-tingling *crunch* as its trachea gave way under the pressure. The Deacon slipped the chain out from under the creature's head and got back up.

The sound of gunfire slackened off and finally stopped. Gore carpeted the rainforest floor for a dozen yards before them. Kimura knelt and checked Farris for a pulse. He muttered a curse as he came up with nothing.

Navarro didn't take his eyes off the surrounding area as he

loaded his M4 with a new magazine. Only when his weapon had been made ready did he speak.

"Grimes, Kimura, Deacon, sound off," he said. "Any of you badly hurt?"

He got a chorus of 'No', 'Fine' and 'Passable' in reply.

"You all right, Leigh?"

"Just a few scratches," she said, as she stood back up. Austen looked over to the Deacon in surprise. "Thank you. For doing…that."

He shrugged. "*Het is niets.*"

"How did you know that chain thing was going to work?"

A grim smile. "An educated guess. I've only used piano wire before."

Despite her feeling of gratitude, his words sent an additional shudder down her spine.

"Jesus H. Christ!" Grimes breathed. "They sure as hell don't show anything like this on those nature documentaries!"

"That's because none of the cameramen would have survived," Navarro said, as he gestured towards the mass of mangled corpses. "Leigh, what the hell caused all this?"

"They're infected with that same strain of *Claviceps,*" Austen said firmly. "It seems that the fungus toxins have a psychotropic effect on animals too, boosting their aggressive tendencies."

"That's an understatement." Navarro tapped repeatedly at his headset. "October, Wanjiru, come in. Come in, damn it!"

He got nothing but static.

Once again, the group heard the gut-churning *throb*. This time it came from somewhere directly ahead of them. As if in echo, a chorus of snarls and howls rose up from the path behind them in the distance.

"That's got to be another pack of animals," Kimura said. "Maybe they heard the sound of our gunfire, and they're attracted to that?"

"Whatever they're attracted to, we need to get our backs up against something," Navarro declared. "We won't be able to hold off another attack like that in the open.

"That flare," Austen said. "It came from up ahead. There might be a dwelling that way."

"I doubt they're going to be friendly, but we don't have much choice." Navarro dug into a pocket. He tossed a set of keys to Kimura and then pointed to the Deacon. "Get him out of those cuffs."

Navarro reloaded his service pistol and pressed it into Austen's palm. "You once told me that you didn't like weapons that put holes in things. Time to put that dislike aside."

"No argument there," Austen agreed, as she took the gun.

Grimes said a quiet prayer under his breath as he took the extra ammo from Farris's still form and split it between him and Kimura. Navarro did the same as he pried a bloodstained M4 from the grip of the other fallen trooper. The Deacon stood nearby, watching silently as he rubbed his newly freed wrists.

Navarro set his jaw as he gave the Deacon a critical look.

Then he handed the weapon over and turned away without comment.

"Come on," Navarro said. "We can't be caught out in the open again. Double-time it forward!"

Navarro led the way at a jog. Austen did her best to keep up with him and his men. Blood dribbled from scratches along her forearms and a shallow wound along one thigh. The cuts stung as if lemon juice had been poured into the wounds. She had to force herself to ignore the pain.

Slowly, the mist began to lighten. The air grew cooler and moister as they double-timed it away from the scene of the massacre. Suddenly, the deep, gut-churning *throb* sounded again. This time it was much closer.

Navarro drew up short. "Hold up!"

A roar filled Austen's ears as she slowed to a stop. The sound of thousands of gallons of cascading water. The mists parted for a moment.

"*Wat is dat in vredesnaam!*" the Deacon breathed. "Look over there!"

They stood at the edge of a small lake. On the opposite

bank, three separate waterfalls thundered over a set of high cliffs, feeding the body of water even as they threw out clouds of sparkling foam.

Something else stood on the far bank as well. A machine the size of a small building had been placed where the two largest falls plunged into the lake. Austen made out a pair of giant scoop-bucket wheels that slowly spun under the weight of the falling water.

The machine threw open a vent with a chest-pounding *throb*. It spit cold water vapor up into the sky, adding to the natural mist thrown up by the waterfalls. Navarro stared for a moment before snapping his fingers as a recollection came to him.

"That's a gravity-feed pump," he said. "They use them on lake fountains…but I've never seen one so large."

"There's something even larger over there," the Deacon said, pointing off to the right. "Another building of some kind."

Austen grimaced. "Something tells me they won't have the welcome mat out."

"Maybe," Navarro acknowledged, as the snarl of a pack of jaguars answered the pump's noise. "But we're running out of options."

Another heart-pounding jog brought them within shouting distance of the building. Sheer-sided walls rose for three stories up to a series of rusty metal catwalks and oblong windows. Austen's chest burned from the exertion as they made it to the base of the walls.

Navarro turned and rested his back against the wall. The surface felt smooth and damp against his shoulder blades. He brought his weapon up, ready to sell his life dearly. So did Austen, the Deacon, and Navarro's two remaining men. The tramp of paws and hooves closed in on them.

Austen heard a *pop*. A second flare arced up from behind the walls and into the sky. There was a *paf!* as it burst. This time, the dazzling shower of sparks and light were tinted emerald green.

The howls and snarls of the approaching jungle fauna cut off as the animals dispersed back into the mist.

"That's a nice trick," Austen breathed.

With a *clack*, a spotlight was turned on from atop the wall. It swiveled down, pinning the group in place. Navarro squinted and made out a trio of riflemen standing next to the light.

A voice boomed at them through a bullhorn.

"Drop your weapons. *Now!*"

Michael Angel

CHAPTER FORTY

Navarro gritted his teeth. He made out three armed men above them, but God only knew how many more were up there. Realistically, they had little chance in an open fight.

It's a long shot, he thought. *But maybe I can improve the odds in the next encounter.*

"Stand down," he said to the others. He knelt for a moment and set his M4 down on the muddy ground. Kimura, Grimes, and the Deacon followed suit.

Austen did the same. She frowned as she saw Navarro adjust something and then tuck it under the collar of his jungle fatigues. Before she could say anything, there was a dull *thump* next to them.

The men above them had thrown down a rope ladder. Navarro reached out to grab a rung where it dangled along the side of the wall. He steadied it before beckoning to Austen.

"Take my hand," he said. "I want you out of this killing zone first."

The squawk of the bullhorn came on again.

"No. That ladder is for you only, Navarro."

That stopped him. He turned and squinted up past the searchlight beam again.

"How do you know my name? Who the hell are you?"

"Neither answer is any of your business, *domkop*."

The Deacon took a step forward, ignoring the barrels of the guns that now trained on him. He shouted up towards the men at the top of the wall as well.

"I know that voice! Erich Zann, that's you, isn't it?"

The bullhorn shut off with a *click*. Now they heard a man's boisterous laughter. That was followed by a shouted reply, without any artificial amplification.

"Johan, what on earth are you doing here? Especially in this motley looking company?"

The Deacon put his hands on his hips. "I'm here because of *you*, old friend! They tracked that weapons system you purchased back to me. Then they wrecked my house, injured my men, and forced me to come out here!"

"That is a right shame, *vriend*. All right, you can come up too. No others."

"Hold on a minute," Navarro said firmly. "What happens to my people if Johan and I take this ladder?"

A pause. Zann's voice took on a distinctly irritated tone. "I can tell you what will happen to them if you do *not*. A single bullet to each of your heads at this range should do the trick."

The Deacon cleared his throat before speaking to Navarro.

"They appear to have us over the proverbial barrel."

"Go on up, Nick," Austen said. "If they wanted us dead, they'd have shot us down already."

Navarro looked around for a moment, as if considering, before he shouted up again.

"All right, we're coming up. But only because you have at least three riflemen up on that wall of yours."

He grabbed a rung and began climbing, the Deacon following behind. Austen watched them as they ascended and then disappeared into the glare of the searchlight.

Navarro stepped over the edge of the wall. His booted feet made a *clank* as they came down on a metal grated catwalk. A trio of guards in black fatigues stood further back, their weapons at the ready. A muscular man with close-cropped blond hair watched him with cold blue eyes.

"So, you're Nicholas Navarro," he said. "I expected you to be taller."

"And you must be Erich Zann," came Navarro's reply. "I don't think I'd forget a face like yours. How do you know mine?"

A rueful shake of the head. "You Americans are so addicted to your technology that you can't see straight. Do you really think all intel has to be gathered by machines?"

"The constant fog your gravity pump puts out certainly hid this place from aerial or satellite recon. You must need fifty, sixty men to guard it?"

"You must be joking. This place is quite secure. I use maybe half that number to hold it."

The Deacon finally made his way over the wall. One of the guards trained his rifle on the man as he stood next to Navarro A flicker of annoyance crossed the Deacon's face.

"There's no need for that."

"Johan," Zann said, "I allowed you up here based on our past association. But I don't trust traitors. Yes, your story about being 'forced' to come here is a good one. Yet I doubt they forced you to carry a carbine."

Navarro didn't take his eyes off Zann even as he spoke to the Deacon.

"Who is this guy? The head of the Zielverkop cartel?"

"Apparently," the Deacon replied. "Surprising, really. His background is all about moving narcotics. Like me. I suppose he's moved into smuggling and bio-terrorism out of boredom."

"Those who ran the Zielverkop cartel were mice that ran and hid when the cats came out," Zann spat. "They built this facility to hide their work. Burrowing like rats in the dirt for gold, or harvesting and refining coca leaves. But I'm taking things to the next level, Johan. Instead of running and hiding, I'm going to be the *overnemen*. The one who runs everything. Releasing this new disease was only a move in the bigger game."

The Deacon shook his head. "I am no saint, friend. But when we killed, we only killed those who came against us. Cops. Rivals. Those who displeased us. Not random civilians. Not women and children. You're releasing the devil into the world, Erich. And we have to grow up."

Erich Zann laughed at that.

"That blonde you married...that oh-so-educated *puta* got into your brain, made you weak. Women, children, they mean nothing. They are nothing more than grist for the mill. But take heart. With that disease, I could have killed everyone in Suriname. Perhaps the rest of the world."

"But you didn't," Navarro said bluntly. "Why?"

"Because I only needed it to stretch your people to your breaking point. So that I could capture someone like *you*."

A distant howl of jungle beasts echoed from down the valley. It was punctuated with the sounds of automatic weapons fire. Navarro looked out into the mist-shrouded forest, his fingers clenched as if still curled around a carbine.

"I see your other squad of mercenaries have encountered our local wildlife," Zann said. "It's an unfortunate side-effect the pathogen has on the animals here. It changes their brain chemistry in many strange ways, making them violent and insatiably hungry. Annoying. We can't even use the west gate anymore. It's helicopter transport or nothing."

"But they're not uncontrollable," the Deacon pointed out. "Those colored flares?"

"We can spur on their aggression, or re-direct it. And if we keep them well fed, they remain in the area and don't turn on each other. It's the best way to keep trespassers out."

"You're a monster," Navarro finally gritted. "My second squad..."

Zann held up a hand as he listened. The animal sounds and the rat-tat of gunfire slowed, and then ceased. He smiled.

"Your second squad is no longer a concern." He pointed to the guard watching the Deacon. "Take him to the guest quarters, make sure he is comfortable."

Navarro watched the man being taken below.

"What about me? Don't I rate the 'comfortable' guest quarters?"

"I'm afraid not," Zann said. "In fact, you don't rate guest quarters at all."

The Zielverkop leader motioned to the other two guards.

One rammed the butt of his rifle into Navarro's gut. The big man made an *uff!* as he dropped to his knees. The second guard cuffed Navarro's hands behind his back. Then he snapped a leather collar around Navarro's throat. A black sphere the size and shape of a golf ball projected from the back.

"There's always the chance that you might waver in your loyalty to your friends," Zann said. "So I've strapped a very special shaped charge to the nape of your neck."

The man took a single-button remote out of his pocket, holding it up for Navarro to see.

"It's just large enough to separate your head from your body," Zann informed him. "That is, without causing too many problems for those around. And lucky you, the detonator's wireless. Such fun toys we get to play with these days, don't you think?"

Navarro got back up. His jaw remained set, and his eyes spat fire.

"*Laten we gaan,*" Zann said heartily, as he strode off.

The two guards nudged Navarro to follow. He did so grudgingly, even as he felt the cold steel of the cuffs on his wrists and the nub of explosive at the base of his skull. Zann took the main catwalk that ran into his facility's central courtyard, shouting orders to the men below.

Navarro heard the low-pitched *whine* of helicopter motors starting up. Looking to the source of the sound, he spotted four Dauphin Eurocopters parked in the courtyard below. The rotors on two of them had already begun to spin.

"Come along, Mister Navarro," Zann said expansively. "It's time that you and I paid a visit to the headquarters of Deep Six in person."

Michael Angel

CHAPTER FORTY-ONE

Navarro did his best to keep a poker face at Zann's words.

It's time that you and I paid a visit to Deep Six in person.

"Deep Six? What's that?"

Zann's eyes flashed. "Keep lying like that, and I'll make your friends pay. As it is, I'm only keeping them alive to ensure your cooperation. Also, I find it entertaining to keep their fate dangling in my hands."

One of the two guards shoved Navarro forward as Zann moved on. The group descended a rust-spotted ramp as they made their way to the waiting aircraft. The smells of grease and aviation fuel blotted out the damp smells of the rainforest.

"I only provide security for Deep Six," Navarro insisted. "It makes no sense for you to go out of your way to capture me in particular."

"I didn't say 'you in particular'," Zann corrected him. "I said someone 'like you'. You, John Redhawk, or Geoffrey Chadwick would have all done fine. I needed someone with the keys to the castle, so to speak."

"Then why not take Redhawk or Chadwick? Why me?"

"*Doelmatigheid*, Mister Navarro. What you would call 'expedience'. Chadwick's a moron, but you always kept him well guarded. I had hopes of taking Redhawk when you sent him to be treated for my disease, but you stuck him on a boat and put a whole squad of your men between me and him."

Navarro watched as a group of eight more Zielverkop gunmen clad from head to toe in black boarded one of the helicopters. Erich Zann headed towards the other one as he continued talking.

"So I was stuck trying to locate and bring you in. You're a slippery one, though. My people couldn't nab you when you went into Goblintown. Or when you visited the sugar plant. So it was kind of you to have yourself delivered to my door."

Navarro considered, then decided to try and keep Zann talking. At least he could find out what the man knew.

"Deep Six is nothing more than a fancy name for a research project," he said, raising his voice to be heard over the rising sound of the rotors. "Just a black box."

"A black box based on the same technology as your Dazzlers," Zann said dismissively. "Only a lot more powerful. It's amazing what a mole can find out for you. For example, I learned that Suriname's become a test bed for an exotic laser weapon project. They've developed a very special ship called the *Archimedes*. Stealthy, fast, shallow-draft, and armed with a multi-gigawatt laser that can burn down or sink anything that flies or floats for hundreds of miles."

Navarro had to fight against expressing surprise. Sweat beaded on his forehead. Erich Zann had seen most of the cards in his hand already.

"That's a pipe dream. The United States military will stop you."

"That would be difficult. I'll be able to shoot down both planes and missiles. As for submarines, they can't go into the shallow waters the *Archimedes* is designed to operate in. But I'm not planning on taking them on ship to ship."

"Who, then?"

"Mister Navarro, you're as limited a thinker as the Zielverkop leaders I disposed of. You see, with the *Archimedes* I'll have the ability to choke off shipments of anything the cartels send from South America northward. Drugs, gold, gemstones…the worth is in the tens of billions of dollars. I'm going to control it all. I'll leave military confrontation out of this. Though I suppose that if push comes to shove, I can always threaten to release my little madness-inducing bug all over the world."

"You haven't changed anything," Navarro said, with a shake of his head. "You'd still just be a drug runner and extortionist, like all the dime-store pushers out there."

One of the guards slid open the helicopter's side door. The other nudged Navarro to board. He did, and Zann sat across from him, waggling the wireless remote in one hand.

"On the contrary! I will be much, *much* richer. All I have in my way is a locked door. The door leading to bridge of the *Archimedes*. A bridge that's armor plated and shielded against an EMP blast. Get me through that, and I'll let you and your friends live."

The rotors completed spinning up with a rising whine. The two helicopters took off, ascending through the mist until the green of the rainforest disappeared below.

* * *

Austen gazed up into the gloom that still surrounded them. The sound of a pair of helicopters thundered overhead and then faded away. A new trio of riflemen stood atop the wall at their backs, looking down at them. She put them out of mind. At least they'd turned off the blinding searchlight.

Kimura slumped back against the wall in utter exhaustion. Next to him, Grimes did the same. The two M&B men left their M4s lying in the dirt only a couple steps away. But grabbing the weapons was a sure ticket to suicide right now.

She noticed a trickle of red coming from Grimes' leg. Austen went over, took off her backpack, and knelt next to the man. He looked up at her in confusion.

"You're wounded," she said. "Let me take a look."

"It's not bad," Grimes said. He had a rough, blocky face that was only softened by a haze of beard stubble. "Don't worry about it."

"If it bleeds like that, it's a problem," Austen insisted. Grimes let out a sigh and shifted his leg. She tore away an already tattered pants cuff and spotted a deep slash in his calf. A quick dig into her pack and she came up with a wound disinfectant wipe.

"Okay," she said, "You know the part where a doctor tells you, 'this is going to hurt a little'?"

"Uh, yeah?"

"Yeah. Well, this is going to hurt a *lot*."

To his credit, Grimes only let out a couple of pained grunts as Austen painstakingly cleaned out his wound. The environment was too moist for adhesive tape to hold, and she didn't have the right material for stitching. Reaching back into her pack, she used a wound adhesive and pressed the edges of the wound together until it took.

"Thank you," he gritted.

"Welcome," she said. "When we get back, you still need to get that checked out. Unless you had a tetanus booster recently, you'll going to be up for some shots."

"If we get home," he gloomed.

"No, *when*." Austen insisted. "Navarro's surprised me more than once."

That roused Kimura enough to chime in. "The lady's right. You haven't served with Navarro long, have you?"

A shake of the head. "I just transferred in with Sims. And Sims bought it in Goblintown. Maybe our turn's coming up."

Before Kimura or Austen could respond, they heard the distant whine of motors from high overhead. Though they craned their necks, none of the three could make anything out in the mist. Austen's heart leapt as she realized that they weren't helicopter rotors.

They were the higher-pitched, quieter *whirr* of robotic drone propellers.

"Get ready," Austen whispered to the two men. "If those are Abbott and Costello, that means October's squad survived. We might need to grab our weapons after all."

A hundred feet overhead, the two drones slowed to just

over stalling speed. A strange looking device the size and shape of an apple box had been strapped to each aircraft's belly. Each device winked on with a flurry of electronic lights indicating that the weapon had gone hot.

Which was perfectly appropriate in this case.

Just as the *whirr* reached its peak, a second noise joined it. An asthmatic *vroop!* echoed through the air. A second later, it cut off.

Then the screaming began.

Michael Angel

CHAPTER FORTY-TWO

The three riflemen who guarded them from above cried out in agony. They danced about as if on fire, though Austen couldn't make out any flames. One flailed at the edge of the wall as he tried to escape his invisible tormentor.

With one more throat-wrenching scream, he fell from his perch.

The man landed with a crunch before them. His neck bent at an unnatural angle and he lay still. The sight galvanized the two remaining M&B men.

They leapt up and scrambled to grab their M4s. Austen got out of the way and retrieved Navarro's service pistol. The screams of the riflemen stopped abruptly as Kimura and Grimes cut them down with long bursts from their carbines.

Austen spotted a flicker of movement in the clouds above. The *whirr* of the drone engines hadn't ceased in all this time. A second asthmatic *vroop!* and yet more screaming came from inside the compound.

A series of rustles came from the underbrush nearby. Before the two M&B men could raise their carbines, October's huge form loomed out of the fog. He was followed by the rest of his squad. They were stained with mud from the jungle and breathing hard, but they all looked unhurt.

"*Sukin syn!*" the big man swore. "I am hating jungle more every minute!"

"October!" Austen cried, as the two groups met. "You're alive!"

"We heard your guns," he said simply. "Not hard to figure out what happened. We take precautions. Put backs against nice solid rock. The drones helped drive off crazy animals."

"Navarro had me install a TDS on both Abbott and Costello before we left," Wanjiru explained, as he made an adjustment to the drone controller unit. "That's a Thermal Denial System. Non-lethal energy beamed at 95 gigahertz excites the water and fat molecules in the skin. Just like a microwave."

"Is very good!" October enthused. "We have our own flying heat rays! Now, follow me. There is gate on west side. We break in there while bad guys getting cooked from above."

Kimura and Grimes fell in at a jog beside their fellow M&B troopers. The group's progress was marked by the continued whirr and wheeze of the drones as they orbited overhead, firing their TPS beams. Screams and sporadic gunfire continued to come from inside.

"How…did you know…about this 'gate'?" Austen gasped, as she moved to keep up with October. The big Russian was bulky, but his long strides covered the ground at a rapid clip.

"Nicholas is clever man," October explained. "He put headset away but kept on transmitting. This Erich Zann is a *zadnitza*. Loves to talk. Told us much of what is inside."

They turned the corner of the big building. As predicted, a large metal gate punctuated the sheer walls. Yet each of the men with her made some expression of surprise as they drew near.

The gate lay wide open.

The Deacon stepped out and beckoned them with a wave. "*Kom binnen!* What are you waiting for? I'm not mailing invites out!"

The M&B men sprinted up to the open gate. Austen trailed

behind, feeling a stitch developing in her side. Reyes and Hagen looked inside the compound, alert for any threats. October let out a booming guffaw of approval.

"Well done!" he beamed. "Is much easier to do job now!"

"I agree…" Austen asked, as she caught her breath from the last sprint. "But how?"

A shrug. "Zann left only a single guard to escort me to the 'guest quarters'. Poor fellow doesn't need oxygen anymore. But I was getting bored in here, so I decided to open the gate."

"Where's Zann? And Navarro?"

"Gone. I saw them take off with an additional armed squad in two helicopters. I don't think there's more than a dozen men left to guard this place."

October grunted. "Then we make short work."

He barked out a set of orders, dividing the men into pairs to root out any of Zann's remaining forces. Wanjiru was to find a sheltered spot on the catwalk above to direct the drones' TPS beams where needed.

"You two need to come with me," the Deacon said, addressing Austen and October. "The corridor I was led down needs to be seen."

"What? Why?" Austen asked.

The Deacon gave a chilly smile. "Because of what they're growing down there. And because I heard someone banging at a door, trying to get out."

October raised an eyebrow as he chewed this over.

"Okay," he finally said. "Sounds interesting enough. You point the way, I take lead."

The Deacon directed them along one set of buildings. Their journey was punctuated by several stops where October peered around corners, checking for anyone who might ambush them. Overhead, the drones continued to orbit, stabbing out with heat beams whenever a target was spotted. The screams that arose from the thermal rays were usually cut short by a burst of carbine fire from the M&B men.

Finally, the Deacon moved up to throw open a set of doors leading to the interior. They descended a darkened stairway.

Air conditioning greeted them, chilling the sweat on Austen's skin and making her shiver. A luminous red light came from below.

Austen let out a gasp as they arrived at the base of the stairs.

The light came from a subterranean greenhouse. The structure was the size of a warehouse, but it had been divided up with transparent walls into four-by-six-foot cells. A potted coca bush sat in each cell under a grow lamp. Many of the plants looked sickly, and all had the same slimy sheen to them as the rainforest plants outside.

Tentatively, Austen walked up to the closest cell. A little electronic screen hung on the glass. She walked across a row, reading each screen with alarm.

"This is a giant test garden," she breathed. "It's where they're breeding more *Claviceps* fungus. They're trying to figure out the best temperature and humidity conditions for it to thrive."

The corridor echoed with a deep *bang* of metal on wood. October made his way over to a door that had been secured with a heavy metal latch. He held his weapon's barrel up by the door's small square window.

"Who are you?" he barked. "Answer, or I shall blast down door like big bad wolf!"

CHAPTER FORTY-THREE

"Don't shoot!" came the scared-sounding reply. "I'm Doctor Marten Tiwari, and I'm being held here against my will. Can you please let me out?"

October reached out and unlatched the door. A beanpole-thin man with square-rimmed glasses and a white lab coat came stumbling out. He looked around uneasily as Austen came up to him and grasped his shoulder, steadying him.

"It's all right," she said. "You're among friends now. I'm Leigh Austen, and I work with the WHO. These coca plants...are they part of your work? Are they the source of this fungus?"

"Yes, they're my work," he said, nodding sadly. "I'm a plant geneticist by trade. I was offered a job to combat a new plant disease that was ravaging crops in this region. When I got to Suriname, I was blindfolded, bound, and flown here. This new disease wasn't affecting grains or fruit crops. They were destroying the coca plantations in this valley."

"I see why they grabbed you," Austen said. "No coca plants, no cocaine for the cartel."

"The pathogen's a fungus. One that affects both plants and animals. I named it *Claviceps kutari*, after the main river that flows into the lake here."

"How did you create this thing?" the Deacon demanded.

"Me? I didn't create anything! The fungus is a natural mutation. It was fragile at first. Ultraviolet light kills it quickly. It only arose here after Erich Zann built his gravity pump. It kicks up enough water vapor to shroud this valley all year round."

"Then what are you doing with these plants down here?"

"Zann's been holding me captive," Tiwari quailed. "I couldn't find a way to stop the fungus from colonizing plants, not without direct sunlight. So he had me growing coca bushes to increase the yield of fungus instead. He's weaponized the bug in pursuit of something bigger."

"You said that you couldn't find a way to stop the fungus from colonizing plants," Austen broke in. "What about humans? Is there a way to eradicate it from the human epidermis?"

Tiwari nodded so fast that his glasses threatened to fly off. "Yes, yes! It's a simple cocktail of three readily available drugs."

"Can you duplicate formula?" October grunted.

"Oh, of course I can!"

"Good. Then we need to be keeping you safe."

The big Russian shoved Tiwari back into his cell and latched the door. The diminutive doctor didn't even have time to cry out. October then turned back to the Deacon.

"You said Zann and his men left in helicopters, yes?"

The Deacon nodded. "I did."

"Are there any other aircraft?"

"Two. Dauphin Eurocopters, if I'm not mistaken."

"Show me where." October beckoned to Austen. "We need to go."

The Deacon led them back up the stairs. October followed, his weapon still held at the ready. Austen sputtered in protest as she brought up the rear.

"What are you doing?" she demanded. "We can't just leave Tiwari down there!"

She got a shrug in reply. "Is quiet. Is safe. Zann may still have men here. And I need to get airborne."

The Deacon pushed through the doors at the top of the stairs. They waited a moment until their eyes adjusted to the comparatively brighter outside light. Then, he led them along a second pathway deeper into the compound.

"There they are," he said, pointing.

A half-empty courtyard lay before them. Two helicopters sat nearby, their skids and fuselages dotted with the same rust spots that afflicted everything in the humid compound. Otherwise, they looked in excellent shape.

The tread of boots to one side turned out to be Reyes and Grimes. The latter trooper limped, but otherwise looked hale enough. Reyes grinned broadly.

"Just checked in with Wanjiru and the other team," he said. "Looks like this place is ours."

"*Otlichno!*" October said in congratulations. "Form perimeter. Have drones circle, watch for returning aircraft. Also, we found a hostage downstairs. Go let him out before he makes *pisayet* in his pants."

With that taken care of, October and Austen made their way to the closest helicopter. The big man yanked open the cockpit door and began fiddling with the controls. He let out a satisfied grunt.

"Is good. Much fuel. I can hotwire to fly, no problem."

"October, *wait!*" Austen demanded. "Where are we going?"

"Not 'we'. Is only 'me'." October opened a side panel under the pilot's seat and began to work on the wiring. "As I said before, Zann loves to talk. He spilled all of Nicholas' beans."

"You mean, he spilled all the beans to Nick. Told him all the plans."

"Yes, yes. Zann used this 'bug' to stretch us thin. So he could kidnap anyone who can get him into Deep Six project."

Austen thought back to her short but unpleasant meeting with Geoffrey Chadwick. "Go on, October. I don't think it matters at this point if you tell me what's going on."

"Deep Six is ship. Special one, hidden in Hoogeveen harbor. Nicholas can get Zann onto bridge and take control."

She shook her head in disbelief. "All this…was over a damned *boat?*"

"Not just boat," October corrected her. "The *Archimedes* carries special weapon. Shoot laser beams. Can take down any plane, any missile. Very powerful."

"How powerful?"

"Can destroy large ships," he said, with a shudder. "Could melt the Suriname navy's only patrol boat. Could burn the Sea Star down to waterline."

"The Sea Star?" she murmured, as prickles ran down her back.

"Is what *Stella Maris* means," October said. He reconnected the wires he was looking for and closed the under-seat panel. "Okay, now I must go."

The revelation hit Austen like a thunderclap. The last piece of advice that DiCaprio had given her finally fell into place. She swallowed hard as she contemplated it.

Save those you can from the burning star.

"I'm coming with you," she said firmly.

"We cannot rescue Nicholas! All I can do is warn Captain Henriks aboard the *Nieuw Amsterdam*. His patrol boat is last thing that can stop the *Archimedes*."

"You won't be in time." Austen yanked open the passenger side door. "You're going to have to drop me off at the *Stella Maris* on the way."

The big man looked at her hesitantly.

"Trust me on this," she urged. "After all, you said that I meant more than vodka and *kletska* put together."

October considered. "Dumplings *are* very good…"

Austen climbed into the seat, belted herself in, and crossed her arms.

"*Bozhe moi,*" he cursed. "You win, crazy American doctor woman!"

With a flip of a switch, October started the aircraft's engine. It coughed to life as he took his seat. He gave a few last orders to his men before switching from the squad radio to the pilot's headset.

A last notion crossed Austen's mind as the helicopter's rotors reached full speed.

Wait a minute, she thought. *What happened to the Deacon?*

But she set that aside as they lifted off into the pale gray sky.

CHAPTER FORTY-FOUR

Zann's pair of helicopters flew due north. Eventually, they dropped out of the clouds as they approached Hoogeveen City. Gray squares of cement and the crumbling red roof tiles gave way to tropical blue water of the U-shaped harbor.

At the far, open end of the 'U' lay the exit to the ocean proper. To the right, Navarro made out the sleek white form of the *Stella Maris*. Further up the docks lay the blockier looking Surinamese patrol boat, the *Nieuw Amsterdam*.

Both helicopters banked to the left, crossing the widest part of the harbor. The one carrying the bulk of Zann's gunmen surged forward to take the lead. Navarro made out a multi-barreled cylinder that had been bolted or welded beneath the second aircraft's fuselage.

The brackish smell of water and salt kicked up by the rotors filled the cabin as the helicopters dropped down to practically skim the waves. The bank ahead drew near. From the outside, it appeared to be a warren of abandoned dock works and rotting wooden piers. Navarro knew it was just more 'security through obscurity'.

And it was about to fail.

"Dolphin One to Dolphin Two," Zann said as he pressed

his headset microphone closer to his lips. "Start your attack run."

The second helicopter bore in at full speed. It pulled up just before reaching the bank. Navarro felt as much as heard a repeated *ka-chow!*, *ka-chow!* Bright flashes and a dull gray cloud of smoke billowed from the cylinder slung under the aircraft.

Arrow-shaped objects flew towards a decrepit building on the shoreline. They burned a series of red-hot arcs as they flew towards impact. One skipped twice before coming to rest, while the others exploded on impact with gouts of white flame.

"Another variant of the weapons system we purchased from our mutual friend, the Deacon," Zann explained. "Those are simply rocket-propelled grenades, modified for range and chemically altered to include white phosphorus."

Navarro gave Zann a look. "Nothing short of a battleship round is going to dent the hull of the *Archimedes*."

"True, true. But those rounds aren't meant to penetrate. They're meant to trigger the hidden base protocol. If Deep Six headquarters catches fire, the valuable experimental combat vessel is to be moved out of harm's way. And it looks like the incendiary we added to the grenades is doing the trick."

Sure enough, each grenade had set sections of old roof tar or rotting wood beams ablaze. Thick black smoke rose as fires grew and joined together into a larger brew-up. For a moment, Navarro made out the blare of klaxons over the sound of the helicopter's rotors.

Suddenly, a pair of seemingly-old metal doors down at the waterside swung open. An otherworldly *vrooo* echoed against a cavernous interior. With a swash of white-curled bow waves, the experimental laser ship slipped out into the harbor for the first time in broad daylight.

"There you are," Zann said, almost cooing. "You beautiful thing."

The *Archimedes* was too angular and severe to win any awards for beauty. In appearance, she resembled a dull gray throwing knife with a triple tip. The prototype used a trimaran design made up of a slender main hull and two outrigger hulls attached by a spidery network of lateral beams. The ship didn't plow so much as slice through the water.

The foredeck was low, flat, and featureless. A grooved silvery cylinder sat atop this level surface, fitted snugly into a rotating turret. To Navarro, the thing looked like a twenty-foot high coffee can with an attached muzzle bore. Instead of ground coffee beans, the polished titanium housing held a neodymium-infused crystal that could pump out up to sixty gigawatts of destructive power in mere seconds.

Just behind the laser, the main bridge structure reared up in a sheer wall of heat-resistant titanium plating four stories high. The remainder of the ship's structure sloped down to a pair of helipads, exhaust ports, and a network of cables to shunt power to or waste heat away from the ship.

"Dolphin Two, go!" Zann ordered. The second helicopter swooped in low towards the helipad just as a dozen M&B men had swarmed out onto the deck to bring their carbines to bear.

Navarro's jaw worked as he watched the battle unfold. Suddenly, he felt the cold touch of steel at his temple. He turned slightly, feeling the coldness slip across his skin.

Erich Zann held the pistol pressed to his forehead.

"Eyes forward," said the Zielverkop leader. "You don't want to watch what's going on below. And I don't want you getting any ideas."

Navarro glared at the man, his eyes burning with hatred. Outside, he heard the thump of the helicopter landing. The sustained rat-tat-tat of assault rifles firing. The sound of men screaming and dying below. After what seemed an eternity, Zann smiled broadly and tucked his pistol away.

"Looks like everything is *gedaan*." Zann raised his voice as he called up to the pilot. "Take us down."

The helicopter landed on the remaining clear pad with a gentle *thump*. Navarro disembarked with the rest of the passengers. He kept his expression neutral, but internally he cataloged what he saw across the *Archimedes'* deck.

Bodies clad in his company's mottled gray fatigues sprawled across the deck, bleeding from bullet wounds. The Motte &

Bailey men hadn't gone down without a fight. Three of Zann's team of eight gunmen lay flat and silent as well. The pilot he'd sent in on the attack slumped behind his cockpit controls, his chest and cockpit windscreen stitched with bullet holes.

The scene must have gotten to Zann as well. The man shook his head as he looked over the carnage. He walked over to the second helicopter and surveyed it with a critical eye. Smoke puffed out the engine mount and the top of the slowly revolving rotor.

Meanwhile, one of Navarro's guards pressed a finger to their ear, concentrating on the transmission in his headset. The man's skin paled at what he heard. Hesitantly, he called over to his boss.

"*Overweldigen*! Home Base just checked in...they've been taken!"

"What?" Zann spun on his heel. "Explain!"

"The transmission said that they were under attack by a squad of men from Motte and Bailey," the man said quickly. "That the west gate had been thrown open and that our men were being overwhelmed. Then the line went dead."

"It looks like my second squad wasn't as dead as you thought," Navarro remarked.

Erich Zann's eyes narrowed. He barked out orders to his remaining men. Five remained to watch the deck for boarders or approaching aircraft. Two more led the way forward. He then gave Navarro a shove.

"Move it," he said irritably. "Time for you to perform the only useful function you have left for me."

CHAPTER FORTY-FIVE

The base of the bridge structure had been shut tight. Yet it only delayed them for a short while. Zann's two men set charges that blew off one of the ship's watertight hatches with a *bwam!* of concentrated explosives.

Inside, Zann ignored the elevator to the bridge level. Instead, he located the emergency stairwell and took the three flights up to the top. Navarro did his best to navigate the stairs, which had been plunged into gloom with only emergency lighting to show the way. With his hands behind his back, any slip or fall would end up with his face smashed against the steel grating that made up the steps.

Finally, they reached the top level. The walls here had a cobalt sheen where polymer plates had been bolted on to protect the electronics from an EMP blast. The dark blue created a strange optical illusion, as if the corridor were deep underwater.

Off to one side of the corridor, a small alcove led to the bridge entrance. A trio of buttons and two screens separated by a keyboard punctuated the wall to the right of the door. Zann gave Navarro a push towards the screens.

"My informant gave me data on the laser weapon and on

one of this door's controls," Zann said, as he jabbed a finger at the trio of buttons. "Open, Close, and Lock. None of which will work on this side of the door now that the alarm has been tripped. Get to work overriding that."

"That requires a retinal scan," Navarro said. "Then I've got to type in today's access code. Finally, I've got to perform a simultaneous biometric scan of my left index finger and right thumb."

"Right. Hop to it, then."

Navarro gave him a contemptuous look.

"How do you expect me to do all that…when you've got my hands cuffed behind my back?"

Zann scowled anew. He spoke tersely to one of the two men with him.

"Do you have any flash-bang grenades?"

A nod. "*Ja, meneer.* I do."

"Get one ready. Toss it in as soon as that door opens. When it goes off, we go in firing. Try and hit the person you're shooting at. If you damage the laser controls, I'll have your head."

Zann pulled a set of keys from one pocket. Then he located the remote for the bomb attached to Navarro's neck and handed it to the second man.

"If he does anything besides touch those screens and keyboards, blow his head off."

With that, the leader of the Zielverkop cartel unlocked Navarro's cuffs. He stepped back as the big man brought his hands back around to his front and rubbed the chafed skin at his wrists. Zann brought out his pistol and crouched at the ready.

Navarro muttered a curse under his breath as he turned towards the panels.

He leaned forward and squinted one eye at the upper screen. It made a *squink*, followed by a green light.

Next, he tapped in a combination of numbers and letters on the keyboard. A second *squink*, followed by a similar green light.

Finally, Navarro moved to press his thumb and forefinger to the lower screen.

He paused.

His fingers froze, only a fraction of an inch from the screen's glassy surface.

"*Vervloek je ogen!*" Zann shouted. "Go on! What are you waiting for?"

Navarro looked over his shoulder.

"The game's up, Zann. How do you think you can win this? My men already took out your home base. You won't be able to infect anyone with your pet disease. Even if you take this ship, how long are you going to be able to hold it? Eventually, *someone's* going to be able to take you out."

"You know what else my informant was able to tell me? The *Archimedes'* price tag. This ship cost your country enough coin to feed every schoolchild for the better part of a decade. I can sell it back to them unscathed for half price."

"I doubt they'll cut a deal over that."

"You think so? Then maybe they'll dig deep into their pockets when I sail this ship to Paramaribo and threaten to vaporize the entire city. Frankly, if they won't pay, every country on this continent with a seaside port will." Zann gestured with his pistol. "Now. Open the door. Or I'll shoot both of your kneecaps out. My men can hold you up long enough to type, if that's the way you want to play it."

Navarro went silent at that.

He set his jaw as he touched his fingers to the screen.

A *squink*, followed by a green light, and the door slid open in the blink of an eye.

Zann's subordinate chucked the flash-bang grenade onto the bridge. It went off a second later with a *BAM!*

"Come on!" Zann shouted.

Gunfire rang out as soon as the two men disappeared into the smoky room. Navarro heard the whine of a ricochet, and he ducked instinctively. There was a shout of pain, followed by the thump of bodies hitting the floor.

Zann's voice sounded from inside. "Get Navarro in here."

The remaining Zielverkop gunman motioned with his rifle's barrel. Navarro noted the bulge in the man's side pocket, which still held the wireless remote. He held his hands up, turned, and moved inside. His guard followed close behind.

Navarro had to fight against coughing as his nose filled with acrid smoke from burning potassium nitrate. Three bodies lay spread-eagled across the floor, blood gushing from body or head wounds. Two wore naval uniforms, one with a captain's insignia.

The third was the gunman who'd accompanied his boss into the room.

Pity that it wasn't Zann, Navarro thought. *I'm going to have to take care of him myself. Just one more thing to handle. Patience. The right moment will come.*

Zann finished tapping in a setting on the bridge's main control dashboard. It chimed and began a countdown with a slight *hum*. The Zielverkop leader stood to one side so that Navarro could see directly out the bridge windows. The panes had been badly cracked by bullet impacts, but the view was clear enough.

Ahead of them was the sleek white form of the *Stella Maris*. It lay all the way across Hoogeveen's harbor, but it was close enough that Navarro could make out the sharp point of the vessel's bow.

"Since your people took something from me, I think it's only fair that I take something from you," Zann gloated. "You see, you can never truly…"

The man went on, but his voice faded out of Navarro's consciousness. His mind focused with crystalline clarity on only two things.

One was the handle of Zann's pistol. It wasn't in his hand. It lay gleaming on the ship's dashboard next to the laser controls.

The other was a fuzzy glimpse in the corner of his eye. The very edge of an assault rifle's muzzle. The man guarding him had moved a half-step too close. A half-step too far to one side.

There's my moment.

Whip-fast, Navarro moved.

He pivoted on one heel and thrust his arms out. His palms slammed into the last guard's chest like twin jackhammers. The cartel gunman let out a pained *uff!* as his rifle flew up and fired a single round with a *bang*. The bullet embedded itself harmlessly in the ceiling's acoustic tile.

The man's feet flew up with the force of the blow. He landed on his butt and skidded backwards on the smooth floor tile, just outside the bridge door.

Navarro leapt forward. He smacked the *CLOSE* and *LOCK* buttons on the door's inside panel with his palm.

A *squink*, followed by a green light, and the door slid closed in the blink of an eye.

The look of shock on Zann's face gave way to one of delight.

"Farewell, Navarro," Zann chuckled, as he waited for the explosive at the nape of Navarro's neck to go off.

It didn't.

Navarro advanced on him with a murderous look in his eyes.

Michael Angel

CHAPTER FORTY-SIX

Zann's look of delight slid into one of alarm in a single second. He grabbed for his pistol, fumbling in his haste. The grip fell into his palm.

Before he could curl his fingers around it, Navarro lunged for him. The bigger man bore him back against the control panel, smacking his head into the main bridge window. Another set of cracks spiderwebbed up the long pane.

The pistol fell to the floor and skidded under a nearby desk.

Zann let out a cry of pain and outrage. He brought his legs up, shoving Navarro back. In a flash, he moved to one side, dodging Navarro's incoming haymaker.

"I don't know why your head's still sitting on your shoulders," Zann said coldly. "But I'll end you all the same. I've beaten men to death before."

He came in like a boxer. A flurry of punches pummeled Navarro's chest and midsection. Navarro gasped at the raw power of the hits, his ribs creaking, his sternum exploding in pain. He threw one punch, then another. Zann blocked one, dodged the other.

Navarro only had time to form one thought.

Good Lord, he's fast!

The Zielverkop leader delivered an uppercut to his opponent's chin with a *crunch*. Navarro felt a pair of his teeth crack. His mouth filled with the slick, iron taste of blood. Zann moved in, punching, pressing him back against one of the bridge's computer stations. His hands shot out and grabbed Navarro's throat.

Navarro's vision went fuzzy as he absorbed the blows. Then tinged black around the edges as Zann began to squeeze his windpipe. Navarro's hands first came up, trying and failing to break the capo's deadly grip. When that failed, he clawed his way further up the man's arms.

Zann leaned back as far as he could. But Navarro's fingers found his cheekbones. They were mere seconds from gouging out his eyes.

He released his grip.

In that split second, Navarro sank down and drove his shoulder into Zann's midsection. The whole bridge seemed to shake as he body-slammed the man into the ship's radar station.

The dual scopes cracked and sparked with the impact. Zann cried out as three of his ribs broke with the dull *snap* of wet two-by-fours.

Navarro's mouth dripped red as he spat his words. "Those men you beat to death. Were any of them able to *fight back*?"

Navarro grabbed Zann's body by the shoulder and waist. He flung him back across the bridge. A *crunch* came from the man's spine as he landed next to the control console. Zann gasped and tried to get up, but his limbs only obeyed him sporadically.

"I don't understand," he moaned, as Navarro loomed over him. "The explosive…the remote…"

"Of course you don't understand," Navarro gritted. "Because you're ignorant. This is an EMP-shielded bridge. It blocks *all* forms of electromagnetic radiation. That includes wireless transmissions."

Navarro ripped the explosive collar from his neck, then reached down and snapped it around Zann's throat. Then, he grabbed the man by the belt and the shoulder one more time.

"But here's the thing. This bridge only blocks wireless transmissions...while you're *still inside of it.*"

Navarro swung the man's limp form around like a shot-putter readying a final throw. With a titanic heave, Navarro launched Zann into the cracked bridge window. The pane, already clouded and shot through with cracks, shattered into a thousand crystal daggers as the capo's body hit it.

Even through the pain of his cracked ribs, Zann had enough breath for one last scream. He screamed as he felt the shards of glass dig into his exposed flesh. He screamed as he fell through the open air and sudden sunlight.

The golf ball sized explosive at his throat went off with a *paff*. Zann's screaming ended for good. High above, Navarro heard two distinct impacts as what was left hit the deck forty feet below.

Then he heard a groan from behind him. Navarro whirled around and located the source. He knelt next to where the *Archimedes'* captain had fallen.

Blood poured from three separate chest wounds. Navarro didn't know where to begin to stop the bleeding. He grabbed a nearby seat cushion and raised the man's head, trying to make him comfortable.

"Captain, listen to me," Navarro said quickly. "Your ship's main weapon has been activated. A civilian target has already been selected. How do I shut it off?"

The Captain tried to speak, but only a bubbling sound came from his mouth. He locked eyes with Navarro and simply shook his head. The message was clear: *No way to shut it off.*

"If I can't shut it off," Navarro insisted, "there has to be another way to stop it. Isn't there?"

The Captain's arm shook as it came up. With the last of his strength, the naval officer managed to point to a section at the far end of the bridge console. He suddenly wheezed, and gore bubbled from his chest wounds. His arm fell to the floor with its last exhale.

Navarro reached out and closed the man's eyes. He

whispered a quick prayer and then got up. He wiped the blood that dribbled from his mouth with the back of his hand as went over to the indicated section of console. A frown blossomed at his brow.

The panel before him simply read *SAFETY STOP LOCKS*.

A series of chimes came from the main weapons dashboard. His chest and skull rang with pain, but he limped his way over. The smell of sea air poured through the open window, which helped clear his head as he read the screen.

Navarro skimmed over the figures for *WEAPONS CHARGE, TARGET LOCK*, and *NAVIGATION*. None of them looked promising. Despite what the Captain had told him, Navarro hit every button and spun every dial to try and change the readouts. To shut down the power to the laser, to switch off the targeting computer, or to change the course of the ship.

Each time, the screens flashed the same message: *ACCESS DENIED*.

Navarro racked his brain. He'd have gladly grabbed a fire axe and smashed the controls, but he'd read the design specifications for the *Archimedes*. The computers that ran the vessel were deep in the ship's gut.

Worse, the damned things were armor-plated. They'd require a string of grenades to disrupt. Zann might already be dead, but he still had a half-dozen Zielverkop gunmen roaming the ship. Navarro doubted that they'd allow him the time and leisure to gather up the explosives and try to put a dent in anything.

A *crackle* came over the bridge speakers. Instantly, Navarro realized that the ship's communications channel had been left open on the emergency frequency. He heard a snippet of conversation from a familiar Russian-accented voice.

"...to patrol ship *Nieuw Amsterdam*. I repeat, Kilo, Kilo, Kilo. Prepare to receive helicopter landing..."

Navarro peered out the broken bridge window and spotted the distant speck of a helicopter in mid-air. It was flying low, fast, and on approach to the *Stella Maris*. He had to tear his eyes away to find the communications console. Navarro dispensed with protocol pressed the transmit button.

"October? This is Navarro. I'm on board the *Archimedes*."

"Nicholas?" October's voice was faint, but the joy was evident in it. "It is so good you are not dead! Leigh is here too. She wants me to drop her off at work."

"Wait, wait! Don't let her go! Zann's dead, and I've taken the bridge. But his men still control the rest of the ship. He powered up the laser and locked it on a target before I could stop him."

"Nick?" Austen's voice broke in. "Nick, I know. He's picked the *Stella Maris* as the first target, hasn't he?"

For a moment, all Navarro could do was stare at the bridge speaker. "How did you…"

"DiCaprio said this would happen. He *knew*, Nick. I've got to save whoever I can from the burning star. And no, you can't talk me out of this."

Navarro cursed under his breath. He knew she was right. DiCaprio had never been wrong. Ever. In the future, they'd have to find out why.

Assuming that they even survived the day.

"All right," Navarro said, hating his words even as he said them. "Do what you can. But this ship's travelling at five knots across the harbor, and the *Stella Maris* is already within its firing range. You've got three, maybe four minutes until that laser weapon kicks off. And then…"

"I know, Nick. Trust me, I know."

The connection closed.

Austen and October were on their own.

Michael Angel

CHAPTER FORTY-SEVEN

"We have problem!" October exclaimed, as the helicopter drew close to the *Stella Maris*. "I cannot land!"

Austen craned her neck to look down at the surrounding area. She let out a curse. Unfortunately, October was correct in his assessment.

The cruise ship hadn't been equipped with a helipad. The pier to which it had been moored was simply too narrow for a landing. Half-finished booths and construction equipment from the postponed Keti Koti festival clogged the plaza area just outside the docks.

But Austen saw one other alternative.

"Come in low over the foredeck!" she said, as she unbuckled her safety belt. Austen shifted in the passenger seat and then unlocked the door.

"*Nu ty voobshche!*" October exclaimed. "What are you doing?"

"Jumping out of a perfectly good aircraft without a parachute, that's what!"

"That is suicide!"

"I hope not!" she shouted back. "Get us over the pool!"

Sailors clad in the blue and white uniforms of the cruise line gathered around, laughing and pointing as the helicopter sank lower and lower. October edged the aircraft so close to the bridge tower that only a few feet separated the structure from the whirling rotor blades.

Austen strained her eyes to make out the depth markers painted at the side of the pool. But the rotor wash had churned the water's surface to foam. At best, she could only tell where the deepest portion of the pool lay by the darker blue of the water.

Her mind raced. *Is it eight feet deep by the diving board? Ten? How high am I jumping from? Two stories? Three? If I hit the bottom and break my legs or spine, everyone's done for.*

The helicopter bucked as the wind picked up, rocking her in her seat.

"Cannot hold for long!" the big Russian called to her. "Maybe I land elsewhere, you walk back?"

"No time! Wish me luck, October!"

Austen didn't hear his reply. She ripped her headset off, kicked the door open, and *jumped.*

Her heart pounded in her ears as she fell through open air. She crossed her arms and drew her legs together, trying to make sure she didn't belly-flop into the water and shatter her rib cage.

Seconds dragged into minutes in her mind.

Glimpse of gold sun and blue sky. The shadowy blur of rotor blades passing overhead.

A flash of red-hot stinging in her legs as she hit the surface with a *FWOOSH.* Water turned into sparkling foam, rushing up her nose as she cringed, expecting her legs to crunch into the pool bottom.

The impact didn't come. Austen kicked her feet and swam for the sunlight, which now seemed impossibly far overhead. She gasped as she breached the surface.

Strong arms grabbed her and pulled her out of the pool. She spit up water even as she heard the reassuring phrases *Va bene!* and *Ti ho preso!*

"Bridge," she gasped. "Please, *emergenza.* Take me to the

bridge."

October pulled the cyclic back and moved the helicopter away from the cruise ship's bridge structure. He looked down as he turned the aircraft and spotted Austen being fished out of the pool by members of the liner's crew. Then he set a new heading towards the Surinamese patrol frigate.

Luckily, someone had picked up his earlier radio transmission. He spotted churning water by the ship's stern and sailors hurriedly casting off lines. By the time he'd landed and switched off the aircraft's engine, Captain Henriks was already waiting for him on the bridge.

"October!" the blond captain exclaimed. "Glad you're here. I've got an unknown ship in my harbor off the port bow. And it's a *verdoemde* big one, too. What on earth is going on?"

"Big vessel is laser weapon," October promptly replied. "Built in secret between United States and Suriname. But it is 'gone rogue' now. Set to kill last cruise ship in harbor."

Henrik frowned. "There's around three hundred people on board the *Stella Maris*. We've got to stop this vessel before it harms them. Are you sure about this?"

October bowed his head as he thought of Navarro's presence on that ship. But he knew exactly what his friend would do if their situations were reversed. Too many lives were at stake.

"*Da*, I am sure."

Henrik didn't waste another second. He got on the ship's intercom and rattled off a series of orders. Two teams of men dashed forward to man the .50 caliber machine guns. The vessel's motors roared to life as the *Nieuw Amsterdam* slid out into the harbor's choppy waters.

* * *

Someone had been kind enough to throw a towel about Austen's shoulders, but she still dripped water from her clothes. Her shoes *squelched* as she stepped onto the bridge of the *Stella Maris*.

Compared to what she'd seen before on small, cramped research vessels, this bridge was a tourist's wonderland. The

273

entire front wall was a single pane of smoke-colored glass with an unparalleled view of the harbor. Each bridge control station twinkled with lights as it if it belonged aboard a starship.

Captain Rosella could've passed for Captain Kirk. That is, had the fictional spaceship captain worn a goatee and a permanently pissed-off expression. But Austen had no time to try and soothe wounded feelings.

"Oh, *grande*. *Grande!*" Captain Rosella said mockingly. "What is it you want now? Perhaps you'd like my aft smoking lounge as your personal sanitarium?"

"Captain, *please*," Austen gritted, as she pointed to a small black shape out in the harbor. "That ship out there is the result of a secret defense project created by my government. It's been compromised by one of the cartels, and this ship is going to be its first target."

Rosella looked to the other members of the bridge crew. They were silent for a moment.

Then they all burst out laughing.

The captain made a circling motion with his finger by the side of his head.

"*Ragazza matta!*" he chuckled, pointing at Austen. "*Primo*, take care of this for me."

The Chief's Mate hesitated. He frowned as the black shape resolved itself into the deadly, sharp profile of a military vessel.

"*Capitano*, are you sure?" he said. "That ship out there…"

"Is not your concern! Get that woman off my bridge!"

"*Sì*, I will do so."

He moved to take Austen's by her still-damp upper arm and guided her back through the doorway. They'd hardly taken three steps when she pulled her arm out of his hand and turned to face him. Austen glanced at the man's name tag – *Togni* – and the triple bar on his epaulette that marked him as a deck officer.

"Primo Togni," she said intently, "You saw that ship out there. You saw that it's coming this way. What does it look like to you?"

The man swallowed uneasily. "It looks like a military

vessel."

"It is, and it's going to destroy us. Help me! Where else can you control the engines and steering on this vessel?"

"That would be the auxiliary bridge, three floors below." Sweat popped out on Togni's brow as he heard Captain Rosella call his name. He reached into his pocket and pulled out a set of keys. He yanked one off and gave it to her.

"This will open what you need," he said quietly. Togni raised his voice as he added, "I am sorry, but what you want is not possible. Please, go! I am needed elsewhere!"

Austen quickly tucked the key away as Primo Togni returned to the bridge. She froze as she caught a glimpse through the open door. The black shape of the *Archimedes* had grown larger in the floor-to-ceiling main window. It had shifted to block the harbor exit. And worst of all, it had pointed its bow directly towards the cruise ship.

The Captain's voice sounded anxious now.

"*Che cosa sta succedendo qui?* What are they doing?"

An otherworldly *vrooo* echoed inside the bridge. Conversation stopped. Austen jerked her eyes away and ran for the stairwell just as a series of blue-tinged flashes emanated from a structure on the *Archimedes'* bow.

A flash of heat turned the air around her burning hot. Austen's skin tingled and her hair singed as she took the steps two at a time. Screams of agony came from the bridge, amplified to ghastly levels as the sound echoed down the ship's hallways.

Michael Angel

CHAPTER FORTY-EIGHT

The screams cut off as Austen swung around the corner and down to the next level. The fire alarm sprang to life as everything flammable – even the paint on the walls – of the bridge floor instantly burst into flame. She gasped for breath as she rounded the last bend in the stairwell and ran for a door marked *PONTE AUXILLERY*.

Her clothes got a second, brief drenching from the ceiling-mounted sprinklers. She fumbled for the key and let herself in just as the water flow from the sprinkler heads died.

Three stories above her, the next series of laser pulses had turned the bridge to slag. Plastic wires and furnishings turned into puddles of multicolored goo while metal pipes burst and then melted in turn.

Austen went to the bank of controls, half of which were lit up in bright emergency red. She began flipping on power switches as her mind raced. While the *Stella Maris* couldn't be steered from here, her main engines could be engaged.

The question was: *How would that help?*

There wasn't any way to evacuate more than a hundred gravely ill people off the ship before the laser burned them stem to stern. But steaming full ahead would only take them directly towards the *Archimedes*, which would kill everyone more quickly.

She glanced out through the porthole window. The former harbormaster's building and a freight warehouse had been placed further back on the dock. Finally, she came up with a plan. It wasn't much, but it would buy them time.

Austen set her hands on a big black throttle marked *ENGINE ORDER TELEGRAPH*. She held down a button set on the side of the throttle and yanked it two, three, then four full stops back. The handle rested at the bottom of the throttle arc, next to the setting *FULL ASTERN*.

For two or three terrible seconds, nothing seemed to happen.

Then the big ship shuddered as the engines began to move her huge bulk backwards. Austen spotted a microphone that jutted out from the next console over, labeled *EMERGENCY PA*. She turned the system on and then mashed the transmit button.

"*Attention,*" she began, trying to keep her voice calm-but-definitely-urgent. "*All crewmen and medical personnel, this is an emergency.*"

She paused as she racked her brain for what to say next. Telling everyone that they were being attacked by a laser ship sounded too ridiculous. She needed to be taken seriously, without a second thought.

"*We have a massive fire at the bow of the ship. Move all patients as far astern or to the lower decks as quickly as possible. I repeat, move all patients astern or to the lower decks!*"

She shut the channel off as the heat from upstairs began filtering down to her level. Smells started to spread through the ventilation system. An awful combination of burning plastic, red-hot metal, and charred human flesh.

Austen pushed her way back out through the door. The main corridor had filled with smoke and steam, choking her. She ran from the bridge structure as the last of the crew fled for their lives towards the stern. Several took the more expedient route of simply jumping over the side.

The stitch in her side returned. Grimacing, she limped on doggedly as she crossed the foredeck and reached the safety of the amidships section. She felt the *Stella Maris* moving slowly backwards as she ran. A skin-rippling series of squeaks and groans came from over the side, where the ship's hull rubbed against the pier.

A metallic *crack* made her stop and turn to look.

An otherworldly *vroooo* sounded again. The four-story bridge structure glowed a molten red. It sagged backwards as if it were made of half-baked bread dough. The radar structures that sat on top turned into rivulets of molten metal that flowed like lava into the foredeck swimming pool.

The hellish *hiss* of superheated steam came from the deep end as the water vaporized. Acrid fumes broiled up as the rows of chaise lounge chairs flared up in puffs of black smoke and then liquified.

Suddenly, a shadow fell across her face.

She gasped as she looked up to see the harbor master's house slip past the side of the cruise liner. If *Stella Maris* continued her movement astern, the three-story house would come to rest between the remains of the bridge structure and the laser ship.

Then came a *jolt*.

The ship's motion stopped. A deafening *scrape* came from far aft, followed by silence. Austen realized that the scrape had come from the ship's propellers churning up silt and rock. The cruise ship had gone aground.

Without shelter, the next hit from the *Archimedes* would turn the rest of the *Stella Maris* into so much slag.

* * *

"*Oh, je neukt!*" Captain Henrik whispered, as he watched the results of sustained laser fire from the bridge of the *Nieuw Amsterdam*. Pulses of barely-there blue light leapt from the knife-edged shape of the *Archimedes* again and again. As for the laser ship's target, the entire forward section of the *Stella Maris* had slumped into a shapeless, sizzling mound.

"Such power…" he breathed. "That thing will wipe us out

before we can even shoot at it!"

"Then we do not shoot it," October growled, from his side. "We ram it."

Henrik traded a glance with the big Russian. He set his jaw.

"Sadly, you are right, my friend. I see no other way." Henrik didn't take his eyes off the spectacle before him as he passed along orders to his bridge crew. "Full speed ahead towards the enemy vessel. And get those gun crews off the forward deck!"

That last order turned out to be unnecessary. The crews manning the .50 caliber machine guns felt the shift in speed and watched as they drew closer to the faintly shimmering energy beam. They quickly stowed the guns in their locked positions and ran aft to safety.

"All clear?" Captain Henrik finally received an affirmative from his crew. "Good. Set the autopilot. And then sound the alarm: *All hands to the life rafts, we're abandoning ship!*"

The Surinamese sailors swarmed the after deck within seconds of the orders going out. Life rafts were lugged out of lockers and inflated as the emergency klaxon wailed in their ears. The first rafts hit the water just as the *Nieuw Amsterdam* took the brunt of a blast from the *Archimedes*.

An unholy *vroooo* cut the air. The ship jounced as if it had hit a speed bump, knocking many of the men to the deck. The bridge windows turned to jelly and sluiced like syrup down the sides of the tower.

Then came several deafening *BANGS!* and *KAPOWS!* On the foredeck, the .50 caliber gun mounts and their ammunition began to cook off in the heat like so many firecrackers.

Desperately, the crew of the *Nieuw Amsterdam* redoubled their efforts at getting their life rafts into the water.

CHAPTER FORTY-NINE

Navarro watched in horror as the *Stella Maris* crumpled under the laser's assault. With an effort he didn't think could be so difficult, he put it to one side with a final thought.

Leigh, I hope you had enough sense to get off that tin can before it got zapped.

The alien-sounding *vroooos* continued to come from the massive powerplant aboard the ship. Up close they were deafening. So much so, that he'd had to stop several times to press his palms against his ears.

Navarro stuck his head out the shattered bridge window to see if there was any way to climb down from the outside. There wasn't, but he did see Erich Zann's remains far below. Several of the capo's men gathered around the body for a moment.

Then they made a beeline for the remaining helicopter.

Like rats fleeing a sinking ship, Navarro though, as the helicopter took off and headed for the far horizon. *Only this ship isn't sinking. Not yet, anyway.*

He called up the ship's blueprints on one of the remaining computer consoles. He'd found where one of the critical cooling lines could be breached from the main deck level. It was big enough to cut the power to one of the ship's two engines. He put together that fact and where the ship's Captain had pointed before dying.

It couldn't be that simple, could it? Well, I've only got one way to find out.

Navarro went over to the panel that read *SAFETY STOP LOCKS*. He flipped the switch to the *OFF* position, which promptly set off an alarm. The screen printed out in scarlet red: *THIS ACTION IS NOT RECOMMENDED. CONTINUE? YES / NO.*

He touched the *YES* portion of the screen. Then he went over to the bridge exit and tapped the *UNLOCK* and *OPEN* buttons. Navarro emerged into the hallway and ran towards the ship's small but untouched armory. Instead of a gun, he grabbed a pair of grenades.

A blast of heat and yet another *VROOOO!* made him stumble as he emerged on deck. He spotted a ship that had placed itself between the *Archimedes* and the *Stella Maris*. The camouflage colors told him that it could only be the *Nieuw Amsterdam*.

His breath caught as he wondered if Captain Henrik and October were on board. The patrol ship's bow had been turned into slag. Explosions then dotted the ship's foredeck, obscuring it with smoke and fire.

Navarro put it out of mind. He turned away and moved to where one of the ventilation shafts had been left open to scoop up cool sea air. It was small, and shielded from where it could be hit by opposing gunfire or a missile strike.

However, it was child's play for Navarro to yank the pins from his grenades and slip the explosives into the vent. He heard them bouncing down the shaft, clanging as they slid down into the ship's innards. Then he ran aft for shelter and braced himself.

The deck plates jumped as a muffled *bang!* sounded from deep below.

Geyser-like, a jet of scalding-hot steam gushed from the vent's opening fifty feet into the air. Far below the deck, the pipe sending that steam to the turbine flew to pieces, spraying shrapnel all through the ship's delicate innards. Deprived of power, one of the ship's two drive shafts ground to a halt. The port-side propeller went still.

Navarro felt more than heard the *wrench* of metal under strain. The *Archimedes* slewed around sharply to the left as the starboard engine continued under full steam. His feet flew out from under him, and he grabbed on to a nearby stanchion to keep from being flung off the deck.

What was left of the ventilation duct came loose with a *thwang*. It left nothing but a gash in the deck that directed a fountain of steam skyward. Navarro struggled to his feet as the plating beneath his shoes began to get hot to the touch.

He groped his way to where an emergency locker lay smashed, its doors dangling free. A second gash in the deck tore open, sluicing vapor mixed with engine oil. Navarro snatched up an inflatable life vest from the locker and slid it over his head.

Navarro shimmied his way across the ship's network of lateral beams. He made his way to the outermost edge of one of the outrigger hulls. His eardrums throbbed as the loudest *VROOOO!* yet made him glance back once more. His heart skipped a beat as he realized that his plan was working just as he'd hoped.

The *Archimedes'* main weapon had remained fixed on its heading. In fact, its last discharge had finally melted the oncoming *Nieuw Amsterdam*, which was now sinking by the bow. Yet even as the ship had pulled around to the left, the laser had kept itself locked onto the *Stella Maris*.

The laser's housing at the flat, exposed area near the bow had been intentional. The designers had given it a 270 degree 'free fire' field. Only the safety stop locks kept the weapon from shooting through its own multistory bridge structure.

And Navarro had turned off those very locks.

He leapt from the burning deck and into the lukewarm embrace of Hoogeveen's harbor. As soon as he hit the water, the big man kicked off his footwear and began windmilling his arms. He strained every available muscle fiber to get as far away from the crippled laser ship as possible.

The *Archimedes* continued its uncontrolled turn so that it was facing almost completely away from its target. Yet the computer-controlled laser continued to fire. The next flicker of blue light began to carve its way through the bridge itself, instantly turning the titanium to glittering metallic vapor.

An avalanche of molten metal cascaded down the rear side of the bridge structure. Unlike the half-molten slag created on the *Stella Maris*, this material ran and spread like quicksilver. It instantly ruptured steam lines, melted wiring, and clogged cooling vents.

The laser weapon fell mercifully silent. The starboard engine shut down with a wheezy rattle. Citizens of Hoogeveen City crowded around the harbor's shoreline held their breath as the ship seemed to collapse in upon itself with a metallic *crinkle*.

Then, with a titanic *KA-THOOM!* the vessel exploded. One of the trimaran's outrigger hulls did a flaming cartwheel across the harbor. It finally came apart in a hail of metal splinters just short of the *Stella Maris*. The other parts of the boat split in twain as the *Archimedes* went down with a gurgle of flotsam-choked water and steam.

Navarro struggled to keep above the surface. His head throbbed from his injuries, and the adrenaline that had kept him going was finally starting to ebb. A bone-deep weariness crept into his limbs as he tried to keep going.

Then he heard the splash of oars and a roar of encouragement.

"*Davay, chuvak!* Do not stop swimming!" came a Russian-accented voice. "You will make it more difficult for us to complete rescue!"

Navarro shifted to wearily treading water. A life raft the color of ripe orange rind approached. Eight Surinamese sailors paddled it along as best they could with equally bright plastic paddles. As the heaviest person, had October positioned himself at the midsection. But he was able to reach out and help pull his friend over the side.

It took a moment for Navarro to stop coughing as he brought up the water he'd swallowed or inhaled during his swim. When he looked up, the sailors around him had reversed course to paddle further away from the steaming cauldron where the *Archimedes* had gone down. The grumble of gas-powered motors came from all over the harbor as rescue launches headed their way.

"*Slava Bogu*," October beamed. "Looks like things shall turn out right."

"It looks like," Navarro said. He sat back against the side of the raft, feeling its blessed solidity against his sodden clothes. "You know, I never really liked the water."

"That, I can understand," October agreed, as he waved down the closest boat. "Water is better in Russia. Most of the year, you can *walk* on it."

Michael Angel

CHAPTER FIFTY

John Redhawk sat up with a groan. His eyes widened as he looked at his fingers, which were free of any grayish-white tinge. Then he looked to one side, where Austen and Navarro stood by his bed, still clad in biosafety suits.

"I was going to ask if you'd found a cure," he grumped. "If you two still have that ridiculous getup on, then I guess I'm still sick."

"A better gauge would be how you feel," Austen pointed out. "Care to tell us?"

"How do I feel?" Redhawk took a full, deep breath and lay back against his pillow. "Tired. Tired, but good. I don't feel like I'm going to go *loco*, anyway. What happened?"

"What happened is that we found a cure," Navarro said. "Or rather, someone who told us how to manufacture it. We're still in these suits because the WHO is trying to figure out how long your fungal infection remains in your system. So be patient. You'll only be in here a couple more days, tops."

Redhawk snorted. "I suppose I can swing that. Can I get some food in here? Something more than gelatin and IV drippings?"

"I'll get right on it," Austen promised him.

She and Navarro said their goodbyes to Redhawk. Once they'd de-gowned outside the medical bay, Austen led the way upstairs. Navarro let out a breath as soon as they pushed through the doors and arrived on deck.

"Thank God," he said. "That's the first time in a while that Redhawk's sounded like…well, himself."

"He's going to be fine," Austen agreed. "All the patients are on the road to recovery, now that we're administering Doctor Tiwari's drug cocktail. Even the longest-suffering patient, Jaime Lucas, is starting to improve. He sat up last night and asked Piper if she could sneak him a cheesesteak with something called 'Whiz'."

"You can take the boy out of Philly…" Navarro chuckled. He paused and sobered up again. "Piper's done well. I think you've got a keeper with her."

They made their way aft. The surviving crew of the *Stella Maris* had set up a makeshift cantina on the cruise ship's fantail as a temporary dining area. Behind them, a repair crew was still busy removing the melted slag and wreckage from the bow section.

"I agree with you about Piper," Austen said. "Whatever her legal problem was with the University, I'm recommending that she gets re-enrolled in the tropical disease program. And speaking of tropical diseases, did you know that she still wanted to visit the rainforest?"

"You're kidding, right?"

"I needed the help, so I granted her wish. Piper left this morning to work with Governor Murken's containment crews at the former Zielverkop base."

"Hope they brought along a couple regiments of riflemen, then."

"They're well enough armed. They've got an unpleasant task ahead of them: performing a controlled burn on that part of the rainforest."

Navarro considered that. "Think they can wipe out this new offshoot of *Claviceps*?"

"Most fungi protect themselves by burying fruiting bodies

in the topsoil, where no fire can touch them. And of course, *Claviceps* has been pumping out spores into the air for weeks now." Austen shook her head. "I don't think we're done with this bug. The good news is that it's easy to spot on plants, and that there is a cure."

"Thank God for that. I'm still trying to wrap my head around the fact that Redhawk's going to be fine. I guess part of me already figured that he'd be checking out. But you saved him."

"We *all* had a part in saving him. You led the way through the rainforest. October finished your mission. And let's not forget, the Deacon got us inside. I still wonder what happened to the man."

Navarro shrugged. "I wouldn't worry too much about that."

"I know that you didn't exactly like him, but let's get real. He slipped away around the time October and I got airborne to follow you. If he's out there, then he'd have to cross almost a hundred miles of rainforest just to get back to Hoogeveen City. And if he managed to return through all of that, there's a standing warrant for his arrest."

"All true," Navarro acknowledged. "Still, I wouldn't count out someone like him. Men like that are like bad pennies. They always turn up again."

"Yeah, about those bad pennies..." Austen groaned, as Geoffrey Chadwick's all-too-familiar face emerged from the dining area. "Here we go."

Navarro scowled as the man walked up to them. To his surprise, Chadwick spoke to Austen first.

"Well, now. It's good to see you're still alive," Chadwick began, in a sympathetic tone that Austen didn't buy for a New York minute. "You should know that I'm requesting a Congressional review board to convene back in Washington this week. Expect to be called up to answer some questions."

"*Me?*" Austen blinked. "What in the world do you need me for?"

"Because your actions in the rainforest and on this ship

indicates that you knew about Deep Six's project here." Chadwick squinted at Navarro. "That was an unauthorized transfer of information, and someone could be looking at serious consequences for it."

Before Austen could object, Navarro spoke in a voice that held more than a hint of a growl.

"Am I invited to this lunch party for bureaucrats as well?"

"Damn straight you are! You're one of the main suspects!"

"Good. Because I want some questions of my own answered. Like how you managed to compromise Motte & Bailey's direct secure line."

Chadwick's face flushed, not with embarrassment, but anger.

"You wouldn't dare! I'll have you in the stockade before you can accuse me of—"

Navarro's fist shot out. The blow made Chadwick reel back for a moment. The man crossed his eyes in pain. His hand came up to pinch his nostrils shut as they began to leak blood.

"You...you broke my nose!" he gasped.

Navarro scowled. The scar at the side of his face seemed to throb as he did so. He leaned forward so that Chadwick could hear him clearly.

"Stick around, then. You can watch me break something *else*. Up close and personal."

Chadwick scurried off with a scared *squeak*.

Navarro watched him leave. Then he let out a sigh. "Leigh, remind me again why we keep doing our jobs."

"We're just slow learners."

"Maybe," he said. Almost shyly, Navarro put his hand out. She took it. His grip was firm, but gentle and warm. "On the other hand, maybe we do it...because some people are worth it."

She looked at him, eyes shining.

"Maybe that's it. I like that, Nick. Quite a bit, as a matter of fact."

They headed into the cantina together, still holding hands.

CHAPTER FIFTY-ONE

French West Indies
Port Sainte Marie
Île Pain de Sucre

The distant hum resolved itself into the gull-winged form of a Pilatus single-engine turboprop. It circled the hump-backed hill known to the locals as 'Sugar Loaf' and came in for a landing along the island's single strip of asphalt. The lone passenger descended the deboarding ramp carefully, making sure not to bump the aluminum hard-shell briefcase carried in hand.

A Citroën waited below, the rear passenger door open and inviting. An offer to place the briefcase in the trunk was politely refused. The car started up with a refined grumble and passed the armed checkpoint with only a nod between driver and guard.

The single strip of asphalt that made up the runway turned into the main road running through Port Sainte Marie. However, the Citroën didn't stop at any of the colorful shops selling trinkets, banana bunches, or freshly harvested conch meat. Instead, it ascended the winding road that led to Sugar

Loaf's summit.

A colonial-style French cottage stood within a grove of sweet-smelling manchineel trees. The cracked paint, weather-beaten shingles, and slight tilt to the door beams made it seem as if the dwelling were about to fall down. The Citroën pulled up slightly past the house, so that the passenger door aligned with a brick walkway leading up to a pergola covered in a blaze of blooming bougainvillea.

The woman who waited at a table under the pergola wore a form-fitting pair of slacks, a tropical blue-and-white blouse, and a wide-brimmed sun hat. Her dark hair hung loose over her shoulders like a drape of black silk. She reclined in her chair, with only the irritated exhale of cigarette smoke betraying her underlying impatience.

A short, gangly-bodied man got out of the car, briefcase in hand, and made his way towards her. He pushed his square-rimmed glasses back atop the bridge of his nose. The skin on his face sagged slightly, as if he'd weathered a great deal of stress.

"Helen Lelache," he said, with a slight incline of the head. "It is good to see you again."

"*De même moi aussi*," Lelache replied.

"This is a very nice retreat you have here. How much does it cost to rent it?"

"It is not rented. My family has owned this entire island from a time when men plied the oceans in sailing ships. Now, I wish to see what delight you have brought me, Doctor Tiwari."

Tiwari set his briefcase down. He opened it and took out a container that at first glance looked like an avant-garde mason jar. Actually, it was a specially designed bioflask that could maintain a specific climate-controlled environment inside its confines.

It also sported a handwritten label: *Claviceps kutari*.

"Very nice," Lelache said, as the doctor carefully placed the flask on the table between them. "You are aware that I collect such delicacies from time to time."

"I'm aware of how much you pay for them. I went through

a great deal of trouble to get this for you."

"I read the news reports. They said that you'd escaped imprisonment after being kidnapped and taken to a cartel compound against your will."

"That's the story I told, yes. But people like you and I must show one set of plumage to the world. Another to those who are like us. Who know the truth of how the world works."

"*Toutefois!* Are you saying that you weren't held against your will?"

Tiwari gave a rueful laugh. "Not at first, no. Erich Zann first hired me to collect the mutated strain of *Claviceps* that showed up in his coca fields and try to stop its spread. When that didn't happen, he had me grow the fungus in order to concentrate its properties. To weaponize it."

"Indeed."

"I'd thought of Zann as ruthless. And yes, he possessed that quality in abundance. But he was also at least half-mad. He wanted me to refine the toxins put out by the fungus to better control how the local wildlife reacted to prompts and cues. Things got unpleasant."

"I heard that he murdered three of your lab assistants. Beat them to death with his own fists."

Tiwari dismissed the statement with a wave of his hand.

"Please. Each of those people meant as much to me as the swatting of a mosquito. The unpleasantness came from my having to feed the animals. And not getting paid."

Lelache took one last drag of her cigarette, exhaled, and flicked away the stub. When she spoke again, there was an acidic bite to her voice.

"*Mon ami*, you didn't get paid because you *didn't deliver.* You failed to stop the fungus from infecting his plants. You failed to change its chemistry to alter its effects on animals."

"I did collect it," Tiwari insisted. "And I weaponized it."

"Collecting is a simple matter. As for 'weaponizing' it? The deadliest organisms are perfect predators already. There is no need to make them any more lethal." Lelache gestured to the bioflask. "What you bring me causes sickness with tremendous speed, to be sure. But it can be cured with a trio of readily available medications. This is more akin to a weak strain of influenza or a common cold virus."

Beads of sweat popped out on Tiwari's brow. He pushed his glasses back up onto the bridge of his nose. Then he leaned forward and spoke insistently.

"I brought what you wanted. I need money. If I don't get paid, then I'll have to talk to other people. People who might like to know about your family's little Caribbean retreat."

Lelache raised an eyebrow. "Very well, Doctor. You shall be compensated fairly."

She raised a hand and signaled to the driver with a single wave. He nodded, went inside the house, and brought over a silver case. Lelache took the bioflask and set it aside before the case was placed atop the table and opened.

Tiwari's eyes lit up. He ran his hands over the stacks of bills crammed inside. A gleeful sound bubbled up from his throat, somewhere between a giggle and a cackle. He closed the case and then grunted as he picked it up.

"It's a bit heavier than I expected."

"That could not be helped," Lelache said, shrugging. "You specified bills in smaller denominations. That makes it weigh more."

"It's harder for the authorities to notice smaller bills. And it makes it easier to spend!"

"On a plane ticket home? Gifts for your expectant wife? Toys for your child?"

Tiwari let out a bark of a laugh. "That was something I told Zann to see if I could gain some leverage. I've no idea when my wife's expecting, nor do I care. I've got a younger, *tighter* girl I've been keeping on the side for months in any case. *That's* where I'm heading next."

"*Au revoir*, then."

The weight of the briefcase was all that kept Tiwari from skipping on his way back to the car. Lelache watched the driver speed off with his passenger. She stretched, catlike, feeling the vertebrae in her spine pop pleasantly as she did so.

Far below, the Pilatus' engine spun up and the aircraft took off. It circled Sugar Loaf once in order to gain altitude before vanishing into a cloudbank to the south.

A flash came from the clouds. Perhaps it was a flash of lightning. Then a distant *rumble*. It sounded close enough to be the grumble of a rising thunderhead.

Both were common enough during the Caribbean's hot and humid summers.

Lelache picked up the bioflask. She hefted it in one hand as if testing its weight. She shook her head as if chiding herself and then headed up towards the cottage.

Such a pity, she thought. *If you must do something right, you must do it yourself.*

EPILOGUE

British Overseas Territory
Caicos Islands
Bottle Creek Cay

Another island, another approaching plane.

This time, the island lay several hundred miles further north and west. A stretch if flying from Suriname. A stretch if flying from the United States.

But it could be done.

With enough planning and persistence, most anything could be done.

A dark-haired man with a strong, bony face waited amongst the groves of palm trees. He watched as the plane banked around to make its approach. His clothes hung loose over his sturdy frame. As if he'd lost a great deal of weight over the last few weeks.

The man rubbed his hands to stave off his nerves. He'd waited long enough to make this happen. A couple more minutes meant nothing.

Finally, the little four-seat island hopper landed. The wheels jounced over the pits and bumps of the rough sand that made up the runway. But the pilot brought the aircraft in safely and shut off the engine.

The passenger door opened. A woman with shoulder-length blonde hair and delicate, birdlike features stepped out. So did a six-year-old girl with golden tresses and sparkling gray eyes. She ran towards the man as soon as she spotted him.

"Daddy!" she cried, as she threw herself into his arms. "I need to find a whelk!"

"Wait, a what-now?" he asked, as he kissed her and set her down. "A whelp?"

"Not a *whelp*. A *whelk*! That's a kind of sea snail. They have them here, and I need to find one."

"Well, I'm not sure what a whelk looks like. But this is an island. You might find one on the beach. Mommy and I can join you down there in a minute."

"Okay, but hurry! Or I'll find all the good ones first!"

"I have a feeling that you will, *liefje*," He sighed happily as she took off in a cloud of dust. Only then did he shift his attention to the woman who'd joined him. "Hailey, what on earth have you been feeding her?"

"Whelks, mostly," came the reply. She put her arms out and let him draw her in for a languid kiss. When they came up for air, she added, "Livia's got a show-and-tell due at the end of the month. She picked mollusks to talk about."

"We better follow her before she drags in a shark by the tail," he said. They followed a sand-strewn path down towards the beach. "I missed you, *schatje*. My little treasure."

"Not so little if Livia keeps getting me to make us pasta carbonara," she joked, before peering at him more closely. "But I'm not the one who's been on a diet. You have. I can see the bones in your face."

"I've been doing a lot of travelling," the Deacon admitted. "Hiking, mostly. It can take a lot out of you."

"Just don't overdo it. I think you've lost what, ten or fifteen pounds? Have you been sick?"

"Not really," he said, as they emerged on the sandy crescent that made up the beach. Livia prowled the shoreline up ahead, a pair of shells already in her hands. "But I've been doing a great deal of thinking lately. And I think it's time."

Hailey put a hand to her mouth. Trembling, she asked, "Do you mean you're getting out?"

The Deacon nodded.

"I'm already out. The arrangements we made...I used them. New name, new identity. We can be together from now on. We can live comfortably. Not as comfortably as I'd dreamed, perhaps, but we shan't be wanting for *alles wat je wilt*."

"I don't care if we end up living under a bridge!" she declared. "Having you out...that's enough."

His eyes lit up at that. "Then that's enough for me, too."

"Can I ask...what made up your mind?"

Johan pursed his lips in thought. He knelt for a moment, picked up a small stone, and then got up before answering.

"Something happened that made me see things a little differently. I suppose you could say that I finally grew up."

With that, the two walked along the warm sand together. Livia's delighted cries echoed up and down the beach. Johan laughed and threw his stone across the cay's shallow water.

It skipped three times before finally disappearing beneath the surface. The ripples kicked up from the splash radiated out into the open sea, becoming part of the waves that would crash upon unknown distant shores.

The End

Michael Angel

AFTERWORD

Thank you for reading *The Reaper's Scythe*! I hope you found it as enjoyable to read as it was for me to write.

There are some research notes involving *The Reaper's Scythe* that I'd like to share. Effort was taken to ensure basic accuracy in many areas of this book. However, most of the story is equal parts speculation and imagination. For example, the mutant fungus *Claviceps kutari* and its horrific effects exist only within these pages.

In general, fungi which attack plants are unable to deal with the different structures found in animal cells. This should be considered a blessing. One shudders to think how dangerous horticulture would be if we could catch a cold or fever from an infected vegetable garden!

But there is at least one case where a plant-based fungus can infect humans. *Sporothrix schenckii*, a fungus that lives on dead rose thorns, can enter the body through a scratch or puncture wound, causing *sporotrichosis*, also known as 'rose-picker's disease'. Those with compromised immune systems run the risk of developing problems with the lungs, eyes, lymph nodes, and central nervous system.

Additionally, the group of fungi that cause ergot poisoning

are real. Perhaps the most prominent member of this group is *Claviceps purpurea*. This fungus attacks many types of cereals, forming black masses of branching filaments. These masses contain ergot toxin, made of alkaloids like ergotamine. Ergotamine is an astoundingly complex molecule consisting in part of lysergic acid, the key component in LSD.

Ergotism, the effects of long-term exposure to ergot alkaloids, is marked by hallucinations, irrational behavior, convulsions, and death. Since rotting grain has been a consistent problem prior to modern agriculture, this phenomenon was unfortunately well-known to early human societies.

Outbreaks of 'madness' and convulsive symptoms from ergot-tainted grains date back to antiquity. However, they were first reliably recorded in south-central France by the 12th century chronicler, Geoffroy du Breuil. During the Middle Ages, this form of poisoning was known as Saint Anthony's Fire and sometimes depicted with dancing skeletons and a skeletal reaper representing death incarnate.

Additional outbreaks have been noted north of the Mediterranean right through the late nineteenth century. There are even theories that ergotism may have affected early American history. Ergot-contaminated rye is suspected to have caused both the hallucinations and convulsive behavior that provoked the Salem witch trials.

The light-blinding 'Dazzler' weapons used by Navarro and his men at the Deacon's island retreat are real. These are directed-energy weapons intended to temporarily blind targets. In May 2006, the U.S. military announced it was using Dazzlers in Iraq as a non-lethal method of stopping drivers who failed to halt at military-manned checkpoints.

Thermal Denial Systems, such as the one used against the Zielverkop compound, are also real. Called Active Denial Systems (ADS), they were designed as non-lethal energy weapons for perimeter security and crowd control. ADS variants have been deployed in Afghanistan as well as at the Pitchess Detention Center in Castaic, California. Prison authorities plan to use ADS in special situations such as breaking up fights between inmates.

The ship-mounted laser weapon system depicted in the last quarter of the book is fictional, but based on designs that are already starting to become a reality. As of early 2019, the U.S. Navy plans to install a High Energy Laser and Integrated Optical-dazzler (HELIOS) aboard an unspecified Arleigh Burke class destroyer.

At 60 kilowatts, HELIOS will be able to burn small speedboats and unmanned aerial drones. Of course, the 60 *gigawatts* laser used by the *Archimedes* is much more powerful, but also a complete fantasy. As a point of comparison, in 2012 the total capacity of all electricity-generating plants in the *entire United States* came out to around 1,000 gigawatts.

The name of the laser ship *Archimedes* is something of a reference in itself. Archimedes of Syracuse was a mathematician, physicist, engineer, and inventor from Greek antiquity. It was said that during the naval siege of Syracuse, he employed a 'flaming death ray' to burn approaching Roman triremes. The 'death ray' was likely a steam cannon or multiple mirror-like lenses directed at a vessel to try and make the sails or deck rigging burst into flames.

Finally, it should be noted that the bioterrorism-embracing Zielverkop cartel and the lawless environs of Hoogeveen City were invented for this story. No disrespect was meant to either the people or the country of Suriname.

Again, thank you for spending time with me, Leigh Austen, Nicholas Navarro, October Shtormovoy, John Redhawk, Niles Bailey, Edward Preble, Emily Piper, Daan de Murken, Erich Zann, and Johan de Diaken.

Michael Angel

Michael Angel

THE PLAGUE WALKER PANDEMIC
MEDICAL THRILLER NOVELS

The Devil's Noose
The Reaper's Scythe
The Blood Zone

The Plague Walker:
(A Leigh Austen Short Medical Thriller)

FANTASY & FORENSICS
BY MICHAEL ANGEL

Book One: Centaur of the Crime
Book Two: The Deer Prince's Murder
Book Three: Grand Theft Griffin
Book Four: A Perjury of Owls
Book Five: Forgery of the Phoenix
Book Six: Assault in the Wizard Degree
Book Seven: Trafficking in Demons
Book Eight: A Warrant of Wyverns
Book Nine: The Conspiracy of Unicorns
Book Ten: Dragon with a Deadly Weapon

Forensics and Dragon Fire
(Fantasy & Forensics Novella)

ABOUT THE AUTHOR

Michael Angel's worlds of fantasy and science fiction range from the unicorn-ruled realm of the Morning Land to the gritty 'Fringe Space' of the western Galactic Frontier. He's the author of the bestselling *Centaur of the Crime*, where C.S. Lewis meets CSI. His many books populate shelves in languages from Russian to Portuguese.

He currently resides in Southern California. Alas, despite keeping a keen eye out for griffins, unicorns, or galactic marshals, none have yet put in an appearance on Hollywood Boulevard.

Find out more about his latest works at:
www.MichaelAngelWriter.com

Editing/Proofing services provided
by Leiah Cooper from
SoIReadThisBookToday.com.

Cover art by
DerangedDoctorDesign.com.